To _

Girls Who Dare, Book 4

By Emma V. Leech

****

Published by Emma V. Leech.

Copyright (c) Emma V. Leech 2019

Cover Art: Victoria Cooper

ASIN No.: B07S1GW5TS

ISBN-10: 1088508073

ISBN-13: 978-1088508077

Table of Contents

Members of the Peculiar Ladies' Book Club   1

Prologue   2

Chapter 1   13

Chapter 2   22

Chapter 3   33

Chapter 4   44

Chapter 5   59

Chapter 6   72

Chapter 7   87

Chapter 8   98

Chapter 9   109

Chapter 10   125

Chapter 11   136

Chapter 12   146

Chapter 13   159

Chapter 14   177

Chapter 15   193

Chapter 16   207

Chapter 17   216

Chapter 18   223

To Wager with Love   235

Want more Emma?   237

About Me!   238

Other Works by Emma V. Leech   240

Audio Books!   244

   The Rogue   246

   Dying for a Duke   248

   The Key to Erebus   250

   The Dark Prince   252

Acknowledgements   254

Members of the Peculiar Ladies' Book Club

Prunella Adolphus, Duchess of Bedwin – first peculiar lady and secretly Miss Terry, author of *The Dark History of a Damned Duke.*

Mrs Alice Hunt (née Dowding)–Not as shy as she once was. Recently married to Matilda's brother, the notorious Nathanial Hunt, owner of *Hunter's*, the exclusive gambling club.

Lucia de Feria - a beauty. A foreigner.

Kitty Connolly - quiet and watchful, until she isn't.

Harriet Stanhope – serious, studious, intelligent. Prim. Wearer of spectacles.

Bonnie Campbell - too outspoken and forever in a scrape.

Ruth Stone - heiress and daughter of a wealthy merchant.

Minerva Butler – Prue's cousin. Not so vain or vacuous as she appears. Dreams of love.

Jemima Fernside - pretty and penniless.

Matilda Hunt – blonde and lovely and ruined in a scandal that was none of her making.

Prologue

London. 28th July 1814.

I perceive, at last, that I must be a very selfish kind of man. Fate has intervened and given me a position in life I neither expected nor feel worthy of. Soon – if I do as Trevick expects and wishes – I will add great wealth to my good fortune. Any other man of my position must look upon such a change in circumstances as the hand of a beneficent god.

Why, then, do I feel so cheated?

—Excerpt of a letter from Mr Luke Baxter to an unknown correspondent. Never sent.

1st July 1800. Ballyhill House, Armoy, County Antrim, Northern Ireland.

Luke ran as fast as he could. He ran away from the large house, with its empty, echoing rooms, away from his weeping mother and his father's fury. Why Father was so cross, Luke couldn't fathom. It was all his fault. They'd lost everything, not that there had been much to lose, but Father had frittered away the only thing left with any value: his honour.

It was a dreadful scandal. What exactly the scandal was about Luke wasn't certain, except *that woman* had been a part of it. He was only nine, so his thoughts and feelings counted for nothing. All he had gleaned through a few snatches of overheard conversation was that his father had disgraced the family. The head of their illustrious line, the Earl of Trevick, was displeased, and so had dispatched his youngest brother, Mr Derby, to deal with Luke's father.

They had been banished within a matter of days, threatened with being cut off from the family and snubbed if they did not leave until the horrid affair died down. Mr Derby said it might take years.

Decades, even.

Years stuck in this faraway place, far from his school and his friends, from anything at all. Those years stretched out before Luke, a vast expanse of nothingness and uncertainty.

The house in which they would live out their exile was dirty and smelled of decay, though it had been grand once. There were mice scuttling in the walls and cobwebs everywhere. They couldn't afford enough staff to right it and run it as it should be run, but those they'd brought had set to trying to find some order in the chaos. The dust still clung to the back of his throat and prickled his nose. Luke didn't like upsets and chaos, or disorder, or change.

He'd liked his life, his school, his pals. He'd liked the predictability of knowing what would come each day, just the same as the one before it.

Scrubbing his sleeve over his face, he scolded himself for crying. He wasn't a stupid baby. He hated his father and couldn't bear his mother's tears, and he'd lost everything, but he wouldn't cry about it. It wouldn't change a thing; that was a lesson he'd learned long ago. His father ignored him whether he cried or shouted, or behaved impeccably. His mother was too busy crying herself, forever at the mercy of her nerves. Luke had a healthy terror of his mother's nerves. Anyway, there was no point in fighting fate; it only fought back harder.

"What's the matter?"

Luke jolted, having believed he'd run into the middle of acres of nothingness and was all alone, a state he must endure for years to come. The soft voice—gentle, with a lilting accent—startled him half to death. He spun around, confronted at once with a girl.

She was slender, with a cloud of thick black curls that surrounded the sweetest face, as delicate as a fairy's. Her eyes were enormous, almost as dark as her hair, and thickly lashed. There was the faintest touch of pink at her cheeks, and her delicate lips were just a shade darker. He thought perhaps she was a year younger than he was; two at most.

He'd seen nothing as beautiful as her in all his life and, for a second, he wondered if she was real. There was a local woman working at the house who'd told him stories of the Sidhe, the good folk who could bless or curse you on a whim. She'd said they were beautiful beyond belief and that, once you'd seen them, your life would never be the same again.

In that moment, Luke believed it.

He would love her and follow her anywhere she led if she asked him.

His heart made an odd little thump in his chest and he hated himself for thinking anything so thoroughly nauseating. She was only a girl, not a tricksy fae, not a beautiful Sidhe princess. His friends would have pounded him if they'd known.

"Why are you crying?" she asked, her accent so unfamiliar and impenetrable it took him a while to comprehend.

"I'm not crying," he retorted, indignant at the accusation, no matter how accurate.

"My, don't you talk funny," she said, her dark eyes bright with interest.

"Not as funny as you," he retorted, stung by the observation.

She watched him for a long minute, as though studying a foreign entity, something she'd never seen before and wanted to understand. Her pretty head tilted to one side.

"Your hair is so red, red as garnets when the sun's on it." Her gaze was full of admiration as she added, "I like your freckles too. You'll be a handsome fellow one day."

Luke blinked as a flush burned over his cheeks. He'd spend a goodly amount of his school life pounding bullies for teasing his red hair and freckles. *Ginger, carrot-top, poison-pated, bran-faced....*

She *liked* them.

He'd hardly begun to get to grips with this strange phenomenon, and the stranger feelings that her reactions provoked, before she returned to her original question.

"So, why were you crying?"

Luke, who was still reeling from discovering he *liked a girl*, and that she thought he'd be a handsome man one day, was appalled to think she'd believe him a crybaby.

"I wasn't," he bit out, clenching his fists.

She gave him a pitying look and moved closer. To his astonishment she took his hand, unfurling his fingers like the sun opening a bloom, and raised it to her cheek, which was every bit as soft as he'd imagined. Luke's breath caught in his throat as he was torn between gratitude and outrage.

"Sure ye were," she said, the words chiding him, though gently. "But it's none o' my business, I suppose. Though if ye tell me, I shall take it to my grave, swear on it."

Her elfin face was so earnest that he blinked in surprise. Perhaps she was fae after all, there was something in her eyes, those dark, dark eyes, something he knew he could trust in. He gave a hopeless sigh and startled himself by replying with the truth.

"We've been banished here, and I've lost everything. We've no money, and I've no friends. I hate it here and… I'm all alone."

"No, you're not," she said, giving him a smile that made him feel a little dazed. "Because I've found you, and you've found me, and so… we shall be together, and never alone again."

***

Four years later

12th September 1804.

Kitty clung to the branch which swayed in a rather alarming fashion.

"Just admit it, Kitten. You're stuck."

She glared down to where Luke was staring up at her, looking so damned smug she reached up and snatched an apple—the reason she'd gone up in the first place—and lobbed it at his head. She missed, and it rolled towards her dog, Khan, a massive brindle mastiff. He sniffed the apple, gave her a long-suffering look and laid his head back on his paws.

"I'm not stuck," she said, stubborn to the last. "I… I just can't see which is the best way down… yet," she added. "But I shall."

Luke folded his arms and said nothing. Khan gave a sigh.

Kitty swallowed as the wind gusted again, large clouds scudding across a sky which had been blue only half an hour earlier. The sharp breeze made the boughs—already heavy with fruit—sway in a manner that made her heart skitter in her chest. She'd climbed a deal higher than she'd intended, but that was typical of her. She rarely thought before she acted, just threw herself headfirst into whatever it was. Luke admired her for that, though he said she frightened him half to death, too. For her part, she wished she had an ounce of his unshakeable calm. If ever you were in a fix, Luke would get you out of it, and Kitty was always in a fix. Like now, for example.

The tree swayed again, harder still. She gave a little shriek, and then saw that Luke was climbing up to her.

"Stubborn little Kitten," he said with a sigh as he drew level with her. "I told you you'd never be able to climb in those heavy skirts, but you just had to prove me wrong."

Kitty felt a strange, rather breathless sensation fill her chest as he got closer. At thirteen, Luke had become a very handsome fellow, just as she'd predicted. His hair shone a coppery red, and she adored the scattering of freckles over his nose. His eyes were blue, bluer than any sky she'd ever seen. Sometimes it hurt to look at him.

She adored him *and* his freckles.

"I know," she said, huffing with frustration. "And I don't see why I must wear the dratted things. They're impossible."

"*You're* impossible," he said, grinning at her. "And you know why. It's so you can be a proper young lady and not a hoyden. Your father wants you to have every advantage, now he can afford to dress you properly."

"I don't want to be a young lady," Kitty replied, a stab of anxiety hurting her heart. Her father wanted to send her away soon, to live with her aunt and uncle in London where she would learn to be a proper lady and grow up to marry some impoverished nobleman who needed her dowry. She'd have to leave Luke and Khan behind. She'd rather die. "I don't want to grow up. I want us to stay here, just like we are, forever."

His face softened and the breathless sensation increased. "But if you don't grow up, I shan't be able to marry you."

Kitty felt her breath catch and hold this time, and she could do nothing but stare at him.

He blushed, the colour vivid on his pale skin. "Unless… you don't want to—"

"Of course I want to!" Kitty exclaimed and threw her arms about his neck, then felt a blush rise to rival his. "You know I do," she added, a little chagrined for her outburst as he was looking smug again.

Of course he knew. She'd never hidden it from him, not from the very first day when she'd found him all alone and miserable. They'd been inseparable ever since. It was her and Luke against the world, it always had been and it was just how they liked it.

"Come along," he said, helping her untangle her skirts and find a suitable foothold. "We can't discuss the future with you stuck up a tree."

"I wasn't stuck," Kitty said, dogged as ever.

"No," Luke said, his tone soothing. "I know. You were just resting."

Kitty held her tongue, too in charity with him to argue the point, and allowed him to help her down. As she jumped the final distance, however, she stumbled, and Luke caught her, steadying her. He was always doing that. Kitty was reckless and pig-headed, and obstinate, with a temper that led her into trouble without fail. Luke was calm, patient, and understanding, and never complained—or at least rarely—when he too ended up in trouble. He was steadfast and loyal, the best friend she'd ever had, and she loved him with all her heart.

He was looking at her a little oddly now though, and Kitty stilled, wondering if she had dirt on her nose. She was about to ask him when he leaned in and pressed his mouth to hers.

It only lasted for the briefest moment, and then he was staring at her again, scarlet-faced and unsure of himself.

"Do you mind?" he asked, breathing hard.

Kitty felt a ridiculous smile curve over her mouth, and she shook her head, her black curls dancing in disarray about her face.

Luke let out a breath and kissed her again, for a fraction longer this time. Kitty closed her eyes and clung to him and knew this was the happiest moment of her entire life.

"Will you really marry me?" he asked, his blue eyes as serious as she had ever seen them.

"Yes," she said, the one word breathed on what little air remained in her lungs, for he'd stolen it with the kisses he'd taken. "Yes, please, Luke."

They sat together, hands clasped, leaning back against the gnarled trunk of the apple tree, making plans to run away as soon as they were old enough to marry. Khan lumbered over and heaved his bulk down beside them, placing his heavy head on her skirts and pinning her in place.

"You know your parents won't allow it," Luke said after a blissful few moments of sitting with her head on his shoulder. "Not now you've got money. So, we shall have to elope," he said, looking troubled by the idea. "I'm sorry for it, as there will be a scandal. My family has scandal enough, so that's of no matter, but yours...."

She watched him shrug and knew how badly his father's disgrace rankled.

"Your family has become wealthy since your father built his mill, and since my father died without making the least effort to...." He shrugged again and her heart ached for him.

As far as Kitty could see, Luke's mother was a miserable woman who spent a deal of energy lamenting their impoverished position and berating his dead sire, but never lifted a finger to do anything useful. Her only purpose in life seemed to be to make Luke as wretched as she was by reminding him daily of everything they'd lost, everything that ought to be theirs.

"I've nothing, Kitten, nothing to offer you, but I won't be like my father. I shall work hard and earn my fortune, like your father has done. My tutor at school seemed to think I've a brain in my head and I won't let you down, I promise I won't."

"I know that," she said, staring up at him and feeling like her heart would burst from happiness and pride. "And I don't care how much money we have, so long as we're together."

"I care," he admitted, the words a little taut. He reached out and tugged at a dark curl, winding it around his finger. "I want you to have everything. Pretty dresses, and carriages, and—"

Kitty snorted and shook her head. "Much I care for such things," she said, giving him an indulgent look.

"You should," he said, frowning again. "If Father hadn't ruined everything, I'd at least still have a name worth a damn, instead of his reputation as an adulterer and a murderer hanging about my neck."

Kitty winced to hear him curse. He rarely did so, but he'd never forgiven his father, and his anger was still palpable. She'd heard the tale, prised out of him a little at a time, once he'd discovered the truth of it. Even out here the rumours had followed them. His father had fallen madly in love with an opera singer, as had another—also married—man. They'd fought a duel and his opponent had died. It had been hushed up, naturally. The Earl of Trevick had seen to that, but they had shipped Mr Baxter, his hysterical wife, and their son off to an abandoned family estate in Ireland before the story could hurt the earl by association. They could return when the scandal had quieted, the earl had said. Except Luke's father had died three years ago, and Trevick seemed to have forgotten they even existed.

"I love you, Luke," she said, gazing up at him and knowing he'd be a fine man one day.

Even now, young as they were, she saw this in him, recognised the strength of his heart and purpose. He always seemed far older than she, far wiser too, and she depended on that—on him—to keep her from falling into folly with her wild spirit and impetuous temper.

"I shall love you always, Kitten," he said, just as solemn.

She knew they ought not say such things, let alone think them, but her parents had let her run amok until recent months, and Luke's mother cared for nothing but her own comfort. They'd been left too much alone and had clung together until the idea of one without the other was too fantastic to contemplate. There had barely been a day since Luke had arrived that they had not spent together.

The words, once exchanged, seemed to alter something between them, the quality of the air about them somehow different.

"I don't want to wait," Luke said, and the vehemence of the words startled Kitty. "I wish we could marry now and go away, far away from all of them. Especially my mother."

"I wish that too," Kitty said, a little cautiously. She was unused to being the voice of reason. "But we're not old enough, Luke. They'd only find us and bring us back, and this isn't so bad for now, is it?"

She looked up at him and Luke smiled, slipping his arm about her shoulders and kissing her nose.

"No," he said, though he sounded uncertain. He was quiet for a long moment. "But... but what if we could marry now?" he asked, suddenly breathless, his eyes bright with excitement.

"Whatever do you mean?" she asked, laughing at his enthusiasm.

"I mean, what if I got a bible, and a ring and we said the words? I know it wouldn't be legal, not really, but... *we'd* know in our hearts it was real, that it was done."

Kitty caught her breath. "Truly?" she said, hearing the tremor in her voice.

Luke squeezed her hands and nodded. "Truly. Right now, today."

He shifted beside her, going down on one knee and looking to her like the most chivalrous knight of old as his blue eyes met hers. "Kitty Connolly, my own Kitten, will you marry me?"

"I will," she said, her throat growing tight. "I already told you so."

He beamed and got to his feet. "Then don't move from this spot," he said, laughing.

"But where are you going?" she asked, laughing too, for his delight was infectious.

"Why, to get a bible and a ring, of course!" he exclaimed, and ran away, back through the orchard and out of sight.

Chapter 1

Ten years later.

My dearest friend,

Tonight is the firework display at Green Park. I am so looking forward to it, especially as I am going with Matilda. I think she is lonely now Aashini is married, so she has invited me to stay with her until we go to St Clair's house party. That too I am excited for. There is much to enjoy in life if one is inclined to look for it, and it is not in my nature to mope as you well know.

I have found some lovely friends during this last season, yet beneath all this excitement and happiness my spirit is torn asunder. Everything is coloured by your absence and I don't know how to mend the tear in my soul.

My heart is still yours, you see, and always shall be, just as we promised that lovely day in September. The ring you gave me is too small now, but I have it still along with the vows we made each other. Please come back to me, dear Luke. I feel my heart grows a little emptier each day that we are apart.

—Excerpt of a letter from Miss Kitty Connolly to Mr Luke Baxter... never sent.

1st August 1814, South Audley Street, London.

Kitty smoothed her gown, feeling unaccountably nervous. The Marquess of Montagu was escorting both her and Matilda to the fireworks at Green Park tonight and the man scared her half to death. She was bound to do or say something outrageous—she always did when nerves got the better of her—and then he would despise her even more than he already did. Why he'd invited her at all, she couldn't fathom, except she suspected it had more to do with Matilda than her. That too was a worry.

At least Mr Burton would also be there. He was a handsome, sensible sort of fellow, a self-made man, which meant the *ton* despised him despite his great wealth.
What nonsense. Matilda would do well to marry a man like that, one who'd made his fortune through his own cleverness and industry, rather than having been born to it.

Kitty's own family was an illustrious one, though her Irish heritage meant she may as well have been born in a bog and raised by wolves as far as the *ton* were concerned. Their fortunes had floundered for a while until the linen trade had flourished, and the family's wealth with it. Her father owned hundreds of acres of flax and three mills now, and he had plans for another.

Her parents, eager for her to snare a titled husband, had sent her to stay with her aunt and uncle. Aunt Clara Henshaw had wed an English gentleman and had become so thoroughly English herself most people had forgiven or even forgotten her Irish heritage. Her aunt had tried hard to erase her accent but Kitty refused to lose it, though she was aware it had lessened over the past years with her aunt and uncle forever correcting her. Still, she clung to it, as stubborn as ever. What did it matter? She had no intention of catching herself an English husband. She already had one.

She'd just… temporarily misplaced him.

The thought made her heart ache, and she pushed it away. She would not allow herself to sink into the dismals. For the first time in a long time, she had hopes of finding him. Matilda's brother had promised to ask about, and Nate Hunter knew everyone.

"Are you ready, dear?"

Kitty looked up as Matilda called out to her and then poked her head around the door.

"Oh, you do look lovely, Kitty," she said, smiling and looking Kitty over. "That shade of blue is very becoming."

Kitty smiled and thanked her, not mentioning that she'd chosen it as it was the exact shade of Luke's eyes. She noted then that Matilda wore a beautiful soft silver-grey gown and fought back a surge of misgiving.

"I understand the Earl of St Clair will be with the marquess this evening?" Kitty said, trying to quell her nerves.

Matilda at least looked as cool and composed as ever, so hopefully the event would go without a hitch.

"Yes, thank heavens," Matilda said with a conspiratorial grin. "So, we need not sit in terror of the marquess' disdain, with St Clair's charm and address to diffuse the tension."

"That is a comfort," Kitty said with a sigh. "Though I suppose it will put Harriet in a pelter. Do you have any idea why she hates him so?"

"No, I don't," Matilda said, looking thoughtful now. "But I don't believe the feeling is mutual."

"Oh?" Kitty replied, delighted with this information. "Whatever do you mean?"

Matilda shrugged and gave her an enigmatic smile. "Just watch St Clair this evening, when Harriet is around. You'll see."

With this intriguing nugget of information, Kitty had to be satisfied, and she followed Matilda downstairs to await the carriage.

***

Jasper Cadogan, Earl of St Clair, cast a curious glance across the carriage towards the Marquess of Montagu. They were not exactly friends, barely acquaintances, yet when the marquess had invited him to attend as his guest this evening, Jasper had been too curious to refuse. The marquess was a mystery, a solitary man who guarded his privacy like a dog with a bone. Jasper suspected no one knew him at all, which naturally made everyone ravenously curious.

"I'm holding a party at Holbrooke House, from the twentieth of the month. Should you like to attend?"

The marquess looked around, his habitually bored gaze settling on St Clair.

"Kind of you," Montagu replied, before returning his attention back to the window. "But I am obliged to return to Kent. I have neglected my affairs for too long and they won't wait any longer."

"Of course," Jasper said with ease, before some urge to play devil's advocate provoked him to speak when he'd do better to hold his tongue. "Mr Burton will be there."

A glint of amusement flickered in Montagu's cold silver eyes as he studied Jasper. "You mean to imply that I risk losing my quarry," he said mildly.

Jasper stared at him, wondering if he was truly as bloodless as he appeared, before giving a nonchalant shrug. "I believe he intends to court Miss Hunt."

The faintest glimmer of a smile played around Montagu's hard mouth. He lifted his hand and snapped his fingers, the sound echoing in the dark of the carriage. "For Mr Burton," he said, and returned his attention to the window.

By God, what an arrogant bastard, Jasper thought, wondering what life must be like when viewed with such absolute certainty. For his own part, Jasper liked Mr Burton and thought Miss Hunt a fool if she turned up her nose at him, though most of the other guests would likely regard him as a mushroom, one of the encroaching newly rich who tried to buy or marry their way into the *ton*. From what he'd seen, Mr Burton could hold his own, though, and he deserved a proper chance to secure Miss Hunt's attentions without the marquess muddying the waters. Jasper could only wish him luck.

The carriage rocked to a stop outside of the smart house on South Audley Street and soon the ladies were ensconced within. Jasper smiled at them both, complimented their dresses and enquired as to their health, whilst the marquess continued to look out of the window. He was a strange fellow to be sure. It was a matter of minutes before they arrived at their destination.

The impressive facade of a fortress dominated their first glimpse of the park in the fading light. Though a temporary structure erected solely for the evening's entertainment, the ramparts were one hundred feet square. A round tower in the centre rose a further fifty feet from the ramparts, and what looked increasingly to be thousands of people were gathering around it. All had come to view the evening's spectacle, from London's hoi polloi to the upper echelons of the *ton*. The masses stood, whilst seating had been arranged for the quality, but all looked on in amazement at the scale of the structure.

"We must hope it doesn't burn down this time," Montagu mused, smiling a little as Jasper laughed.

"This time?" Miss Connolly enquired, eyes wide.

"I believe Montagu refers to the last such event, some sixty years ago. As I understand it, the first fireworks caught the structure alight and all the remaining fireworks went off at once. Some tens of thousands of them," he said as Miss Connolly looked somewhat alarmed.

"I'm sure it's all under control this year," he said, with a soothing smile which fell as the rest of the guests joined them... including his nemesis, Miss Harriet Stanhope.

"What ho, Jasper."

Jasper nodded as his best friend and the nemesis' brother, Henry Stanhope, hailed him with his usual jaunty grin.

"There's a devilish lot of people here," Henry said as he drew closer, before becoming all stiff and formal to greet Montagu.

The marquess had that effect on people.

Soon, everyone was gathered. Mr Burton had made a beeline for Miss Hunt, Jasper noted, an event which the marquess had not yet deigned to notice, though Jasper felt certain he was perfectly aware of it. Countess Culpepper looked bored and resigned to behaving herself, as her husband was accompanying her. Mrs Manning, a rather fine-looking widow who'd made unmistakable overtures to him at their last meeting had no such restraints on her, and cast him a flirtatious smile to which Jasper politely inclined his head.

"You lucky devil."

Jasper looked around to discover his younger brother, Jerome, and sighed. "What are you doing here?"

"I was invited," Jerome replied, grinning broadly as he knew this would irritate Jasper. Jerome's life work was irritating Jasper. "Now, do me a favour and introduce me to Mrs Manning."

"Damned if I will," Jasper said with a bark of laughter. "She eats little boys for breakfast."

Jerome glowered at him. "I'm only three years younger than you."

Jasper returned a quelling look, one he'd spent years perfecting.

Jerome narrowed his eyes.

"Fine," he said, and stalked off, no doubt to find another method of ruining Jasper's evening other than flirting wildly with Mrs Manning and making a spectacle of them both.

Jasper watched his brother's progress, and the smile which lit Harriet's face as she greeted him. He suppressed a vicious stab of jealousy which he knew was beneath him. Harriet then introduced Jerome to her friend, Miss Bonnie Campbell. The young Scottish woman was a curvaceous bundle of trouble if ever Jasper had seen one, and he recognised the gleam of interest in Jerome's eye all too well.

Jasper suppressed a sigh and wondered when he'd become so ruddy old. At that moment, Harriet looked up and his heart stuttered in his chest as her cool, bespectacled gaze met his. Wide brown eyes that were even larger behind the glass of her spectacles settled on him for a second, during which time all the warmth and laughter chilled to arctic temperatures before she looked away again.

"Would it kill you to smile at me, Harry?" he murmured, before pasting a smile to his own face and attending to his friends.

***

Kitty stared at the skies until her neck ached, amazed and delighted by the spectacle above them. The festivity, intended to celebrate the centenary of the House of Brunswick and the peace with France, had been done on a scale Kitty had never experienced. The faux fortress was like nothing she'd seen in her life. Rockets thundered from the battlements, at once impressive and beautiful and yet giving the crowd a tiny taste of the power and horror of everything the men involved in the conflict must have faced. Smoke and noise, flashes and fire as explosions rocked through the spectators, drew startled gasps of wonder from even the most jaded onlookers.

For a moment, she allowed her attention to drift away from the sparkling skies as flurries of golden stars fell to earth, and focused instead on those below. Hundreds and thousands of people. As she always did, she searched their faces, though it was impossible to see in the crush, and beneath the light that changed in a moment from brilliance into darkness and back again. Was Luke here somewhere? If he was here, why hadn't he come for her, or at least sent word? Had he forgotten her, had he found another? Perhaps he was married now.

Had the words he'd spoken with such gravity meant nothing to him?

She knew it was foolish, or at least that anyone else would believe it so. She'd attended a real wedding earlier that day, when Viscount Cavendish had married Aashini. It had been an informal affair and yet with all the attendant solemnity and intent it ought to when two peoples' futures joined together—till death them do part.

She and Luke had been children: innocent, silly children with no notion of real life and responsibilities. Yet it *had* meant something to her, and to him. Kitty knew in her heart he'd felt the weight of his promise to her, and he'd meant the words. So why hadn't he come to her? Why hadn't she been able to find him? How could a boy who'd told her he loved her with such devotion disappear, and never so much as send her a note of explanation?

A barrage of sound drew her attention back to the fortress amid a violent display of flame and smoke and the thunder of artillery. The giant edifice was slowly transformed by the removal of giant screens to expose the Temple of Concord beneath the layers of the fortress. The rockets continued to fire overhead, and the temple was revealed like a butterfly from a chrysalis. Each rocket contained a multitude of smaller rockets that burst and burst again, brighter than any star, illuminating the scene beneath. An ethereal blue light was cast over the world around them, everyone from the lowliest to the grandest dipped in silver and, for one transient moment, appearing equally magnificent.

At last the skies subsided, and the land grew quiet again, until the crowd erupted with cheers and laughter, clapping and exclaiming about all that they'd seen.

Kitty stared still at the heavens, at the billows of smoke that drifted over the clear night sky. The stars began to appear, one by one, shining tentatively now the gaudy display was done. Though it was foolish, Kitty searched for and found the north star as she'd done with Luke when they were children, usually with one or other of them wishing for nonsense—a pony or a puppy, or that Papa shouldn't discover who'd broken the vase in the dining room.

"Let me find him," she begged, focusing on the tiny light and feeling the ache in her heart with as much sorrow as she'd done the day she'd discovered him gone. "Please. *Please* let me find him."

Chapter 2

Dear Bonnie,

We are leaving tomorrow for St Clair's House Party!

I'm so excited. Aren't we lucky to have found such generous friends, for surely neither you nor I would have a hope of attending such an event without them? You would be destined for Gordon Anderson for certain, and my father would be haranguing me for not having found a husband, but now we have a chance to live a little longer and hope for better things.

We must grab the chance and hold on tight!

—Excerpt of a letter from Miss Kitty Connolly to Miss Bonnie Campbell.

19th August 1814, South Audley Street, London.

"It's so good of you to take me with you," Matilda said, embracing Harriet as the young woman's eyes widened at the number of valises and hat boxes assembled in the hallway. "Oh dear," Matilda added, seeing Harriet's alarm. "I've packed far too much, haven't I? You don't have space?"

Harriet laughed and shook her head. "No, indeed. We have plenty of space, only… you've brought three times as much as I have, and now I feel anxious I didn't pack enough."

"Well, I'm sure you barely have a trunk full, once you discount the two you filled with books," her brother Henry remarked as he oversaw the servants trooping back and forth. "I never knew a girl less interested in clothes," he added, shaking his head. "You're an oddity, Harry, no getting away from it."

Poor Harriet blushed scarlet and Matilda took her arm.

"Don't listen to him, you're certain to have just the exact right amount of everything. You're always so organised. I'm afraid I'm horribly vain and can't make a decision to save my life. Packing is torture so I just cram in everything I can and hope for the best."

Harriet smiled though she didn't look entirely reassured, but at that moment Kitty came thundering down the stairs.

"Harriet!" she exclaimed, throwing her arms about the young woman's neck.

Matilda hid a grin; Harriet was clearly overawed by Kitty's boisterous nature. It was a little like living with a puppy, she reflected, having spent the past two weeks and more in her company. Kitty bored easily and was constantly looking for diversion. Once occupied, she was tranquil, happy, and easily pleased, but heaven help you if she took it into her head to entertain herself.

"Come along, come along," Henry said, now all the baggage had been safely stowed. "Let's be having you."

Obediently, they all hurried outside, where a smart coach awaited them.

"I'm afraid we'll be a little snug," Harriet said, pitching her voice low. "Aunt Nell insisted we must be chaperoned on the journey."

"Well, that's your own fault," Henry said tartly. "You would tell her I couldn't chaperone a sponge cake, so... hoist by your own petard, Miss."

Harriet laughed at her brother's indignation and they were soon settled inside.

They made a merry party. Henry was always a cheerful soul and he and Harriet, or Harry as he called her, seemed on very good terms. Kitty was in good spirits, too, and looking very fetching in a new bonnet crowned with cherries. Her dark hair framed her face with glossy ringlets and her eyes sparkled. Matilda prayed she'd be able to find her some news about her childhood sweetheart soon, though, for she knew Kitty was optimistic of hearing results and knew too how quickly optimism could fade when no news was forthcoming.

She worried that it was a hopeless case though. If Mr Baxter had wanted to write to Kitty, had wanted her to know of his whereabouts, he could have written a hundred times and more over the past years.

They made a brief mid-morning stop to change horses, and arrived at Holbrooke House in the early afternoon. It was an impressive sight.

"Good heavens," Matilda exclaimed.

Despite having been warned of its scale and opulence, the Elizabethan prodigy house was more than a little intimidating.

"Interesting, isn't it?" Harriet said, looking at the building with a smile. "It was influenced by the Classical style of building popular in France and Flanders during the sixteenth century. Especially by Hans Vredeman de Vries." She pointed out the window, warming to her theme. "It was damaged in the Civil War when Cromwell's forces bombarded it, so the 6th earl inserted those arched windows to enclose the gallery. The 10th earl employed Capability Brown to modernise the gardens and parkland. He also built the stables, which are rather magnificent, and an orangery, as well as a Gothic summerhouse."

"Our house is about five miles in that direction," Henry said, gesturing into the distance. "We used to spend all our time here, though. We played in that grand Gothic summerhouse as children," he added with a wistful smile.

Harriet, who had become quite animated whilst speaking of the building, fell quiet.

"What fun we had," her brother chuckled, apparently oblivious to her change in demeanour.

They were greeted by the Dowager Countess St Clair and the earl himself, as well as his younger brother Jerome Cadogan. She'd met Jerome at the fireworks and had liked him at once. There was a mischievous glint in his eyes she appreciated, though she knew he was the bane of his older brother's existence. He was a handsome fellow, like his brother, though a broken nose gave him a rakish, disreputable air.

The young man had a reputation for falling violently in love with quite unsuitable women and making something of a spectacle of himself. As the St Clair family's wealth was staggering, the earl lived in daily terror of finding his young sibling married to a fortune hunter. Rumour had it he'd already had to buy off a courtesan and placate a married lady threatening to tell all to the scandal sheets.

"How lovely to see you here, Miss Hunt," the Countess St Clair said, greeting her warmly. "I was so pleased to hear you were coming, and Miss Connolly, you are most welcome."

The countess was a glamourous woman, and it was clear where her sons had inherited their looks from. Dressed in a pale green gown trimmed with delicate lace, she looked far too young to be St Clair's mama. Her golden hair had faded a little, but it did nothing to diminish her beauty. Her vivid blue eyes were bright and full of intelligence. Jerome had the same intense blue colouring, Matilda noticed, whereas St Clair's were an unusual shade, almost aquamarine.

"I always forget how handsome the earl is," Kitty whispered to Matilda as they followed their hosts into a breathtaking entrance hall.

The sheer scale of the building was meant to impress upon its guests the wealth and power of the family who owned it. Matilda thought it was doing a wonderful job.

"He is a beautiful man," Matilda said with a smile, as Harriet rolled her eyes.

"Do you not agree, Harry?" she asked, too curious not to ask.

Harriet looked from Kitty to Matilda and put up her chin, a stubborn glint to her eyes. "He has arms and legs in all the correct places, all his own teeth and a head of hair. Add that to his title, and I should think any young lady would think him the epitome of male beauty."

Kitty frowned at her. "But I have no interest in marrying him and gaining his title, or all this," she added, gesturing around her as they followed the family up one side of an impressive double staircase. "So that has no bearing on *my* decision. But for you, Harry dear—objectively, as if regarding an artwork—do you not think him a thing of beauty?"

Harriet paused and Matilda bit her lip, aware St Clair and the others had gotten some distance ahead.

"If I regard him as an artwork, a Grecian urn, for example," Harriet said, an impatient tone to her voice, "then yes, I should say he is as lovely an example of the art as ever existed. Close to perfection, if I must be truthful. Unfortunately, he is not a Grecian urn, though his mind bears a close resemblance to the contents."

With this rather unvarnished assessment, Harriet turned and hurried up the stairs.

"Gosh," Kitty said, wide-eyed.

"Quite," Matilda agreed with a sigh. "We can only hope she doesn't kill him before this party is over."

***

Luke Baxter regarded Mr Derby on the opposite side of the carriage. As stern and severe as always, he was a handsome man, tall and broad despite the years weighing heavier on him now, and a heart condition that his doctor had warned him to manage with care. His hair was iron grey, but there was plenty of it, and his eyes contained the energy and strength of will of a man twenty years his junior.

Luke had hated the man for most of his life, but hatred was an emotion that took a great deal of energy and Luke was too good-natured to allow it to embitter him. So, hatred had faded, though not expired. Instead, it was overlaid by the knowledge that he must do his duty and that Mr Derby was a fount of knowledge about how this ought to be achieved. There were many people who relied upon Luke, and upon what his future held.

That Mr Derby didn't give a tinker's cuss whether or not Luke had wanted the position thrust upon him was something he had no choice but to set aside. He had endured too many arguments, too many bitter quarrels, all of them ending the same way—with his capitulation.

What choice did he have?

The Earl of Trevick was an unlucky man. In fact, it was said the men of the family were cursed to die young. The earl and his youngest brother, Mr Derby, had made a mockery of this old wives' tale as the earl had reached his three score and ten, and Mr Derby seven and sixty. The rest of the family had lived up to it admirably, however, with every son, grandson, nephew and cousin succumbing to war, disease, carriage accidents and—on one notorious occasion—a jealous lover.

Mr Derby himself was the father of six daughters. Having discovered his first wife was barren, he lost no time in marrying again, within mere weeks of her demise. This later union had, much to his disgust, produced six females. Indeed, the Trevick family was littered with female progeny, but not a single male survived. As his youngest surviving brother was not far behind him in years, this was a problem the earl could not ignore if the family was to endure.

Sensing impending doom, Trevick had acted when his last but one remaining heir had succumbed to a fever of the lungs. That action had been to pluck his last chance—Luke—from obscurity and wrap him up in cotton wool.

His mother had been in transports; finally the recognition and position in society she'd always craved was hers. What did she care that her son was miserable as sin? He'd be the next Earl of Trevick in one day, a circumstance any young man in their right mind ought to rejoice over. Everyone seemed well pleased with the arrangement… except for Luke.

He'd fought it, to begin with, desperate to return to Kitty and the life he'd planned for them both. He'd run away, bribed staff to write letters, and generally made himself ill with frustration and anger but, in the end, it had been for naught. What else could a boy do against the wishes of a family as old and powerful as Trevick? The staff were loyal to a fault, the grand estate so vast it would have taken him days to leave its grounds, even if he'd remained undiscovered. Besides, his mother's fury and reproaches—combined with the cold disdain of the earl himself—had been more than a very young man could endure.

Still, he'd known that Kitty would wait for him. One day he'd be a man and his chance would come to escape, and he'd take it.

Mr Derby had guessed his intent, however, and issued an ultimatum. If Luke failed to do his duty, the earl would ruin Kitty's family, destroying their fortunes and the prospects of their only daughter. Trevick had many interests in Ireland, Mr Derby reminded him, especially in the rapidly growing flax business. If that wasn't threat enough, Mr Derby made another that he promised to keep if Luke even considered fighting his fate….

He'd ruin Kitty.

It could be done easily enough, Luke knew. A woman's reputation was a fragile thing. You only need breathe a word in the right—or wrong—ear and a rumour would begin. It wouldn't matter whether or not there was any foundation, or proof... a girl like Kitty would not survive it.

It wasn't blackmail, Mr Derby said with a smile. Only a warning. He knew Luke would not forget himself, or what he owed the title, for what should happen to the women of the family. He'd often gesture to sweet little Sybil at this moment as if Luke's actions would see her out on the street. She was Luke's favourite cousin and had the misfortune to accompany them on this journey, as if her presence could guarantee Luke's capitulation. There seemed to be dozens like her in the family, her sisters and nieces and cousins, all of them dependent on the head of the family.

From then on, Luke had cared for nothing. He'd stopped fighting the future and making plans, he stopped caring about anything at all. His feelings were buried, smothered, forced away to a small corner of his being where they could no longer trouble him. Luke had few acquaintances and no one he regarded as a friend, but was regarded by all who knew him as a placid, level-headed man who did his duty uncomplainingly. He was charming—if rather dull—and handsome, too, though he lacked a certain something... whatever it was that made a man stand out from the crowd.

He knew what it was. He was dead inside. His heart still beat in his chest, but his life had ended the day Kitty had been taken from him.

By the earl's decree, Luke had been educated by tutors and sheltered from life's vicissitudes until the age of nineteen. Then he'd been sent off on a grand tour and had gone without a murmur. He'd wanted to be far away from the girl he couldn't have without ruining her and everything she loved, far enough that he could try to pretend she'd been nothing more than a childish dream.

Now he had returned after four years abroad, ready for the final stage of the earl's plan.

He was to marry.

A suitable bride had been selected, naturally. Nothing left to chance. It would be the match of the decade. Lady Frances Grantham, a duke's daughter no less, an heiress with an impeccable blood line and an older sister who had already birthed three sons. Her fertility was all but guaranteed, and her blue blood would purify anything lacking in Luke's, as he was merely a distant branch of the original Trevick line. They'd gone back three generations for his line.

The earl was beside himself with glee.

Luke wanted to put a gun to his head, or possibly the earl's.

Either would do.

Lady Frances was beautiful, accomplished, and popular. Well, of course she was, she was beautiful, accomplished, and the daughter of a duke with a dowry large enough to sink the English fleet. Popularity had been handed her on a plate.

Luke didn't like her.

To be fair, he'd only met her three times to date, so it was unkind of him to have made up his mind already. He knew he must try harder, not that he had a choice.

Yet she was all wrong. Her eyes were blue, her hair blonde, and she was always utterly composed. She never did or said anything she ought not, never laughed so loud he thought his eardrums might burst, never snorted or got stuck in trees or....

Stop it.

The fleeting image of a pair of sparkling dark eyes flickered somewhere in the depths of his soul and he slammed the door on it. *Damnation.* He hadn't thought of her in months, had banished the memories and the ache in his heart. He'd thought he'd cured himself.

Sybil caught his eye and sent him a sympathetic smile, full of understanding. Sometimes he wished he didn't like her or her sisters—that he could hate her, hate all the family—but she was just as much a victim of her father and uncle's tyranny as he was. They all were.

Luke took a deep breath and studied the landscape beyond the carriage window. He was going into English society at last; that was something to be grateful for. Luke had become adept at counting his blessings. Though he'd not met St Clair or anyone else who would be there before, having been kept away from English society, he'd read the scandal sheets. The earl sounded an interesting character, at least. A man who'd seen life, rather than being coddled like an egg.

Going abroad had offered Luke a little more freedom than he'd experienced since the man opposite had snatched him from his idyllic life in Ireland, which was something. That the bastard had exiled him there in the first place, damning his father and the rest of them by default to obscurity was ironic, but it *had* been an idyllic life.

Don't think of it.

He forced the memory away. He would not allow himself to remember the pretty orchard in spring with the scent of newness in the air, the taste of green, everywhere bursting, budding, full of life and hope and....

For Heaven's sake!

"What's that?"

Luke jolted as Mr Derby addressed him, a suspicious scowl in his eyes.

"N-Nothing, sir," he said, appalled that he'd spoken aloud. God, he hadn't slipped like that in years.

"Hmph." Mr Derby folded his arms and looked away from him. Sybil stared at him in alarm before returning her attention to the scenery once more.

Luke let out a slow breath and told himself to get a grip. No more memories, no more wishful thinking or what-ifs or daydreams. Kitty was gone, his love for her nothing more than maudlin sentimentality. He'd banished such thoughts many years ago when he'd realised nothing but madness and misery would come from them.

He was resigned. He had been for years. He was duty bound, and would do his duty. Marriage to Lady Frances first, beget an heir and a spare second, and then….

Then he would run.

Chapter 3

Dear Kitty,

*Ruth and I are so looking forward to seeing you
and all our friends. We hope to be with you at
Holbrooke House on the 22nd so pray do not
have too much fun before we arrive. Do get all
the best gossip for me though!*

**—Excerpt of a letter from Miss Bonnie
Campbell to Miss Kitty Connolly.**

20th August 1814, Holbrooke House, Sussex.

Kitty smiled at Matilda's maid, Sarah, turning her head this
way and that.

"Goodness, I would never tell my Aileen, as she's such a
darling old thing, but you do have a wonderful way with hair," she
said, admiring her reflection. Her dark curls were piled up in an
artful tumble at the top of her head, with a few glossy locks
allowed to fall at her temples.

Sarah beamed with pleasure. "Well, Miss Hunt is so stylish I
have to keep up to date, Miss Connolly. Always looking for
something new, we are."

"Heavens," Kitty said, laughing. "Poor Aileen would have
palpitations at the idea."

"'Tis a shame, miss, when you've such lovely hair."

Kitty shrugged, casting her reflection one last wistful look. "Yes, but she dotes on me you see, and… well, she's such a comfort I should be lost without her. She's been with me since I was a baby and quite regards me as her own. My uncle mentioned retirement last year and she wept so piteously he swore never to mention it again. I was glad of it too," she admitted, before giving Sarah a mischievous look. "But it *is* fine to look the high kick for once."

"And you do indeed," Matilda said as she entered the room, giving Kitty an approving once over. "What a beautiful gown."

Kitty smoothed her gloved hands over the white satin fabric. It was the finest she'd ever worn. It had little puff sleeves trimmed in blue with a pale blue drapery of delicate crape over it, pinned at the shoulder with a sapphire studded clasp.

"My father is feeling generous, as it appears as his new mill is proving a huge success," she said, smiling a little. "When he heard of the invitation Harriet had given me, he insisted I must have a dozen new gowns. No doubt he means me to ensnare an earl with it," she added with a bitter laugh. "As if St Clair would look at me! He'd be roasted from here to London for selecting an Irish bride, and one with a dowry from *trade,* no less," she added, with a theatrical tone of horror in her voice.

"Stuff," Matilda replied with a sniff of disgust. "But should you want him to, anyway?" she asked.

Kitty looked about and Sarah bobbed a curtsey, before discreetly leaving them alone.

"Of course not," Kitty said with a wistful smile. "I've told you. I've no interest in anyone but Luke. Everyone tells me I must forget him but it's impossible, and I believe it's wrong to try." She paused then before admitting. "My family think I *have* forgotten him, but I cannot, Matilda. I won't. I love him."

"I have concluded that love is the most wretched thing," Matilda said, taking Kitty's hands in hers. "It either comes at the wrong time, or not at all, with the wrong man or with the right man who doesn't know you exist, or disappears," she added with a wry smile. "How are we to survive such caprices?"

Kitty laughed and squeezed her friend's hands. "With fortitude and friends to keep our spirits up," she said, forcing a cheery determination into the words. "I shall find Luke, and all shall be well, and you shall fall desperately in love with Mr Burton."

Matilda returned a sceptical look and sighed. "Well, I am quite as determined to try to fall in love as you are to find your missing man. So… let us put our minds to it."

They had gathered for the evening in one of the state rooms on the south side of the house. As the party was at present friendly and intimate, this *smaller* drawing room—still on a lavish and opulent scale beyond anything Kitty had ever experienced—was nonetheless a little less overwhelming than some of the grander and larger rooms used for more formal occasions.

Kitty looked around at the guests. St Clair, the dowager Countess and the earl's brother Mr Cadogan were excellent hosts and had put everyone at ease. Mr Burton had been made welcome and was already conversing Matilda, who appeared to be hanging on his every word. Harriet too, looked to be taking an interest in Mr Burton's conversation, while her brother Henry was chatting with St Clair… who was stealing covert glances at Harriet.

Kitty's eyes widened as she remembered Matilda's words on the night of the fireworks, that the animosity between Harriet and St Clair was not mutual. She'd noticed nothing that evening, too enthralled by the fireworks to pay them much mind but now….

So, that's how it was.

Tucking that intriguing bit of information away to mull over with Matilda later, she carried on perusing the guests as Prue and Robert, the Duke and Duchess of Bedwin entered the room.

Though she looked every bit the duchess now, Kitty didn't doubt that Prue's fingers were ink stained beneath her pristine white evening gloves. A writer of some renown, she had met the duke when she'd cast him—rather cruelly—as the villain of her romantic story.

Prue grinned as Matilda and Harriet and Kitty hurried to meet her.

"Hello, darlings," she said with a bright grin. "How wonderful to see you here! I am looking forward to this. Have I missed any gossip yet?"

Matilda laughed and slid her arm through Prue's. "Not a thing. We were waiting for you so you could write it all down and make a scandalous novel about us."

"Oh, you can smile, Tilda," Prue said with a wicked glint in her eyes. "But I shall be taking notes."

Matilda laughed as Prue turned her attention to Kitty.

"So, Kitty, the dare. Are you all prepared?"

Kitty grinned and nodded. The dare she'd picked from the hat had been to dress St Clair's taxidermy bear—which lived in his study—in evening clothes. Harriet had filched some of Henry's old clothes especially for the occasion.

"Harriet's organised everything," she said. "So, I don't feel I can take much credit, but yes. Later tonight when the men have their port…."

***

Dinner was an informal affair, and yet the table was still the most lavish at which Kitty had ever sat. They were a little late in sitting down after some last-minute adjustments when some of the guests had failed to appear.

Jerome—Mr Cadogan—had explained that a Mr Derby, his daughter, Miss Sybil Derby and a cousin of theirs—the heir to the Earl of Trevick—had sent word that they would be late. The cousin was something of a mystery, Jerome informed them, plucked from obscurity as the earl's last remaining heir. No one seemed to know a thing about him. He'd been abroad for many years and had only just returned to England. Jerome was interested to meet him as they were of an age, but their carriage had broken an axle en route and so they would not arrive in time for dinner whilst repairs were being made.

Kitty was more interested in the meal than another nobleman. There were enough lofty titles about the table to make her feel like an imposter as it was.

The first course alone was awe-inspiring, with dozens of dishes including crawfish soup, fillet of veal, loin of beef, petit patties, five roast chickens, pigeon fillets in a rich sauce, a turkey, and a ham.

Kitty accepted a bowl of soup and endeavoured not to look as overwhelmed as she felt. She'd been to some grand dinners over the past season, but none with so illustrious a family.

"Do you ever feel the need to pinch yourself?" Mr Burton murmured to her in an undertone.

Kitty looked up and smiled at him. "Not usually, but tonight…." She glanced around to see the Duke of Bedwin sitting a little to her left—to the right of the dowager countess and up to the head of the table where the Earl of St Clair was speaking to Lady Frances Grantham, daughter of the Duke of Lymington. "Yes, tonight it seems a little daunting."

"I'm glad I'm not alone," he said, giving her a conspiratorial grin. "Lady Frances has already refused to speak with me."

Kitty's eyes widened with horror. "She never did!"

Mr Burton nodded, his expression wry. "Oh, it was expertly done, with the least amount of stir, but after we'd been introduced, she pretended not to have heard my opening gambit and turned to speak to Mr Cadogan."

"What an ill-mannered wretch," Kitty said, a touch too loudly. Matilda, who was sitting opposite them and next to Lady Frances, widened her eyes in a warning gesture that made Kitty blush.

Mr Burton smothered a laugh by pretending to choke on his beef and took a hasty sip of wine. Putting the glass down, he turned back to her. "I'll think you'll find her manners are just what they ought to be when faced with conversation from an encroaching mushroom of my stamp," he murmured.

"Well, I think it's nothing but ignorance and rudeness. Bedwin would never act in such a shabby manner, and he's a duke."

Kitty simmered on Mr Burton's behalf. She'd been snubbed for her Irish heritage often enough, and because her father's fortunes were growing through trade. It mattered little that their family was an ancient and distinguished one; gentlemen did *not* dirty their hands with such things.

Apparently, it was better to let your family starve than lift a finger. What idiocy.

"We so enjoyed the fireworks at Green Park," Matilda said to Mr Burton, giving him a warm smile.

Kitty hid a grin at the undisguised pleasure in Mr Burton's eyes at being addressed by her.

"They were very impressive," Tilda added. "Beautiful, too, like the sky was full of golden stars."

"Were they?" Mr Burton said, gazing back at her with undisguised admiration. "I didn't notice."

Matilda blushed and turned her attention back to her dinner.

"Did you enjoy the fireworks, Miss Stanhope?" St Clair asked, picking up the conversation and drawing Harriet into it.

It had amused Kitty to discover Harriet seated to St Clair's left. She wondered if the countess was oblivious to Harriet's animosity, or if she'd done it on purpose when arranging the table.

Harriet, who had barely spoken since they'd sat down, lifted her head.

"I'm not sure," she said, her tone thoughtful.

St Clair raised an eyebrow, considering her with interest. "Why ever not? Either you did or you didn't."

Harriet looked at the earl and scowled. "No, it is not that simple."

St Clair sighed, returning a rueful smile. "No, Harry, it never is with you. Please, won't you explain?"

Harriet blushed scarlet at St Clair addressing her in such an informal manner before company. Kitty could see it had unnerved her. They were childhood friends, of course, but others could interpret it as an intimacy she would never have allowed him.

"The fireworks represented the Battle of Waterloo," she said, her tone rather stern. "And as lovely and impressive as they were, I could not help but imagine the men who suffered and died during that terrible battle. The noise, the smoke, the chaos and terror—"

Harriet broke off and looked suddenly horrified. Such subjects were not suitable for the dinner table, especially not from a woman. Mr Burton was frowning too, and Kitty wondered if he thought women ought not consider such things. She hoped not, for she would think less of him for it.

"What an imagination you have," Lady Frances remarked, one blonde eyebrow arched a little. "I just saw the beauty of the evening and enjoyed the convivial atmosphere. I had no idea of the morbid undertone."

Kitty decided she didn't like Lady Frances. Judging by the way St Clair's jaw tightened, he didn't approve of her comment either.

"Harriet has a superior intellect, Lady Frances," St Clair said, his expression frigid. "She feels things rather deeper than most."

Lady Frances gave a dismissive sniff and turned back to her dinner. St Clair was still regarding Harriet.

"Must you think so hard about everything?" he asked quietly. The words were gentle, his expression one of consternation, as if he was trying terribly hard to understand her.

"It's better than thinking of nothing at all," she snapped and then closed her mouth, looking appalled. Kitty could almost hear her cursing herself for the outburst. "I'm sorry, would you excuse me for a moment...?"

Harriet got to her feet, causing all the men to stand as well, as she walked from the room.

St Clair started forward, as though he would go after her, which would have been quite inappropriate.

"I'll check she's all right," Kitty said, halting the earl before he could set tongues wagging. She smiled at him in what she hoped was a reassuring manner. "She had rather a headache earlier," she added with sudden inspiration. "I expect it's still troubling her."

Kitty hurried from the room, catching up with Harriet and sliding her arm through hers.

"Are you all right?" she asked, tugging her to a halt.

Harriet took a deep breath and nodded. "Yes. Yes, I'm fine, I.... Oh, damn my tongue. Why can't I just make small talk like everyone else? I mean to, I swear I do, but it always seemed so... so stupid not to say what one really thinks or to consider a question properly rather than giving a glib answer." She turned a pleading expression on Kitty. "Why couldn't I just say 'yes, Lord St Clair, it was a very pleasant evening?'"

"Because you're honest and clever, and that night was about far more than fireworks, as everyone in a brain in their head surely knew. I knew it, and I certainly don't consider myself an intellectual," Kitty added with a laugh.

"But I promised myself I'd be good and sociable *and* polite to St Clair," Harriet said, sounding so mournful that Kitty felt wretched for her. "I promised Henry, too. He'll be so cross. I... I don't know what comes over me, truly I don't. Jasper—Lord St Clair—seems to have a knack for making me behave badly."

"You've known him a long time," Kitty said, wondering if she could get Harriet to tell her what the problem was. "Since you were children?"

Harriet nodded. "Yes, we grew up together. I probably spent more time here than at my own home as our parents were often away. The countess liked having us about as playmates for Jasper and Jerome, so...." She shrugged and they walked on, arm-in-arm.

"Did you always hate him?"

"I don't *hate* him," Harriet said with a huff of annoyance. "That would imply he holds far more of my attention than he does. I simply don't like him. He's like an irritating bluebottle. Once you know it's there, you simply have to get rid of it."

"Did you always *dislike* him, then?" Kitty pressed, determined to get an answer.

"No," she said, sighing. It was a rather wistful sound, sorrowful even. "No, we were friends once."

Kitty smiled, feeling a sudden kinship with Harriet. "Did you love him?"

"Good heavens, no!" Harriet exclaimed, looking alarmed by the idea and shattering Kitty's romantic ideas of having found a kindred spirit. "He was always a beastly boy and I was always the butt of his jokes. I don't think I ever did more than tolerate him, or him me, but there was no animosity there until later. I was sixteen when I realised what a smug, self-centred coxcomb he really is. I simply don't understand why everyone fawns over him so."

"Don't you?" Kitty said, raising one eyebrow and quizzing Harriet with her most sceptical expression.

41

Harriet sighed and pushed her spectacles up her nose, a gesture of irritation Kitty had become familiar with. "Oh, very well. Yes, he's handsome and charming and rich, and he has a title, but that falls a long way short of impressing *me,* I can tell you."

"Clearly," Kitty said with a laugh, and feeling desperately sorry for St Clair. If he did have feelings for Harriet, he was doomed to disappointment. If that gorgeous man with his wit, his fortune *and* an earldom couldn't impress Harriet Stanhope, she wondered what on earth he'd need to do. She wondered if Harriet had any clue of his feelings for her. "I think you rather impress *him,* though, Harry."

Harriet stopped in her tracks and glared at Kitty. "Now, this… this is what no one understands," she said, her eyes flashing with annoyance. "It's all a game to him. He expects the world to love him and fall victim to his charms, and when they don't, they become a challenge. He can't bear it that I won't fall at his feet like the rest of the world, that's all. If I changed my mind and was actually *nice* to him, he'd be onto the next challenge so fast my head would spin."

Kitty frowned. She could see what Harriet was saying, and it made complete sense. She'd met men like that herself, but… but something in the way St Clair had looked at Harriet made Kitty believe that wasn't it.

"Why not be nice to him, then?" Kitty said, curious what would happen if Harriet did just that. "If you're so certain. Then he'd stop bothering you."

Harriet looked at her as if she'd started speaking Chinese. "I'd never give him the satisfaction," she said, revolted.

With a sigh, Kitty put the conversation to one side. "What did you think of Lady Frances?"

"I think she's a duke's daughter," Harriet replied, her tone suggesting this was not a compliment. The two women glanced at each other and burst out laughing. "Oh, Kitty, I am glad you came," Harriet said, grinning at her.

Kitty felt a surge of warmth for the rather prickly young woman at her side. She'd not liked her much at first, a little intimidated by her intelligence and rather cool demeanour. It had become clear that wasn't who Harriet was once you got to know her, however, she was simply reserved. Kitty was pleased to discover she'd made a good friend.

"I'm glad you invited me," she said.

"Oh, Kitty, the bear," Harriet said, grabbing hold of Kitty's arm, her eyes alight with laughter. "They're all at dinner. It's the perfect moment."

"Let's go!" Kitty gave a laugh of delight, and they hurried off towards St Clair's study.

Chapter 4

Dear Bonnie, you desired gossip... I have it.
Only you must not breathe a word of it to
anyone. I cannot be absolutely certain as it is
only from observing the man since we got here
but Matilda has suspected the same thing for
some time.

St Clair is in love... with Harriet!

—Excerpt of a letter from Miss Kitty Connolly
to Miss Bonnie Campbell.

Still the 20ᵗʰ August 1814, Holbrooke House, Sussex.

Kitty leaned back and regarded the massive brown bear with a frown. From her position—standing on a chair—before the great beast, she looked down at Harriet.

"I can't get his cravat right," she said, shaking her head.

"Here, let me have a go. I've done Henry's before now. He says I'm better than his valet."

Kitty laughed and climbed down. "You do know this is supposed to be my dare," she said, giving her hand to Harriet as she took her place. "I feel like I should take another one."

Harriet grinned. "Only if I can claim this one is entirely mine."

"Oh, no, that won't do," Kitty said, wagging a finger at her. "You don't get out of it that easily. I have all the dares packed safely away and the bear is only borrowing the top hat. You're going to pick yours before we leave here."

"Ugh," Harriet said, pulling a face.

Kitty chuckled and watched as Harriet's deft fingers made short work of the cravat.

"Oh, I say, Harry, your brother is right. What a splendid job!"

Harriet jumped down and they stood back to regard their handwork. "He does look rather dashing," she said with approval. "I do like the rakish angle of his hat, too. If St Clair was a bear, he'd look just like that."

Kitty snorted and unfolded a hideously garish waistcoat of violet and yellow stripes. "Would he wear this monstrosity?"

Harriet chuckled. "Lord, no. He'd rather die than commit such a crime against sartorial elegance. Henry, however, has no taste whatsoever."

She arranged the chair to the right of the bear. "You'd best bring that chair to other side, Kitty. Even with the all the ties at the back of the waistcoat undone, we're going to have the devil's own job getting it on him."

"Never mind that, what about his pantaloons?" Kitty asked, before dissolving into giggles.

Harriet bit her lip, laughter dancing in her eyes. "We'll have to figure that one out when we get to it."

"This is going to take a deal longer than I'd anticipated," Kitty admitted, looking at the clock. "I think I'll have to cut the pantaloons in half and sew them onto him."

They'd already missed most of dinner, as wrangling the shirt on had been nigh on impossible. In the end they'd cut it up the back and pinned it back together. That Harriet had thought to provide a sewing kit for the affair showed her superior intellect in Kitty's opinion.

"Good," Harriet said, looking like she was thoroughly enjoying herself. "I've no desire to go back, and I've done nothing like this before in my life. If you think I will leave the job half done, you don't know me very well. We'll just have to say the headache you lied about turned into a megrim and you stayed to look after me."

Kitty sighed and gave a sad shake of her head. "Harriet Stanhope, now you're telling lies as well as behaving like a hoyden. I do believe I'm leading you astray."

Harriet snorted and climbed back onto the chair with the hideous waistcoat clutched in one hand. "Oh good," she said, her tone somewhat defiant. "It's about time someone did."

***

Jasper looked up as his butler, Temple, sidled up to him and gave a discreet cough. The men had just returned to the ladies after their port, and his mother was serving tea.

"Mr Derby and his party arrived half an hour ago, my lord," the man said in an undertone. "I have had them all seen to their rooms and they requested not to join the guests at this late hour. However, Mr Derby is desirous of seeing you as soon as is convenient."

"Oh?" he said, surprised. "Very well, I'll come at once."

Mr Derby was a rather humourless devil and no doubt wished to give his apology for their late arrival in person. Not that a broken axle was anything anyone could have foreseen, but it gave Jasper an excuse to leave his guests and search for Harriet. Neither she nor Kitty had returned to the dinner table, which was most out of character for Harry. He hoped she was all right.

He was unhappily aware he'd upset her, though he'd not meant to. Not that it made a difference; she always took offense whether or not he was deliberately provoking her. Admittedly, sometimes he couldn't help himself, and riling her was so easy. He far preferred it when she was furious and raging at him, though, it was better than being ignored. Her indifference cut him far deeper than any angry words ever could, though he'd never admit that to another living soul.

"I had him shown to your study, my lord," Temple said as Jasper got to his feet.

Jasper nodded his understanding, apologised to his guests, and went to deal with Mr Derby.

On entering his study, he was a little taken aback to find not only Mr Derby and another young man he did not know, but... but....

"Good heavens," he said.

Mr Derby turned a disapproving expression upon Jasper. "Good evening, Lord St Clair. I am relieved to discover this is not the usual state of affairs to be found in a room designed for more serious matters."

Jasper felt his hackles rise a little at such stuffiness, but caught the glimmer of amusement in the younger man's eyes and forced himself to reply with tact. He had relatives himself.

"Indeed not, Mr Derby. I suspect foul play." At that moment a slight movement caught his eye. The curtains covering doors that led out to the grounds beyond had been closed for the night. A glimpse of pink silk had been unmistakably visible for just a moment, before being whisked out of sight.

Harriet had been wearing a pink silk gown.

His lips twitched. The little wretch. Who would have thought it?

His bear— a recent gift from some of his more idiotic friends —looked as if he'd had a jolly good evening. Dressed fully in evening clothes, his waistcoat looked like some nightmarish thing Henry would delight in tormenting Jasper with, and the bear's hat was set at a rakish angle. Somehow, she'd even fixed an empty bottle into its massive paw.

Jasper found himself delighted by the discovery that Harriet—always so serious and disapproving—had a ridiculous sense of humour.

"My brother, no doubt," he said with an easy smile, feeling not the least qualm in blaming his sibling for any diabolical behaviour. It was the sort of thing Jerome *would* do when in his cups, anyway. "Young men find amusement in such things, I believe."

Mr Derby looked increasingly disturbed and glanced at the man beside him, whom Jasper judged to be much the same age as Jerome. It looked as if Mr Derby regretted bringing Trevick's heir—for Jasper assumed that was who the fellow was—to such a den of iniquity. Rumour had it that, after years of untimely deaths and catastrophes, the earl was taking no chances with the last in his line.

"Well, I'll take your word for it," Mr Derby said as Jasper willed himself to return a polite smile. "I shan't take much of your time. I realise you have guests, but I thought it only right and proper to inform you that there will be an announcement later this week. Mr Baxter here will become engaged to one of your other guests, the Lady Frances Grantham. We have her father's approval, of course, but your house party seemed a convivial moment to make the news public."

There was a slight scuffling noise by the curtains which Jasper studiously ignored and spoke quickly to keep their attention fixed upon him. "Of course, Mr Derby. How delightful."

Jasper was perfectly conscious of the fact Mr Derby would be well aware of his own reputation. What the fellow was really saying was *Lady Frances Grantham is off limits, so keep your sticky paws off her.* Jasper was only too happy to comply.

Lady Frances had made her interest in him known from the beginning of the season and he'd have not invited her if his mother hadn't insisted. All he could feel was relief at not being chased around his own home for the next two weeks or more, while trying to avoid getting himself leg shackled. She struck him as the kind of woman who would set a trap without thinking twice about it.

At that moment, a knock sounded at his study door.

"Come," Jasper called, eager to be done with this interview so he could deal with the woman hiding behind his curtains. He was thoroughly looking forward to it.

To his surprise and chagrin, Lady Frances herself bustled in, with her companion Mrs Drake in tow.

"Oh, it *is* you, Mr Derby… and Mr Baxter," she added with a shy smile. "I do beg your pardon for the intrusion, my lord," she said, turning a melting gaze on Jasper. "But when Mrs Drake informed me of the accident, I knew I wouldn't sleep a wink until I assured myself they were unharmed."

"As you see, Lady Frances," Mr Baxter said with a smile that Jasper thought did not quite meet his eyes. "We are perfectly well and—"

Jasper's heart flew to his throat as there was a sudden burst of activity behind the curtains… and Kitty Connolly stumbled through them. She was staring at Mr Baxter as though she'd seen a ghost, and then an expression of such joy dawned on her face that Jasper's heart felt squeezed.

"Luke!" she exclaimed, and flew across the room, throwing her arms about Mr Baxter.

The young man made a choked sound, but there was no doubting his expression was the twin of Miss Connolly's.

"Kitten!" he breathed, the one word husky with surprise.

For the briefest moment he embraced her as if he'd never let her go again, before realising where he was and in what circumstances, and hurriedly setting her away from him. A blush stained his cheeks, but he squared his shoulders and faced her.

"Oh, Luke," Kitty cried. "Where have you been all this time? Why did you never get in touch? And… and tell me you're not truly thinking of marrying that… that *woman*?"

"Indeed, he is," Lady Frances said, her tone icy. "And I should like an explanation right now, Mr Baxter, this minute. Who is this creature and why was she hiding behind the curtains?"

Mr Baxter went to open his mouth but Mr Derby spoke over him.

"It's obvious enough: the woman is clearly deranged. No doubt she was lying in wait, setting a trap for the first eligible man to come through the door," Mr Derby said, an expression of deep distaste on his already severe features. "Lady Frances, please do not upset yourself. If you would just leave it to me we will deal with this outrageous creature, I assure you."

"Mr Derby!" Mr Baxter exclaimed, looking furious.

Jasper didn't think Lady Frances looked upset. Rather, she looked murderous, especially when her soon-to-be-betrothed spoke in Miss Connolly's defence. He glanced around to see that Harriet too was emerging from the curtains and shook his head, glaring at her, silently commanding she return to her hiding place before anyone noticed her presence. Heaven alone knew what this could do to her reputation. Kitty had just ruined herself, and he'd not let her take Harriet down too.

Harriet hesitated, defiance in her eyes, wanting to go to her friend.

Trust me, he told her with his eyes, willing her to do so for once in her life. With a glower that told him he'd better not mess this up, Harriet slid back behind the curtains.

Jasper felt he might breathe again, except for the fact the atmosphere in the room was becoming increasingly combustible.

Mr Baxter was ashen, so rigid with tension Jasper worried something might snap inside him at any moment.

"I insist this young woman is removed from the premises at once," Derby thundered.

"This *young woman*?" Miss Connolly said with a sneer. "You know very well who I am, Mr Derby, and you know Luke loves me too, no doubt, as it was clearly you that separated us. Besides which, he has no intention of marrying your Lady Frances."

"I know no such thing! They are engaged. We will make the announcement this week!" Mr Derby bellowed.

"Oh, no you won't!" Kitty yelled back, her slender hands curled into fists and sounding very much like she'd break Derby's nose at the slightest provocation. "Because he's already married— *to me*!"

The silence that greeted this announcement was so absolute that the hairs on the back of Jasper's neck prickled. Well, this house party was off to a flying start. Curse his mother and her hare-brained ideas.

He looked around a fraction too late to see Lady Frances crumple to the floor. No doubt she'd expected him to catch her, but he'd not been paying her the least bit of attention, too riveted by the drama unfolding before him.

With a shriek of alarm, her companion Mrs Drake fell to her knees beside her in a flurry of skirts.

"Luke," Mr Derby said, staring at Mr Baxter, a menacing glint in his eyes that chilled Jasper to the bone.

Mr Baxter closed his eyes for a moment before opening them again and staring back at Miss Connolly. He was struggling, fighting some inner battle. Jasper could see it, sense it, and every instinct told him that the girl had spoken true. Mr Baxter had loved her, he still did, but it wouldn't make any difference.

"Luke," Miss Connolly said in a whisper, looking close to tears. "Tell them, Luke, please. Tell them it's true."

For a fleeting moment Jasper saw a flicker of acute misery in the poor man's eyes, but he swallowed and stood a little taller. "We were children, Miss Connolly," he said, his voice gentle. "It was only play acting, as I'm sure you recall."

The words hit the young woman so hard he may as well have struck her.

Ah, hell.

Jasper's heart ached for her, for the desolation he knew she felt.

"Liar!" she said, the exclamation torn from her, broken and wild with pain. It rang about the room and Mr Baxter could not look at her. "This is your doing," she said, turning on Mr Derby. "You've got your claws in him, I know you have. You've blackmailed him into it," she said, her fury palpable. "What did you threaten him with? What hold do you have on him?"

"You're insane," Mr Derby said, looking bored, as if the whole affair was very much beneath his notice.

Jasper felt an increasing desire to break the fellow's nose for her.

"Miss Connolly," Mr Baxter said gently. "We're not children any longer. Please... you must not...."

Miss Connolly put up her chin. "Tell me you didn't mean it," she said, a quaver in her voice. "Look me in the eyes, Luke. Tell me you don't love me, that it was just a childish game."

Mr Baxter's chest was rising and falling too fast, his turmoil palpable. Jasper held his breath, willing the man to stand up for her, no matter the cost. He watched Mr Baxter force himself to look into her eyes and open his mouth, and Jasper knew, *knew* that he would deny her with his next words... only he didn't.

He didn't say anything at all. He was lost in the girl's eyes, his expression one of such longing there was no possible way of denying it with words. It lasted barely a second before he pulled himself together, but Miss Connolly had seen it, just as Jasper had.

"Miss Connolly," Mr Baxter said. Now he'd collected himself, he was trying to return to his previous cool demeanour, but it was too late.

"If you marry that girl, I'll sue you," Miss Connolly said, a triumphant glint in her eyes.

"What?" barked Mr Derby, looking such a startling shade of red that Jasper began to worry for his health.

"For breach of promise," said Miss Connolly.

Jasper could only admire her spirit. There she stood, all alone and facing a powerful man who clearly had some hold on her beloved, and yet she'd not back down. She loved him, and she would fight for him. He smiled.

"No, Kitten, you can't," Mr Baxter said, panic in his eyes now. He shook his head and took a step forward as if he'd go to her, before holding himself in check one more. "You don't understand—"

"If you wish to deny that we ever married, that is one thing," Miss Connolly said, raising her chin and looking altogether regal with her dark eyes flashing fire. "But tell me you never promised to marry me, or that you never begged to marry me, to run away with me to Gretna Green the moment we could. Tell me I'm lying."

Mr Baxter stared at her and Jasper knew he couldn't do it. The poor bastard's throat worked and he opened his mouth and then closed it again.

"I thought not," Miss Connolly said, smiling.

"This is the outside of enough," Mr Derby said in fury. "St Clair, I demand you remove this... this *madwoman* from the premises at once."

Jasper stiffened and returned a cool look of disdain. "Miss Connolly is a guest in my house, *sir*," he said, giving Derby a look that reminded him he was dealing with the Earl of St Clair, and not some wet behind the ears boy. "Furthermore, I do not believe her to be in the least mentally impaired."

He hesitated for a moment, wondering if he'd lost his mind but… damn it, he wanted to see if such a thing as true love really existed, if a childhood romance could survive into adulthood.

"In fact, Mr Derby," he said, moving to stand beside Miss Connolly. "If Mr Baxter has made promises to this young lady—which he has not tried to deny—then I feel honour-bound to support her in any legal endeavour she may undertake."

Miss Connolly turned an expression of bewildered amazement on him, and Jasper smiled a little.

"My Lord St Clair," Mr Derby said, the words low and furious. "May I remind you that the Earl of Trevick is a powerful man? Luke Baxter is his last living heir and he has gone to great lengths to get the boy to this point, and to arrange this marriage. The Trevicks and the Lymingtons are eager that the two great families be joined by this union and I assure you the earl will not take kindly to your support of this mad female, dragging the family name through the dirt at such a moment."

He took a breath, and Jasper could see him trying to arrange his face into something less confrontational, perhaps realising too late that intimidation was the wrong tack.

"Her family is *in trade*," said Mr Derby, holding his hands out in supplication. "Surely you can understand…?"

He spoke this last in a cajoling manner, as though a man of Jasper's bloodline should understand such niceties.

It was a rare thing for Jasper to lose his temper, but he had never warmed to Mr Derby and now he felt his instincts had been spot on. He was a vile bully. Anger surged through him at the temerity of the man, threatening him in his own home.

"I might remind you that *I* am also a powerful man, Mr Derby," Jasper said, feeling increasingly like a dog marking his own territory and growing angrier still that such ludicrous words were being forced from his lips. "And if promises have been made to Miss Connolly, then those promises ought to be kept. I suggest you refrain from any further remarks about the lady's sanity or her family background, or *I* will not take kindly to it, as I do not take kindly to being threatened."

Mr Derby stared at him, his expression suggesting he ought to lie down and loosen his cravat if he didn't want to turn up his toes in the next few minutes. He was purple in the face, his eyes bulging, and he looked as if he hadn't taken a breath for some time.

"Come, Luke," he said through gritted teeth. "There is nothing more to be said tonight. We shall speak of this again when everyone has had time to think about their actions."

The words were snarled more than spoken, his eyes never leaving Jasper's until he turned and stalked from the room.

Mr Baxter hesitated, apparently torn between helping Lady Frances who was clutching Mrs Drake and sobbing quietly, and going to Miss Connolly, who was staring at him with such hope in her eyes.

"Luke!" Mr Derby bellowed, making everyone jump, but none more so than the man himself, who paled.

He turned to Jasper and bowed.

"My lord," he said, his voice strained. "Please forgive the disturbance."

He turned back to Miss Connolly, such despair in his eyes that Jasper knew both his instincts and Miss Connolly's were right. Derby had some hold over him.

The young man turned and left without another word. Jasper saw Miss Connolly's eyes fill. He moved to her and grasped her arm, shaking his head. She must not break down yet, not until Lady Frances was gone. To her credit, the girl squared her shoulders, understanding.

Jasper pulled the bell, relieved when Temple appeared at once. Bless the man, he could smell trouble a mile off.

"Please fetch Lady Frances' maidservant. She has been taken unwell and needs to retire at once."

It seemed an eternity before this had been accomplished, but finally the woman arrived, and she and Mrs Drake helped Lady Frances to her feet. Jasper was just about to let out a breath of relief when the woman paused at the threshold and turned to give Miss Connolly a look of utter disgust.

"He'll ruin you," she said, the words stark. "My father is a duke and the Earl of Trevick wants this marriage badly, and you...." Lady Frances put up her chin. "Irish trade," she said with a snort, as if that was enough.

In the circumstances, she was probably right.

"That will be all," Jasper said coldly, earning himself a look of deep reproach from the woman.

"You've made an error of judgement, my lord," she said, her tone icy. "I pray you do not live to regret it."

The door closed and Jasper let out the breath he'd been holding as Miss Connolly made a choked sound. Harriet flung back the curtains and hurried out, enfolding her friend in her arms.

"Oh, Kitty," she said as Miss Connolly dissolved into shuddering sobs. "Oh, dearest, whatever have you done?"

Jasper turned away to give them a little privacy and went to pour some drinks. When he looked back Miss Connolly had composed herself a little and he could only admire her fortitude.

"Here," he said, handing her the glass. "It will help."

Miss Connolly accepted it from him and took a sip before looking up at him with tear stained eyes.

"I don't know why you did it, my lord, but I'll never be able to thank you. My parents will be horrified when they discover what I've done. They… they would never support me."

Jasper smiled, feeling a little uneasy. He could feel Harriet's scrutiny, feel her confusion as to why he'd acted as he had.

"Are you sure you want to go through with it, Kitty?" she asked, her voice full of concern. "There will be such a dreadful scandal, and even if you win… would you want to marry a man who was forced—"

"He loves her," Jasper broke in, the words rather harder than he'd intended.

Harriet frowned at him, her scepticism quite obvious. "You can't possibly—"

"I know what a man in love looks like," he said, interrupting her and wishing he hadn't sounded so bitter. "Derby has some hold over him."

"You *know* this?" Harriet pressed, a surge of irritation in her voice that Jasper well recognised.

"Yes!" Jasper snapped, finding his own impatience rising at it always did when she acted as if he was a dumb brute. "I do. I saw the despair in his eyes, Harry, and he could not deny Miss Connolly's words, he could not say it wasn't true."

"It *is* true," Miss Connolly said. "Though he's right, we were only children, but… but I saw it too, Harriet. He doesn't love Lady Frances. He's trapped. If I thought for one moment his feelings for me were dead and gone…."

Her voice broke and she covered her mouth with her hand.

"I think you'd best take Miss Connolly to her room, Harry," Jasper said. He felt exhausted. "She must get some rest before she decides for certain what she wishes to do. I will support you, Miss Connolly, whatever you decide."

Harriet looked at him with confusion in her eyes. "Very well," she said, still staring at him as though he were a puzzle.

Not for the first time, he sensed some war going on in her mind, that incredible brain of hers forcing itself to consider his actions and make sense of them. Jasper wished her luck as he didn't have a clue; all he knew was that he had a tendency to act like a lunatic when she was around.

"I'm not yet sure if it was for the best, my lord," she said, sounding troubled. "But I do realise you stood up for Kitty when you didn't have to. Mr Derby is a foul tyrant and no one else would have done it, so... thank you. I shan't forget your kindness."

Jasper looked back at her, at a face he knew as well as his own. She wasn't especially beautiful—most would say she was merely passably pretty—but most people didn't know her. Most people would think her eyes were brown, but they weren't. Her eyes were a rich bronze, flecked with gold and green, and they could see right through him and find him wanting in every particular.

He nodded and watched as Harriet escorted her friend from the room.

Chapter 5

My dear friend,

It appears I am going to provide more gossip than you could ever have believed. I'm so frightened I'm numb with it. Oh, Bonnie, what have I done?

—Excerpt of a letter from Miss Kitty Connolly to Miss Bonnie Campbell.

The early hours of the morning, 21st August 1814, Holbrooke House, Sussex.

Matilda listened, open-mouthed as Harriet explained everything that had happened.

When the two young women had failed to return after dinner, she'd been anxious and had gone looking for them to no avail, until she'd seen Harriet escorting a white-faced Kitty back to her room.

Now they sat on Kitty's bed, the three of them huddled together.

"I can't believe it," Matilda said for the third time. "To see him again after all this time, and in such a manner. It's like something from Mrs Radcliffe."

Kitty sniffed and gave a wan smile. "Mr Derby is certainly perfect casting for the villain in a Gothic novel. If only we could dig up an ancient prophecy or find a mad monk, it would be perfect, though the weather is too fine," she said, wiping her eyes. "We're in dire need of a thunderstorm."

Matilda's heart ached for her, for her bravery and courage.

What would it be like to love so fully and with such passion, to stand up to a man who would keep her beloved from her, and not to be cowed by his power and rank; to love so fiercely that no thought or fear of her own ruination even entered her head? Matilda felt rather in awe of her, in awe of an emotion that could overpower fear and uncertainty.

"Kitty," Harriet said, the voice of reason amid such desperate romance. "I believe you must take a moment to consider what you are doing, what effect it will have on your family. Even if you and St Clair are correct and Mr Baxter does love you, he's made it clear that it's impossible, that he *cannot* marry you." Harriet took her hands and Matilda watched the spark of anger growing in Kitty's eyes with trepidation. "He's the heir to an earldom, dear. Men of that stamp rarely marry for love, only for power and wealth. Lady Frances is a brilliant match, and one Trevick will not let go lightly. You must accept that… that perhaps Mr Baxter… despite his feelings he… he may *want* this."

"No!" Kitty snatched her hands from Harriet's grasp. "Luke cares nothing for material things, for titles and power. I know him… I know—"

"You knew him ten years ago, Kitty," Harriet pressed, and Matilda could see the anguish in her eyes, her desire to protect Kitty when she was so lost to emotion she could not protect herself. "You knew a boy. He's a man now, with a man's thoughts and feelings. You don't know what influences have worked on him over the past decade. Trevick and Mr Derby will have done their best to mould him, though, that's for certain, to make him in their own image."

"Never!" Kitty cried, getting up from the bed and pacing the length of the bedroom. Her eyes flashed, wild with grief and anger.

"I will never believe him so changed. I can believe they tried to, I can believe they've bullied him and threatened him and made him so miserable he's trapped and doesn't see a way out, but there *is* a way out, and we shall find it."

She stared at Harriet, rigid with fury, and then all the passion seemed to drain from her at once. Her shoulders slumped, her face crumpled, and she burst into tears.

***

Dawn. 21ˢᵗ August 1814, Holbrooke House, Sussex.

Luke stared out of the window as dawn lightened the horizon. Holbrooke House was a stunning location and in ordinary circumstances he would have been eager to explore it, especially the beautiful grounds, which beckoned him as the golden light of a summer's morning crept over the landscape.

Nothing about this morning was ordinary, however. She was here. Kitty Connolly, his own Kitten. She was here, and every bit as bold and beautiful as she'd always been.

He'd not slept. How could he, knowing she was there, so close to him after so many years apart?

It had stunned him when she'd appeared in St Clair's study. He'd been so shocked that it had been the most natural thing in the world to hold his arms out to her, to pull her to him and hold her tight. He'd wanted so badly to never let her go.

How strange it had been to hold her close, the lithe, slender girl he'd once had the right to call his own, now a woman. She was softer now, with curves that had not been there before. He realised now that in his mind she'd still been a girl, their love the innocent, perfect thing it had been then. She was a girl no longer. Even now he could feel the warmth of her body through her gown, feel the soft press of her breasts against his chest as she'd clung to him.

He'd not lived like a monk all these years. Mr Derby was not foolish enough to believe that a good idea—quite the reverse, in fact. He'd no doubt hoped Luke would forget his sweetheart in the experienced embrace of the most talented courtesans. He'd been encouraged to make hay with any number of willing young women put conveniently in his path. Loneliness and a young man's desires had driven him into their arms often enough, yet always it had felt like a betrayal. Always, he'd been left feeling wretched and dissatisfied. Any desire he'd felt for those women had been nothing, though... nothing to the grand sweep of emotion that had hit him when Kitty had thrown herself into his arms.

It was like holding up a match in the blaze of a forest fire.

He was still in shock, he thought, dazed and dazzled by the way she'd appeared like a spirit ... or a fairy princess. He smiled at the idea. Yes, his own tricksy fae, come to lead him into her fairy fort, and how he longed to follow her. His mind still couldn't take it in.

She was here. She was here, after all this time. It was too extraordinary.

Yet it made complete sense when you added the bear in evening dress to the equation. That was the kind of ridiculous thing that Kitty delighted in. Even now, as his chest burned and ached with a surfeit of emotion, his lips quirked at what she'd done.

He'd thought the first years after they'd been parted had been the most painful of his life. He had believed that he could die of it, from the misery and loneliness, but he'd been wrong. Life had carried on and he'd lived until the pain had become something he was used to. Each year it dulled a little, along with his senses.

Once Mr Derby had made his threats against her, on realising Luke's passion for Kitty was not waning as he'd hoped, Luke had died a little more each year, cared a little less what happened to him next.

Nothing—*nothing*—he'd experienced in those wretched years, compared to the pain he felt now.

He knew now that Kitty was no longer the pretty girl he'd loved with an innocent passion. The one thing that had comforted him as he'd matured was that their love had been pure, unsullied by anything. It had been as simple as the happiness of being together. It had been sweet and honest, and something he could remember with a poignant smile when he was an old man, when the pain of losing her would have long since left him.

Seeing her yesterday, all those old feelings had flared to life, harder and stronger, but now with that forest fire blaze of desire. All the breath had left him at once when he'd held her to him. He'd realised in an instant that the feelings he'd had for her had been a prelude, a gentle introduction to a magnum opus of such grandeur and power that it would sweep him up in its grasp and hold him enthralled until the day he died.

There would never be another in his heart and, if he couldn't have her, he was doomed to misery. Just as he'd been from the first time he'd laid eyes on her, he'd been spellbound. Bewitched.

She'd been magnificent.

Her dark eyes had flashed with fury and pride as she'd faced Mr Derby, her dark hair had tumbled from its pins and now all he could think of was sinking his fingers into those thick locks. He wanted to search out every pin until her hair fell over her shoulders. It would look like black silk falling over a white cotton pillow, her lovely skin blushing as he took her mouth and….

Oh, heaven help him.

The memory of Mr Derby's furious tirade in the hours after that meeting chased away any surge of desire. Trevick could ruin the Connolly family if he put his mind to it. He had invested heavily in the linen trade—though in such a way that no one could accuse him of dirtying his hands—and if he boycotted their mills and forced his colleagues to follow suit….

Luke put his head in his hands. He wished he was a different sort of man, a man of action, someone bold and brave and clever;

someone who deserved to win a woman like Kitty. A man like that would find a way… maybe he'd even murder bloody Derby and run away with the woman he loved.

It wasn't an unappealing idea, but even in the overwrought state Luke was in, murder was beyond him.

She'd made him feel as if he could be that man, once. Kitty had made him brave, had shown him the beauty of a world that had looked dark and dismal. When she'd looked at him, he'd felt he could conquer the world with her at his side, even though he'd been just a boy. Now, after so many years of being lectured at by Mr Derby and the earl, of having his every word and deed scrutinised, of being forced to avoid anything resembling a risk… he felt like a dried-up husk, old before his time. They had sucked the life from him, the joy in living taken away from him in their fear of his dying and leaving the Trevick name to crumble to dust with his bones.

Just those brief moments in her company, though….

He'd remembered what it was to live.

For the time he'd held her in his arms, he'd come alive, his heart beating again after so many years packed away and gathering dust, forced back to life with the power of a lightning strike.

Only now he wanted that feeble organ packed back away in the dust again, back in the dark and gloom he'd forced it into. He didn't want to feel it thudding in his chest, reminding him he was young yet and alive—so bloody alive—not when it beat for her and her alone, and she… she was everything he could not have.

Mr Derby had made no idle threat. Lady Frances' father, the Duke of Lymington, wanted this match every bit as much as the earl. If Luke disobeyed them and married against their wishes, Trevick would destroy the Connollys. Their mills would be boycotted, and the family bankrupted. Then there was Kitty, Derby would ruin her somehow, and take pleasure in it—not that she needed the help, with this outrageous scheme of hers. When all that was done, Lymington would ruin him.

Somehow, he had to make her change her mind. He had to see her and make her understand, except she would never understand. She wouldn't care about the dangers, she wouldn't even contemplate them. Kitty had always charged ahead, feet first. She jumped without looking, climbed without considering… she lived with her whole heart.

The only thing that would stop her was if she believed he didn't care, didn't want her.

Luke's heart—the wretched thing that he'd not allowed to feel or experience or so much as beat with anything resembling an emotion—now it swelled in his chest, pain and sorrow and hurt expanding to push at his ribs and crush the air from his lungs. He couldn't do it. He couldn't look at her and tell her she was wrong, that she meant nothing and that he didn't care.

Yet he must. He must for her sake, for his, and for those who depended on him.

It wouldn't be so bad, he told himself, the same as he'd told himself these past ten years. Trevick would be dead one day—soon, he hoped, as wicked as it was to think it. The man's health was failing, and Luke was certain it was little more than spite and ambition keeping him alive.

He'd live to see Luke married to the woman he'd picked out, perhaps long enough to see his heir born, he was that desperate for surety. Derby would follow him soon enough. The man's vile temper would provoke another attack, like the one earlier this year, and his heart would give out.

Then Luke would be Trevick, powerful enough to protect those he loved, but too late to protect Kitty. Still, once his heirs were born, he'd be free to do as he pleased, to live as he wanted, he could… he could….

He could watch Kitty marry another man and bear his children.

Oh, God.

***

Jasper made his way down to breakfast at some appalling hour of the morning he'd not seen in years. There were birds singing, for heaven's sake, and he'd startled his valet half to death by yelling for his attention, instead of waiting for the fellow to waken him with coffee like any sensible man of his rank.

He rarely rose much before noon. His lifestyle was comprised of late nights, overindulgence, and sleeping away as much of the day as he could. You could avoid a great deal of unpleasantness— not to mention *thinking*—by keeping such unsociable hours.

Last night's emotional scenes had left him all on edge, though, and he'd not drunk nearly enough to calm him, as he'd promised his mother to be on his best behaviour for this entire blasted party. So, sleep had eluded him.

All he could see when he'd closed his eyes was the devastation and determination in Kitty Connolly's expression. It was as though her heart had been carved from her chest and exposed to his gaze and he'd realised... he had one just like it.

What revolting drivel.

Despite experiencing a bout of nausea at such romantic twaddle, Jasper was aware of a surge of resentment towards Mr Baxter which was both inappropriate and inexplicable. Yet the object of the man's youthful passion still returned his feelings, and with such fierce and unalloyed joy that Jasper could not help the surge of jealousy that welled in his chest whenever he thought of it.

He wanted that. He wanted to be wanted like that, damn it.

Telling himself he was a blasted fool didn't seem to help a bit, and he felt irritable and befuddled. Coffee, he decided. Coffee and a brisk ride would set him to rights. With that in mind, he headed to the breakfast room and paused on the threshold as three sets of eyes looked up at him in surprise.

His mother, Miss Hunt, and Harriet were already at the table, and deep in conversation.

"Goodness, how long have we been here?" his mother said in alarm, swivelling her head to stare at the clock on the mantle. "Oh," she said with relief, and then frowned, turning back to Jasper. "Are you ill, darling?"

"No," he said, though why the question annoyed him he didn't know. Except that Harriet didn't need the idea that he was a useless good-for-nothing enforced any harder, even if it were true. "I am quite well, thank you."

"Well, I can't wonder at it if you couldn't sleep," his mother said, pouring herself a cup of tea. "Harriet has been telling me everything that occurred last night, and I was never more shocked. Poor Miss Connolly, and poor Mr Baxter."

Jasper snorted before he could think better of it.

"What?" his mother said, instantly on the alert. "I know you support Miss Connolly's claim, though I admit I was never more surprised to see you involve yourself in what is likely to be a shocking scandal, so it must be Mr Baxter you disapprove of. Why, dear? Do you know him?"

"No," Jasper said, reaching for the coffee and wishing he'd had the forethought to have a tray sent to his study.

"Then what is it? Have you taken him in dislike?" she pressed, frowning at him. "One does get a feeling sometimes, doesn't one? I know I do, which is quite unfair of me, but it's like with Mrs Richards," she said, reaching for a fresh roll and carefully tearing it in two. "I took one look at her and her purple turban and thought… *oh, dear, no.* Which is ridiculous, for why should a purple turban have anything to say to a person's character? Though," she added, with a thoughtful expression, "it *was* the most lethal shade, especially for a woman of a... certain age."

Jasper sighed and wished he could turn around and walk out again but he was stuck now.

"No, Mother. I do not know why you dislike Mrs Richards. I know nothing of Mr Baxter, nor did I get a *feeling* about him."

"Oh, but you did," his mother persisted, and Jasper gritted his teeth. Damn her, she acted like a frivolous and forgetful creature for the most part but, as he and his brother knew, she had the most unerring sixth sense where her sons were concerned. Drat it. "Otherwise you shouldn't have made that odd snorting noise."

"It does seem as though you have an opinion," Harriet said, a glimmer of amusement in her eyes.

Well, that was typical, she'd never miss an opportunity to make him uncomfortable or, better yet, make him look like an idiot—not that he didn't offer her numerous opportunities. The uneasy sensation that had kept him from sleep and left him so irritable resurfaced with a vengeance.

"Well, if you must have it, he seems like rather a wet blanket to me."

Harriet stared at him. The glass in her spectacles magnified her eyes a little and made him feel like she was peering at him under a magnifying glass... like some revolting insect she was studying.

"So, you didn't think he was trying to stop her from ruining herself, or that perhaps there were things to consider that he could not discuss with everyone present? That perhaps there were responsibilities and obligations, things we are not aware of?"

Despite promising himself that he would not let her rile him, would not let her make him look like an idiot, his temper got the better of him and he did both.

"No," he said, knowing he sounded terse and angry when she'd made some perfectly valid points which of course—*of course*—he'd known. "I thought he was quite obviously in love with her, and she with him, and yet he stood there like a great lummox instead of sweeping her into his arms and carrying her off to Gretna bloody Green," he said, ignoring his mother's tut of reproach for his language.

"Which—I collect—is what you would have done in the circumstances," Harriet said, her scorn apparent.

Jasper got to his feet. To hell with good manners, if he stayed here a moment longer, he'd say something he'd regret—like, for example, *Yes, it is bloody well what I'd do*—and stalking out of the door in high dudgeon.

He was all the way to the front door before he realised he'd done just that.

***

Matilda watched St Clair storm from the room with no little surprise. During her acquaintance with the earl, she'd never once seen him lose his temper with anyone. Harriet had accomplished it with ease. The earl was always urbane and charming, and exuded sophistication, yet around Harriet he got all prickly and put Matilda in mind of a small boy with his favourite girl—as likely to pull her hair as to be nice to her.

She would never have guessed he had such a romantic nature.

Harriet watched him go with an intent expression before giving a huff of laughter and returning to her breakfast. "There speaks a man with the confidence and weight of an earldom at his fingertips," she said under her breath, buttering a slice of bread with sharp angry motions. "He spends too much time drinking and carousing to be in any danger of falling in love, but I bet *he'd* never get himself into such a position or fall for someone when the circumstances were impossible—no matter how idiotic he is."

Matilda caught her eye and glared at her, reminding her that his mother was in their company. It was common knowledge that the countess doted on her sons and would hear no criticism of them.

Harriet went scarlet, turning her head as she caught sight of the dowager Countess St Clair's look of mild surprise.

"Oh," Harriet said, setting down her knife with a clatter. "I... I do beg your pardon," she said, looking utterly mortified. "I didn't... I mean.... Excuse me... I think I'd best check on Kitty."

Matilda watched as Harriet flew from the room, and heard Lady St Clair give a heavy sigh. She turned, meeting the woman's eyes.

Lady St Clair gave a rueful smile. "He's not at all the careless libertine he's made out to be," she said, reaching for her teacup. She held it in both hands, staring across the room to some place far out of sight. "I'm certain half of what he does and says is purely to get under her skin. He wants her attention, and he'll get it anyway he can."

Matilda's mouth dropped open, unsure of what to say in the face of such an admission.

"Oh, come now," said Lady St Clair. "We are old friends by now and you're no fool. It must be as clear to you as it is to me. He's in love with Harriet, has been for many years now, but the poor fool keeps messing it up, and he's clearly said or done something Harriet finds unforgiveable." Her eyes glittered and she blinked rapidly, giving a sad little laugh of frustration. "I wish his father was here. He'd know what to do... how to advise him."

Matilda reached out and took Lady St Clair's hand, squeezing her fingers. The older woman took a deep breath and composed herself. After the Marquess of Montagu had shredded Matilda's reputation, Lady St Clair had supported her. She had scotched the stories and called them nonsense, and made it very plain that Matilda was blameless. For that, Matilda regarded her with deep affection and gratitude, and it pained her to see the woman's sorrow.

"You know, when it became clear that Harriet would never come around, I did harbour hopes that you and he…." She laughed as she saw Matilda's look of astonishment. "Yes, well, I can see now that there's no spark there, though I can't help but think it might do you both a deal of good to pretend there was," she added with a sly smile.

"Oh, no," Matilda said, shaking her head. "No, no. There's no way I'm getting in the middle of a situation like that."

"No," Lady Clair said, the word spoken on a sigh of resignation. "I'm sure you're right. Well, never mind," she said, brisk all at once. "The problem most pressing is Mr Baxter and Miss Connolly. I can't help but think the two need a little time alone to… to see if they cannot decide on a way forward, whatever that might be."

"I agree," Matilda said, relieved to change the subject. St Clair was gorgeous and eligible but there was nothing between them other than friendship. In any case, it was out of the question when his heart was set on another woman. She returned her attention to the problem at hand.

"From what Harriet told me, Mr Derby is nothing but a bully," she said. "And it's impossible to think straight when there is such a dominant force in the room. At the very least, Mr Baxter should have time to explain his actions to Kitty, and to either change his mind or say goodbye. Then, even if it were not what she wanted to hear, she might come to terms with it."

Lady St Clair looked at her with approval. "You are a wise young woman," she said, giving Matilda such a penetrating look that she blushed. "The question is, how is such a thing to be achieved?"

"Well," Matilda said, smiling a little. "I do have an idea."

Chapter 6

Dearest Matilda,

I do hope that you and the other peculiar ladies are enjoying St Clair's house party. I should probably say that I wish I was there too, except it would be a dreadful lie! I miss you, of course, all of you, but life is too utterly blissful. Silas is such a darling and he and Dharani squabble constantly, like a couple of bad tempered cats. She's in heaven. Do write and tell me about everything you are doing, though, I don't want to miss a thing!

—Excerpt of a letter from Lady Aashini Cavendish to Miss Matilda Hunt.

21st August 1814, Holbrooke House, Sussex.

Luke made his way to the breakfast room with some trepidation. He wondered how many of the guests knew of the altercation last night, and if he would have to face Kitty and make polite conversation. He almost laughed then. Kitty ignoring the situation and making polite conversation was too farfetched. She'd never manage it. She couldn't dissemble to save her life. Her emotions were always raw and exposed in those flashing dark eyes, eyes that had spoken to his soul from the first moment he'd looked into them.

He allowed himself to remember, as he'd not allowed himself for many years. He remembered the years he'd spent with her as his only and best companion. They'd been inseparable. His mother had been a disinterested parent, caring little for her son's whereabouts unless it affected her own comfort. The few servants they kept were ill-paid and badly managed, and so he had unprecedented freedom.

Kitty's parents were lackadaisical too, though not from a lack of feeling. Her father was up to his neck in turning the family's fortunes around, totally focused on the building and running of his new mill. Kitty's mother was often away, spending months at a time with her younger sister, who had given birth to twins barely a year after having her second child and was on the verge of a nervous collapse. Kitty, who was a sunny and robust child, was judged well able to stand her absence.

She stood it very well indeed, spending every second of every day with Luke. In the summer they even spent nights together, though with hindsight Luke knew it had been an outrageous thing to do. He'd not known that then, though, and had been too young to consider anything approaching impropriety.

His throat closed as he remembered nights toasting bread at campfires and hours staring at the stars, making impossible plans for a future that had seemed full of hope and wonder. He remembered Kitty's slight frame hugging him close as she slept, her dark curls tickling his neck. Luke paused and took a shaky breath. If only he'd known then how special those times were, how magical… except he had known. He'd known from the start and he knew it still, and that was what made it so bloody unbearable.

To his relief, the breakfast room was quiet. His cousin Sybil was there, and a beautiful blonde woman whom he didn't know. Sybil introduced them at once, and the woman greeted him so warmly it was clear she couldn't know about last night's drama.

"Luke, this is Miss Matilda Hunt. Miss Hunt, my cousin, Mr Luke Baxter."

"Good morning, Mr Baxter, I am very pleased to meet you."

Luke did his best to appear delighted by the introduction and sat down, realising at once that he couldn't stomach a bite of food. He poured himself a coffee, more for something to do than with any intention of drinking it. His guts felt tied in a knot.

He'd barely sat down when another lady entered. Her age and the remarkable resemblance to her handsome son marked her out as Lady St Clair.

"Ah, Mr Baxter," she said, giving him a welcoming smile before sitting at the head of the table. "I was sorry to hear about the problems with your carriage. We missed you at dinner. Still, there is plenty of time now you are here."

Luke managed some kind of polite reply, though he couldn't have said what it was the minute he'd stopped speaking. It seemed to please Lady St Clair, though, and he relaxed a fraction, hoping they'd breakfast in peace now. A look passed between Lady St Clair and Miss Hunt then, and Luke got the distinct impression they'd been plotting something.

Nonsense, he told himself. Even if they had, it would be nothing to do with him. They didn't know him from Adam.

He allowed his thoughts to wander, returning inevitably to Kitty, and to how she'd looked in the moment she'd flung back the curtain. There had been such joy in her eyes. His heart clenched.

"Mr Baxter?"

Luke jolted, torn from his thoughts so fast he almost spilt his coffee.

"My lord," he said, coming to his feet at once. "Forgive me, I was wool gathering."

"Quite understandable," Lord St Clair replied with a rather taut smile. "I wonder if you might spare me a moment of your time?"

"Of course," Luke said at once, though he had a sinking feeling that he and his companions were about to be ejected—very politely—from the premises. "A pleasure."

Luke turned to excuse himself to the ladies just in time to see Lord St Clair direct a dark and accusing look at his mother. It was quickly gone, replaced by an affable smile.

"I thought perhaps we might go for a ride," St Clair said, striding away from him at quite a clip. "I find it clears the mind, and I think there are things we must discuss."

Luke's heart sank. He could only imagine what kind of unfeeling bounder the earl believed him to be. Yet he was glad the man had taken Kitty's side. Heaven knew someone had to. It had broken his heart to see her standing all alone, so brave and defiant, but then that was his Kitten.

They didn't speak again until the earl had selected a mount for him, and they clattered out of the cobbled yard and into the grounds of the magnificent estate. They rode hard for ten minutes or more, until the earl drew his horse to a halt on top of a rise that looked down upon the grand house.

"It's stunning," Luke said, with honest admiration.

St Clair nodded. "It is," he agreed, frowning a little. "Not that it's any of my doing. Generations of St Clair's before me must take the credit. I shall just hope not to ruin any of it. That will be my epitaph if all goes well," he said, the words bitter. "He didn't do much harm."

Luke opened and closed his mouth, a little taken aback.

The earl turned to him and laughed. "Forgive me," he said, the black mood falling away in an instant and the legendary charm the man was known for immediately becoming apparent. "I'm in a devilish mood this morning."

"I can hardly blame you after last night," Luke said, struggling to meet the man's eyes. "I can't tell you how sorry I am that you have been dragged into this... this—"

"There's no need for that," he said, his expression a little harder now. "What's done is done, but I will have the truth from you, sir. Mr Derby is not here now to curb your tongue and I hope that I'm not mistaken in believing you an honourable man? Miss Connolly seems to think so."

Luke felt an unwelcome surge of colour stain his cheeks, but he nodded. "It's the least I owe you," he said stiffly. It was mortifying to know that the earl thought him weak and spineless and in awe of Mr Derby, but what else should the man believe?

"Good," said the earl. "Then tell me this: are you in love with her still?"

The question caught him off guard. Even after his demand for the truth, Luke had not imagined the man would strike directly at the tender core of the problem. Men, especially those of St Clair's rank, avoided any discussion of subjects where feelings and emotions were required, and spoke instead of practicalities, of reasons and motivation.

It was perhaps this unexpected frankness that explained his unvarnished answer.

"Yes," Luke said simply. "With all my heart."

The earl's expression didn't soften. If anything, it grew harder.

"And yet you stood by and said nothing, did nothing, while she fought for you?"

The starkness of the accusation stole Luke's breath, as did the fury in the man's eyes. All at once, Luke was furious too, even as he drowned under the weight of guilt, under the knowledge that the earl had said nothing that wasn't true. Yet, how dare this man who knew naught of him, of his circumstances, stand back and judge him

For perhaps the first time in his life, Luke appreciated the earl's training, the time spent learning how to act like a nobleman, like those gilded souls who—just as the man before him—had been born to power rather than having to pretend that it came naturally.

"You don't know a damn thing about it," Luke replied, startling himself with the cold anger of his reply.

"Then explain it," St Clair countered, equally cool, unperturbed at such an answer.

Luke stared at him, for a moment wanting nothing more than to drag the man from his horse and break his perfect bloody nose. Damn him and his smug superiority. It didn't last. Luke's anger never did. Instead, he laughed, though it was a harsh sound.

"Kitty knew last night," he said wearily. "She can read me like a book. She always could. I've never been able to keep a secret from her. Never wanted to," he added with a hopeless smile.

"Blackmail," St Clair said, his expression grim.

Luke nodded, relieved not to have to put it into words himself. "I can't have her. No matter how much I want to. Trevick will ruin her and her family, and Lymington… he'll ruin me."

To his surprise St Clair swore, low and harsh, a vicious rant of angry words. His horse sidled and fretted, uneasy at his master's displeasure. The earl quieted the beast with ease before turning back to him. Luke felt sure he'd come to some decision.

"Come along, then," he said tersely. "You'd best follow me."

Luke did as he was asked, though he did not understand where they were going. He didn't have to wait long to find out.

The Countess St Clair, Miss Hunt, and another young woman he did not recognise were waiting a few minutes farther on, beside a small thicket of trees.

Not that Luke saw them; the only thing he could see was Kitty.

She sat upon a neat bay mare, dressed in a pale blue riding habit that hugged her figure and made his mouth grow dry. Her dark curls clustered about her face beneath a stylish little hat with an ostrich feather dyed to match the gown. Her dark eyes were huge in her face, which was pale and wan, and made him want to cut out his heart for the pain he'd caused her.

"I take it I have your word as a gentleman you'll keep your hands to yourself if we allow you some privacy?" St Clair asked, giving Luke a hard look.

Luke's heart leapt. Privacy? With Kitty?

"Yes," he said at once. "Word of honour. I... I can't thank you enough."

St Clair nodded and looked like he would turn away, but he didn't. When he spoke, he seemed almost reluctant to, as though he knew he ought not. "Don't mess it up," he said, somewhat tersely, though there was sympathy in his eyes. "Love doesn't come along when and where you want it to. It's worth fighting for."

"I know," Luke replied, a little startled by the man's passionate words.

He also knew that if he loved Kitty, he'd have no choice but to walk away from her.

"There's a summerhouse just over the hill there," the earl said, gesturing away from the trees. "We'll be waiting there for you both. If you walk into the thicket here, you'll find a path which leads to a small lake. It's private and no one will disturb you. It's... a romantic spot," he added with a smile. "Good luck, Baxter."

"Thank you. You've been very kind." Luke nodded and forced a smile he wasn't feeling, but he was grateful to the earl and wanted him to know it. He needed the chance to explain things to Kitty and... to tell her goodbye.

"Don't waste the opportunity," St Clair muttered, before turning his horse and riding away, up the hill. His mother and the two other ladies followed him, leaving Kitty alone.

Luke swallowed and wished he had the slightest clue of what to say. He dismounted and tied his horse in the shade before moving towards her.

Kitty said nothing, just watching him as he drew closer. He reached up, putting his hands on her tiny waist and helping her down. How many times had he done this in Ireland? How many times had he taken the little intimacy for granted and believed it would always be his right to do so?

She slid to the ground, her hands coming to his shoulders, her eyes fixed on his. They were so close, close enough to kiss, and the familiar scent of her stole over him.

In an instant, the present fell away and they were back in Ireland. He remembered picnics and adventures, laughter and a world free of cares. There were rainy days hiding in camps and telling each other wild stories, endless sunny days fishing in the river and trips to the sea, to the Giant's Causeway.

He remembered Kitty telling him the story of the terrific fight that legend told had created them, spoken in her lilting accent. Any words were instantly more romantic and intriguing when she spoke them, but the story of the giant Fionn mac Cumhaill, who was challenged to fight the Scottish giant Benandonner, had caught his boyish imagination. That day was one of those perfect remembrances that remained forever in his mind, where the sun had shone and happiness had filled him to the brim. It gilded the memory with joy and glowed all the brighter as he knew such things were lost to him.

Kitty stared up at him, everything she felt clearly expressed in her eyes, just as he remembered.

"Oh, Kitten," he said, his own heart breaking.

She moved towards him, to embrace him and he moved back at once. He'd given St Clair his word as a gentleman and if she touched him… if she touched him, he would be lost.

"We don't have long," he said, trying to smile at her, and holding out his arm for her to take. "I understand there is a lake within. Shall we go and discover it?"

She took his arm, still saying nothing, though the hurt in her expression at his rejection clawed at his soul.

St Clair had been right, though he could curse the man for it now he saw the danger. It was romantic here. The sun glinted on a small lake bounded by large rocks. On one side of the lake was a clearing, alive with wildflowers and the drowsy hum of insects. Butterflies flew from bloom to bloom, their colours catching the sun as they moved to the meadow, flying beneath the dappled shade of the trees on all sides, drawn by the lure of the sweetness beyond.

It was the perfect setting for lovers: beautiful and intimate, set away from prying eyes. Luke wanted to weep.

There was no point in putting off the inevitable, though. He must tell her his feelings had changed; he must at least try to make her believe it. If she was angry with him, it would be all the better. She could forget him then, and move on.

His every instinct rebelled against it, but….

"I was never more surprised to see you last night," he said, trying to smile but too afraid to meet her eyes. "Though that bear ought to have given me a clue," he added, able to smile honestly for a moment, for that was nothing but the truth. "I'm sorry that I didn't write to you and explain after I'd left. Everything happened so fast. I was swept up in this exciting new world and I suppose I believed you would have forgotten about me just as I—"

"Stop it," she said, the words full of impatience and scorn.

Luke hesitated, knowing he had to persist, but she stopped and turned to face him, pressing her finger to his lips.

"You never could lie," she said, those fierce eyes holding his, stripping away the man he'd forced himself to become, and finding the lonely boy he'd once been. "Don't try to tell me everything has changed, and that you have forgotten me, for it's obvious that isn't true."

"Kitty," he began, his heart thudding with fear and longing and so many damned emotions he couldn't begin to make sense of the tangle in his chest. "Kitty," he said again, except this time her name caught in his throat and it sounded like a plea.

She threw herself at him then, the movement so unexpected that he stumbled and fell to the ground, taking her with him. Why he'd not expected this, he didn't know; it was just like her to do something so bloody rash.

It was like sun burning through glass to have her in his arms. He'd locked everything away for so long. All his emotions, every hope or dream he'd ever had he'd forced into the dark to gather dust, and then Kitty came along with the intensity of a heatwave. She put a magnifying glass to all the dusty corners and the light shone through it and set fire to the dried up emotions. Those fires were blazing now, hot and urgent.

The weight of her was upon him, her lithe body in his arms, her hands at his face as she lowered her head and pressed her mouth to his.

He almost cried out in alarm in the moment before their lips touched, knowing he'd be done for, that any will to fight, to stay away from her, would be devoured by the flames. There wasn't time, wasn't thought enough in his head before it was too late. Her lips were every bit as soft and sweet as he remembered, but they were so much more.

The last time he'd kissed her it had been a gentle press of lips, an innocent, childish exploration of the feelings they'd shared, but now… now he was a boy no longer and knew what else there was, knew all the ways he could show her his devotion. He wanted them all.

"Oh God," he said, unsure whether he was praying for divine intervention or not.

Perhaps if he was struck by lightning the pain of his love and desire would burn away and leave him be.

There was no lightning strike to save him, though, and he turned her onto her back, teasing her mouth open with his tongue. She opened at once, eager for him as her hands sank into his hair. The first tentative touch of her tongue against his rocked him to his soul, and he knew he was lost.

She tasted like home, like where he was always meant to be. Yet, as familiar as it was, the newness of discovering her was intoxicating. She was always a contradiction, his kitten with the heart of a lioness; she was both the calm and the storm. She was his safe harbour and the power of an unpredictable sea. Luke groaned as she moved beneath him, shifting to accommodate his weight, pressing against him with the desire to get closer, closer than this, as close as two people could get.

So much for bloody honour.

"Kitten," he gasped, trying to move away as the promise he'd made St Clair brought him back to his senses. "Kitty, stop, we must—"

But Kitty didn't seem to agree and drew his mouth back to hers. She'd enslaved him with the first touch of her lips and now he could deny her nothing.

"You're mine," she whispered against his mouth. "You've always been mine."

"Yes," he said, the word torn from his heart. "Always."

She laughed then, the sound so joyous that he didn't know whether to laugh with her or to cry, for there was nothing to be happy about.

"Kitty," he said, trying again, holding her face between his hands, but then he got lost all over again, drowning in those dark eyes, in the astonishment of having her close. "I've missed you," he said, helpless to give her anything but what was in his heart. "I've missed you so... so terribly."

It was all him this time. His mouth fell upon hers, and it wasn't sweet or gentle but desperate. He gathered her close, his hands hard upon her, pulling her sweet body into his. He grasped the back of her knee, fighting through acres of material until he could bring it around his hip and press his aching cock between her legs. Even with far too much fabric between them, the sensation was a shock to his senses. Kitty gasped and arched against him as desire addled his brain and sent anything resembling a coherent thought tumbling into an abyss.

He felt dazed and overwhelmed, as if he'd been hit in the head. All he could think of was how to get closer to her, how to get all this bloody material out of his way and make her his in the only way left to them... except it wasn't the only way.

Somehow, the thought found its way through the fog of desire, and spoke of gold rings, a church, and the sanctity of marriage, and he forced himself to get control.

"No," he rasped, wanting to sob with the unfairness of it. "No, Kitty, we can't. It... it isn't right."

"Of course it's right," she whispered, tugging at his cravat, pulling it free and pressing kisses to his neck. "We married before God, we love each other... what could be righter?"

"No!" he said, pushing away from her, horrified at himself, at what he'd done... almost done. "No, Kitty, we are not married, not really. You know we aren't, not in any way that counts."

Luke scurried away, crablike, frantic to put some space between them. He sat on the ground, breathless and hot and aching, and wanting nothing more than to return to her, but it was impossible. For a moment he just sat there, his breath coming in great ragged gasps, his head in his hands. God forgive him. God help him. Someone help him, *please.*

It was a long moment before he could bear to look at her again. She lay in the grass still, and Luke had to lean forward again to see her. Kitty stared at him. Her hat had fallen among the grasses some distance away, the jaunty feather moving in the breeze and looking like some exotic wildflower, just like her.

Sweet mercy, but she was lovely.

Her black curls fell upon the plants they'd crushed in their passionate embrace, the honeyed scent of a summer meadow rising about her. He watched as her chest rose and fell too fast, saw the flush at her cheeks, the swollen red of her lips, and the dark, dark fathomless depths of her eyes. She looked like something wild and barely tamed, something that would capture him and lead him into danger and he knew it was true, but by God how he wanted it.

"Didn't you mean it, when you read the marriage ceremony?" she asked, her voice low, that achingly familiar accent wrapping itself around his heart. "You promised to have and to hold."

"I know," he said, the words fraught with frustration and misery. "And I meant it, of course I did, but it wasn't legal, Kitty. You know it, I know it, so don't be obtuse. We are not married, so stop pretending that we are. We aren't. We never were and… and we never will be."

There, he'd said it.

She watched him in silence, and he wished she'd get angry. If she would only get angry, he might stand a chance.

It was always like this, though. The tranquillity surrounding and inhabiting her was deceptive. She could be so still, the most peaceful person to lie beside for hours on end, staring at the clouds

84

and just enjoying the experience of being alive. Then there would be a sudden burst of energy, the devilish glitter in her eyes that would lead them both into mischief.

Good God, perhaps Trevick had done them both a favour in taking him away. They'd had so much freedom, never a chaperone in sight, and they'd taken every advantage. As children they'd come to no harm, but with feelings like this between them…. With her passionate nature and him being a green fool, he'd likely have got her with child before she'd reached sixteen. The thought was sobering.

"I'm to be the Earl of Trevick," he said, infusing the words with every ounce of pride he could muster, trying to make her believe it—trying to believe it himself. She must understand that he'd changed. She must see what he'd been turned into. He wasn't the foolish boy who'd tumbled into love with her and followed wherever she led. He couldn't be. Luke would be Trevick. "I have a responsibility to the title, to the family. It's my duty to marry well and—"

"Do you love me?"

The question barged into his well-ordered explanation, destroying his concentration.

"What?" he asked, though he'd heard her well enough and was only buying time.

If he told her the truth, she'd never give up, she'd destroy them both.

She sat up and pushed an errant curl from her eyes. "I asked if you loved me."

Her gaze on his was intent, unblinking.

"We're too old for fairy tales, Kitty," he said, forcing the words to sound cold and hard.

"Ah," she said, sounding thoughtful. "You've forgotten the tale of Fionn mac Cumhaill."

"Of course not," he said, impatient now, though he ought not have answered at all. "Though he was hardly a fairy."

Luke cursed himself for the observation. *Just stick to the facts, you damn fool.*

She smiled at him. "So, you will marry a duke's daughter and be the Earl of Trevick and live happily ever after. That sounds more like a fairy story to me. One that you tell yourself because you're too afraid to break the rules."

There was no malice in her words, yet they struck at his heart. They both knew she was the bold one. She was the one who'd taken his hand and dragged him inside an abandoned house, rumoured to be haunted. She was the one who'd taken him searching for pirate treasure, hunting in caves along the shoreline and going home soaked to the skin, when the tide had come in too fast and nearly drowned them both.

He felt that same terror now, as if the sea was rushing at his heels, tugging at his feet and tearing the shingle from under him, forcing him to his knees. Except it wasn't the sea, it was her, with her dark eyes so deep with love and wanting that he wanted to drown. He prayed for it, though he'd take her down with him.

"That's not fair," he said, hearing pain roughen the words and make them jagged with anger.

"No," she said, soft and sorrowful. "I don't suppose it is."

They stared at each other for a long moment.

"Well, then," she said, sitting up and arranging her skirts like the young lady she was, as if the wild creature who'd taken him to the ground and would have taken him inside her was another girl altogether. "Don't you think you'd better tell me the truth? All of it."

Chapter 7

*I'm so glad to hear you are happy, though it is
no surprise whatsoever. It was clear to the
world that Lord Cavendish was mad in love
with you, you lucky thing.*

*There is much to tell you too, but I will answer
your questions first. Yes, I am well and
Holbrooke House exceptionally grand. Yes, Mr
Burton is here, and yes, he is paying me marked
attention. He wishes to court me. I've not given
him a definite answer as yet, but I have
promised to do so before we leave here.*

*He is handsome and kind and interesting, and
I'm going to try to fall in love with him. I like
him already, so perhaps fondness should be my
first goal. Can you fall into fondness with a
man?*

**—Excerpt of a letter from Miss Matilda Hunt
to Lady Aashini Cavendish.**

**The Summerhouse. 21ˢᵗ August 1814, Holbrooke House,
Sussex.**

Jasper turned his back on the summerhouse and stared down
the sweeping expanse of green to the lake beyond. Unlike the lake
he'd taken Luke to, this one was an open vista with views for miles
around. No privacy here. The summerhouse was private enough,
though, if you had a mind to use it.

It was a strange little building, an odd combination of simplicity and excess. An unpretentious rectangle, it was plain on three sides with full height arched windows in the front façade. On the top, however, it was all Gothic frills and spikes, and looked like someone had gone insane with the sugar icing on a bride cake. There were doors within the middle window that opened into a single room. Inside was a fireplace, oddments of furniture scattered about, musty smelling blankets, a tinderbox, and candles. He'd camped down here with Henry often as a boy, and they'd used it as their own personal kingdom, dragging Harriet with them more often than not. Henry always protested, not wanting his sister in tow, but back then Harry hadn't seemed to mind Jasper's rough and tumble treatment of her. He thought she'd rather enjoyed it.

It was all a muddle in his mind now. He'd spent too long analysing his memories, trying to pinpoint when it had all gone wrong. It had been here, though, in the privacy of the summerhouse. He just didn't know why.

"Shouldn't we go and—"

"No," Jasper said, sending Harriet an impatient look.

She worried for her friend, he understood that, but they needed time. Whether that time would bring a decision to run away together, or for Baxter to force Kitty to accept the situation, he didn't know. He wished they'd run; it would give him hope to see them overcome the odds, or to face them together head on. They loved each other, though. Whatever happened, that desire to be together was between them.

His chances were rather less favourable.

He could *hear* Harriet thinking, he was certain of it. His terse answer had annoyed her, naturally, but he couldn't help himself. Whenever she was near, he existed in a constant state of frustration, as snappy and short-tempered as a small, belligerent dog, nipping at her heels. He was always aware of her, aware of her moods, of where she was in relation to him, in the same way he didn't need to look at the sun to know it was there.

"If anyone finds out, if Mr Derby—"

"No one will find out," Jasper said, wishing he didn't sound so damned impatient. "Mr Baxter went out for a ride with me, and my mother escorted Kitty with you and Miss Hunt. We went in different directions and did not meet. Unless the man will accuse the Dowager Countess of St Clair of being a liar, he's got no option but to accept it."

"He'll still figure it out," Harriet said, as dogged as always.

"Good!" Jasper muttered. "He's blackmailing Baxter, keeping him from marrying the woman he loves. What right has he to do so?"

Harriet returned an expression with which he was all too familiar. It said *you're an idiot* without her having to go to the trouble of saying it aloud.

"Men of your rank don't marry for love and you know it," she said, every bit as terse as he'd been. "Whilst my heart breaks for Kitty, I think it is wrong to give her false hope. It will only cause her more pain, not to mention dragging her and Mr Baxter through a public court case...." She shuddered and closed her eyes. "To have everyone talking about them, knowing the details of their affair... it would be hideous, unbearable."

Though he knew he was doing himself no favours, Jasper could not fight the helpless swell of emotion that rose in his chest. "Have you no notion of love, Harry?" he said, knowing she'd hate him for using the name forbidden to him, the name he'd been allowed to speak once upon a time. "If you gave your heart to someone, wouldn't you fight for them, wouldn't you do *anything*, anything at all, to be with them?"

There was nothing but cool contempt in her eyes when she looked back at him.

"I could never love a man who would act without thought for the consequences, who could be so thoughtless as to ignore who else might be hurt by his actions. We are not animals, to act upon our desires as and when they arise with no thought of feeling. Otherwise a man could lead unsuspecting women astray, falling in and out of love at a moment's notice and casting aside dozens of lovers, leaving them abandoned by the wayside as he went." Her gaze never wavered as she stared at him. "I suppose some men *do* live this way," she added. "Acting as though they are in love in one moment, and casting it aside like an unfashionable coat the next."

He felt the words rather than heard them, felt each one like a small knife paring away another slice of his heart, though he didn't understand why she attacked him so. Was this her opinion of him? Oh, he knew his reputation, of course he did, though it seemed blown out of all proportion to him. Yes, he'd had lovers, plenty of them, but he'd never pretended love, never felt it for any but one woman. He never dallied with anyone he thought might read more into his attention than a mutually agreeable way to spend some time, and he never ended an affair on bad terms with any of the women he took to bed. This was because he never lied, and he chose his lovers with care.

"Harry," he said, knowing at once there was too much emotion in the way he spoke her name. "I've never—"

Harriet turned her back on him before he could say another word and walked away. He moved to follow her, but she called out to his mother, who was speaking to Miss Hunt by the edge of the lake. "Lady St Clair, do show Matilda the summerhouse. It's such a sweet little building, and it will be cool out of the sun."

"Harriet!" he said again, willing her to turn back to him, but she kept on walking.

***

As she'd known he would—*eventually*—Luke told her everything.

He told it in a brief and concise manner, with no embellishments. He said nothing of his feelings on discovering Mr Derby waiting for him at his home the day they had taken him from her. After having spent the day with Kitty and arranging to meet her early the next day, he'd been stuffed in a carriage with no explanation and taken away. He said nothing of his loneliness and confusion at being torn from the place he'd made home and the girl he'd loved, and subjected to an endless procession of tutors and daily lectures from Mr Derby or the earl himself. He went from days of fishing and exploring, and skinny-dipping in the freezing river to being taught everything from the history of the Trevick family to Greek and Latin, to etiquette and the proper comportment of a future earl.

For a boy who'd already been torn from a school with dozens of friends—a place where he'd been happy—and dumped next in the middle of nowhere with not so much as a nanny in sight, it was yet another bewildering change in circumstances.

Not that Luke said as much. There were no disclosures about his isolation, about his mother's indifference to his misery, but he didn't need to give such revelations. Kitty could hear it in what he didn't say, in the brittle, emotionless way he told the story, and she understood. If he allowed emotion to enter his words, they would both flounder in sorrow and no sensible decisions would be made.

Yet her heart broke for him, for his courage, and for his desire to protect her from the tyranny of the Trevick family.

Kitty had always disliked Luke's mother, though as children she'd appreciated the woman's selfishness as it allowed Luke so much freedom. Yet she was in raptures over Luke's inevitable elevation to peerage. The wretched woman cared nothing for her son's happiness, only her own consequence, and Kitty knew well the woman would make him suffer if he turned his back on everything the earl was offering him.

"You did try to contact me, didn't you?" she said, once he stopped speaking.

He was staring at her, his expression resigned. She knew he was waiting for her to agree that it was hopeless, that they could never fight an earl and a duke.

Darling Luke, always so naïve.

"Of course I did," he said with a huff of laughter. "I bribed the staff to post them, but they had been primed. Mr Derby rewarded them for every letter they handed in. The earl's pockets were rather deeper than mine, sadly. Once I realised, I tried to run away. I tried countless times, but I never got far. I was too well chaperoned."

He paused, staring down at his hands, which were occupied with shredding an oxeye daisy, one petal at a time.

"I was desperate to get back to you," he said, and this time she could hear all that he hadn't said before. "I missed you so badly and it hurt, Kitty, like they'd cut you from my chest with a knife. I couldn't sleep for fear that you'd think I'd abandoned you. I couldn't bear to think it."

Kitty smiled at him, blinking back tears. "I never thought that, eejit," she said, though her voice was soft and teasing, the way she'd used to speak to him when he'd said something she thought silly. "But no one could tell me where you'd gone. It was like fairies had spirited you away, or like I'd dreamt you. I begged my father to make enquiries, but all he could discover was that you'd left Ireland, not where or in whose company. For all I knew, you'd gone to America."

She knew he wouldn't move, wouldn't close the gap between them, so she did, crawling on hands and knees, careless of her skirts and grass stains, until she sat beside him.

"I thought I'd die of misery," she said, taking his hand and lacing their fingers together, as they'd done countless times before. "But I knew I'd find you. I knew we'd be together again, and the knowledge kept the worst of the pain at bay, else I'd not have endured it."

"Kitty," he said, and there was anguish and frustration in the sound of her name.

"Luke," she said. "I won't give you up. I won't let them win. They're bullies, that's all, and you have to stand up to bullies, or they'll rule you forever."

He covered his eyes with his hand, and she reached out, pulling it away, forcing him to look at her. She knelt in front of him, leaning forward, her voice barely more than a whisper.

"I won't let them steal our future, not if you still want it too. Tell me you don't love me anymore, Luke, tell me it was just a childish idyll and that you're a man now and I'm not what you want. If you can do that, then I'll walk away and not look back, I swear it."

Even though she knew the answer, her heart gave a sharp, terrified series of thuds, until she saw his eyes darken and his gaze fall to her mouth.

"I can't," he said, his desperation audible. "You know, I can't. Damn it, Kitty!"

Before she could say anything, he reached for her, pulling her into his arms, his hand grasping her hair, holding her in place and kissing her as if his life would end if he didn't touch his mouth to hers. It was such a kiss, fierce and angry and passionate and filled with despair and love, such love. She'd hadn't known such kisses existed. The innocent boy who'd pressed his mouth to hers with gentle affection was gone and she wondered who'd taught him those skills, only to push the sudden spear of jealousy away. He'd been alone, when she'd had family and friends; she should thank any woman who'd given him some respite from his isolation.

As fast as he'd reached for her, he let her go, cursing and stumbling to his feet, moving away from her.

"Do you want to see your parents bankrupted?" he demanded, fury in his voice. "You'd have us all in the gutter, would you?"

Kitty rolled her eyes at him. "Stop being so melodramatic and think a moment, Luke," she said, remembering this about him. His sudden descents into pessimism and despair were no doubt the result of living with his mother's histrionics for too long. "You *will be* Trevick. Perhaps not today, perhaps not for a year or five, but you will be, and no one can stop that. You told me yourself the earl's health is deteriorating, and that Derby suffers from a heart condition. They won't live forever, but you'll be married to a woman you care nothing for, and for the rest of your days if you don't act. Soon enough, you'll be wealthy and powerful and well able to right any wrongs. Would you forget all your responsibilities if we married? Would you leave all the female relatives who rely on you to starve?"

"Of course not," he said indignantly, but she saw first flicker of hope in his eyes. She smiled at him, hoping her words were as reassuring to him as they were to her.

"Besides which, you should not write off my family so easily. My Da's a cunning one where there's money to be made, and once he knows the prize is an English earl, he'll think the risk worth it. He'd have not stirred himself to help me marry *Mr* Baxter, or to drag our family through the courts if you opposed me, but if the future Earl of Trevick wants *me* for his wife? Good heavens! Just try to stop him. No, the threat the earl poses is a real one, but not insurmountable. It's her who's the danger. Lady Frances, not the duke. I think he'll only go after you if she's humiliated, but the engagement has not yet been announced. It *must not* be announced, Luke. She'll still want revenge, perhaps... but there are other noblemen and she'll not be lacking, with her beauty and wealth. We both know she doesn't love you; she just wants your title." Kitty paused. "Or one like it."

There was silence for a moment, but only a moment.

"How do you do that?" Luke demanded. He ran a hand through his hair, paced around in a circle and then stared at her in wonder, utterly bewildered. "How do you *always* do that? You make the impossible seem a perfectly ordinary problem, a meagre mole hill instead of Ben bloody Nevis. This is how you get me. *This* is how I was persuaded into haunted houses, and up mountains, and into caves in search of treasure."

Kitty shrugged. "You can't blame me if you've no imagination."

"No imagination?" he exclaimed, outraged. "Oh, I have imagination aplenty, love. I imagined us falling to our deaths, murdered by cutthroats, and drowned, and that last one was very nearly a reality, thank you very much."

"Oh, you're not still bleating about getting a bit wet?" she said, purely for the delight of seeing his indignation. It had been so long since they'd bickered like this, fighting for the fun of it, for the delight of making up again afterwards.

He glared at her. "*A bit wet?*"

The words were almost a growl and she delighted in the low timbre of his voice. It sent shivers chasing over her. Such a man he was now, a fine big, strong man. Desire simmered beneath her skin, but she just sighed dramatically and shook her head. "Now you're just repeating everything I say."

"We nearly drowned," he flung back at her, throwing up his hands.

"I love you," she said, smiling at him like a fool. Her heart was alight with it, with the joy of being with him despite everything they faced, with the knowledge that he loved her still and they would find a way to be together.

Whatever he might have said next was forgotten as a crooked smile caught at his lips, tugging it up at one corner. His red hair gleamed in the sun, and his eyes had never been so blue.

"I love you," he repeated obediently, knowing at once the game she played, as they'd done it a hundred times before. "I do, Kitten," he added, a little rueful now. "But we must go back now, before they come looking for us. St Clair and his mother have done us a great kindness in helping us meet like this; we cannot exploit their generosity."

Kitty huffed and pulled a face but got to her feet and walked towards him. "Why must you always be so nice and polite?"

"You're nice," he said, bumping her shoulder.

"No, I'm not," she said, laughing. "You of all people know it. I've a horrid temper, and I won't be thwarted once I've set my heart on something." She sent him a warning glance.

"I remember," he said, giving her a grin that sent her tumbling back in time a full ten years.

There was the Luke she'd fallen for, right there, with his freckles and his cheeky smile and his willingness to follow wherever she led. He would save her without a murmur of resentment, he'd get her down from trees and from the clutches of an angry sea when she misjudged and got them into trouble, but he never failed to follow on the next adventure, no matter how reckless she was.

She took his hand, marvelling at how much bigger it was now, how strong and capable. Her own appeared slight and delicate in comparison. Kitty lifted it to her mouth, pressing her lips to the back where the skin was bronzed from the sun, his freckles darker patches against the gold.

He stared at her, a look on his face that made something inside her quiver with anticipation. She'd always thought him handsome, but she'd never experienced appreciation of his looks with the heat of desire burning under her skin. It burned now, though, hot and needy.

"For God's sake, don't look at me like that," he said, the words somewhere between a curse and a tremor of laughter. "I promised St Clair I'd be a gentleman, word of honour. Don't make me a cad, I beg you."

She laughed but took pity on him and walked on. She knew there was time now, time for desire and stolen kisses. While a part of her wanted to rush headlong into the future and make up for all the lost years, she knew the value of waiting to get what you wanted. How sweet it was.

When she'd heard his voice and known in her heart that it was him, she'd been overwhelmed with joy. So, kisses and stolen touches would tease and torment them in the most delicious way, for now. They were her weapons against his fears and doubts, a reminder of what he fought for and why, and something Lady Frances did not have, for all her beauty, and her father's wealth and power.

Kitty's father had once told her that you must use the weapons at hand to your best advantage when in business, and not regret those you did not have. It had been a rare moment when he'd spoken to her of his work and his battle to succeed, and she'd not understood at the time.

Now... she thought perhaps she did.

Chapter 8

I hate him. I hate him. I hate him.

—Excerpt of an entry from Miss Harriet Stanhope, to her diary.

21st August 1814, Holbrooke House, Sussex.

Jasper regarded the young man riding beside him. Mr Baxter was deep in thought, which was hardly surprising.

"You're going to fight for her," he said, finding a grin curve over his mouth.

Baxter turned his head, as though he'd forgotten Jasper was there at all, but his lips quirked in the semblance of a smile.

"Yes, she's leading me off a cliff and into a raging sea, and not for the first time," he said, amusement and something like pride in the words.

"Good for her," Jasper said with approval.

He'd been certain Miss Connolly had persuaded Baxter; the satisfied look in her dark eyes had told him that much. If perhaps he'd gloated a little and sent Harriet a smug look of triumph, he could hardly be blamed for it.

Mr Baxter regarded him more closely then, curiosity in his eyes. "Why do you care?" he asked, and Jasper felt the weight of his scrutiny. "Because you do, don't you? You stood up for Kitty when no one else in their right mind would do so."

"Are you suggesting I'm touched in the upper works?" Jasper remarked, with the nonchalant lift of one eyebrow. He'd rather not consider his own motivation too much, let alone discuss it.

Baxter chuckled. "No more than I, but…." His blue eyes were suddenly intent. "Yes," he said, letting out a breath. "Of course. It's the same manner of madness that's afflicted us both. I can see it now."

"Whatever do you mean?" Jasper tried to make the question cool and aloof, a warning not to probe any deeper, but it didn't come out right and Baxter's face softened with something that looked horribly like compassion. Jasper looked away but felt the sudden urge to unburden himself, to confess his darkest secret—the one he'd hidden for so damn long—for what felt like an eternity.

"Is she unsuitable?" Baxter asked, his voice full of sympathy.

Jasper gave up as a bark of laughter escaped him. "No, not in the least. Indeed, it would make both of our families very happy."

"Then why—?"

"She hates me," Jasper said, the words escaping him before he could think about the wisdom of baring his soul to a stranger, when he'd never told his closest friend.

Then again, as his best friend was her brother, that wasn't terribly surprising.

"Why?"

"I don't know."

"Did she always hate you?"

Jasper allowed himself to remember a day when Harriet hadn't hated him, a day when she'd seemed to like him very well, before everything changed.

"No. Not always. For a brief time, I thought… I hoped, perhaps…." He shook his head in irritation. "Never mind."

99

Mr Baxter frowned at this and they rode on in silence for a moment. "Have you never asked her what changed?"

Jasper rolled his eyes with impatience. "Of course I asked her, but I never could get her to explain, and now… now it all feels…."

Too late. It felt too late, as if any chance he'd ever had was slipping through his hands like the finest grains of sand. No matter how tightly he held on, they kept falling away.

"I thought I'd lost Kitty," Baxter said. "Trevick and Derby between them threatened me with all the dire things they would do, until I was so bloody terrified I couldn't think. I believed it was hopeless, but she never gave up. She's so much braver than I am. So bloody reckless," he added with a laugh. "I hadn't lost her at all. She was there all the time, waiting for me."

"Because you both feel the same," Jasper said, wishing he'd kept his mouth shut. Talking about it only made it worse, made him see how impossible it was. "I can't make Ha— *her* love me. I can't even make her like me, when the mere sight of me makes her furious."

Baxter frowned at him. "The sight of you?"

Jasper nodded. "I need only enter a room and her face darkens. She can appear perfectly content and laughing, and the moment I appear it all goes away. It's a talent of sorts, I suppose," he said bitterly.

The young man had fallen silent and was studying Jasper, and to his infuriation he felt a tinge of colour stain his cheeks. What the devil had he been thinking, confessing such a thing to a complete stranger?

"That's a strong reaction," Baxter said, disregarding Jasper's embarrassment. "So, she's certainly not indifferent to you. Do you know what happened? Was there an incident, something that precipitated her change of heart?"

Jasper's jaw tightened. He wished he could take his confession back. It was pathetic enough, this mooning for years on end after a woman who didn't like him, let alone want him, but at least no one had known about it.

"I'm sorry, I ought not pry," Baxter said, sounding apologetic. "None of my business."

"I kissed her." He blurted the words out as if he was a ten-year-old admitting to stealing cake.

"Oh." Baxter looked wretchedly uncomfortable now too, not that Jasper could blame him. Good God, how mortifying. "And... she was unwilling?"

"No!" Jasper exclaimed, stung by the suggestion. "Not in the least, but... but the next time I saw her...."

Everything had changed. She'd been stiff and formal, as cold as ice, and he'd never been able to comprehend why, or what he'd done. What had happened between the time he'd left her—all smiles and blushes—and seeing her again? She would never tell him, never give him an explanation, and Jasper was all at sea.

So many times, he'd wished he'd never kissed her. It might be easier, not knowing what perfection tasted like.

"Perhaps you need someone to intercede on your behalf," Baxter suggested. "Someone to discover the truth. I take it... I mean, is she here, now?"

Jasper frowned. It was bad enough having Baxter know of his unrequited passion for a woman who thought him an imbecile, let alone being around the object of his devotion *and* having an audience.

"Yes," he said, though the reply was unwilling.

"Does Kitty know her?"

Jasper turned to look at Baxter who smiled at him. "There's no better person to have in your corner than Kitty Connolly, my lord. I can vouch for that."

That was true enough. Jasper had seen and admired her bravery, her spirit and strength and, above all, her loyalty and determination. Not to mention, she thought well of him for having supported her. If anyone could get to the truth, maybe even put in a good word....

He was clutching at straws and he knew it, but he didn't care. He would have to marry soon and do his duty by the title. An heir and a spare was ingrained into every nobleman as the very least expected of him. Spending the rest of his days with anyone but her, though, the girl who knew and loved Holbrooke just as well as he did....

"I need to know who it is," Baxter said, giving him a reassuring smile. "I can promise you neither of us will tell another soul. Though... I'd lay money Kitty already knows. She's very observant."

Jasper scoffed at that. "Impossible," he said as the idea that he'd given himself away made heat crawl up the back of his neck.

He hesitated, drawing his horse to a halt and taking a moment to look down at the vast building that lay before them, the same view they had admired earlier. Jasper wouldn't give it into the hands of a woman who wouldn't care for it and love it like Harry did. He couldn't give his heart to someone else either, not when it had been hers for so long.

"Your word of honour, Mr Baxter, you'll speak to no one else but Miss Connolly and you'll ensure that she holds her tongue? I have no wish to become a subject of pity or ridicule."

"My word, Lord St Clair, though I should be honoured if you'd call me Luke."

He nodded, giving a smile which felt strained, as if it was fraying about the edges. "Jasper," he said, by way of reply. "Very well. I… I would appreciate it if Miss Connolly could make some… *discreet* enquiries on my behalf."

"I'm sure she'd be happy to. I believe she holds you in some esteem, but who is the lady she needs to speak to?"

"Harriet," Jasper said, his heart pounding in his chest as he admitted his feelings for her aloud for the first time in his life. "Miss Harriet Stanhope."

***

Speaking to Jasper about the complications of his own affairs had temporarily diverted Luke's mind from the horror of what he was facing. Sadly, it didn't last.

"Where the bloody hell have you been?"

Luke stiffened as Mr Derby's voice rang out across the drawing room of the elegant suite St Clair had assigned them for the duration of their stay. Determined to conduct himself with all the self-assurance and pride that Trevick and his brother had drilled into him over the past years, Luke turned but did not show any reaction to the man's angry demand.

"Lord St Clair requested my company for the morning, sir," he said, with icy civility. "As I am to be his guest for the next two weeks, I felt compelled to accept."

Derby snorted. "Don't give me the high and mighty Trevick act, boy. I'm the one who taught you it. You must think I was born yesterday. I take it the subject never touched on your pretty little hoyden, that grasping bog-born nobody who would make herself a countess if you're fool enough to forget what you owe."

For a moment, Luke almost forgot himself entirely and hit the man. As it was, his fists clenched and he felt the colour rise over his skin as his anger burned. Yet a decade of hiding his feelings—of allowing no one to know what he was truly thinking—rose to the fore.

"Mr Derby," he said, hearing the measured tone of his words as though listening to a stranger, as inside he was screaming with fury. "Whatever you think of me or my behaviour is a topic you are welcome to comment upon. Miss Connolly and your opinions of her, however, are a subject you touch upon at your peril. She is a lady, and someone I care for deeply. If you hurt her, I will retaliate."

Luke saw the surprise in Derby's eyes. He'd long since given up fighting the man. A boy of thirteen had no power again a full-grown man who had the mind of Machiavelli and few scruples in manipulating a child. Mr Derby alternated between bullying, instilling guilt and—on a couple of truly disturbing occasions—a frank *man-to-man* attitude where he adopted the role of jovial uncle.

As an adult, Luke had learned to agree with Mr Derby and rarely contradict him, no matter his own thoughts or feelings. Until he inherited the title, he had little more power than he'd had as a boy. Trevick paid for everything; Luke had no independent finances, and a gentleman could not work. Not that he cared a damn about the rules, but they had moulded him into the shape of a gentleman and he was now ill-qualified for anything else.

He was trapped.

Of course, he could have just walked away from it all. He'd been tempted many, many times. Once, he'd even threatened to do it. The results played in his mind now.

His mother had... not taken it well.

Hysteria was too mild a word for the tempest that had raged in the hours after he uttered those fateful words. She'd thrown things, smashing whatever came to hand, and then flown at him, hitting him and scratching like a cat, all the while shrieking an incomprehensible litany of abuse. The gist of it had been clear enough, though. Luke was an unnatural child, an ungrateful wretch who wanted to see his mother die of shame.

They had called a doctor to sedate her. Luke had been forced to hold her down for the doctor to accomplish the job. Mr Derby had said nothing. He hadn't needed to. His expression was eloquent enough. *See?* it said, *this is what happens when you disobey the rules.*

Luke knew a similar scene would greet him when his mother learned of his refusal to wed Lady Frances in favour of an Irish nobody whose family's revival in fortune came from trade.

Now, however, there was a difference. Now, the taste of his beloved's kisses were still upon his lips. He remembered the feel of her in his arms, and the promise of all there was to come if he faced the appalling prospect like a man and did not flinch, did not turn from his purpose.

"You dare oppose me?" Derby said, his words dangerously quiet. "You dare to threaten *me*?"

"I do, sir," Luke replied. "I have done everything you asked of me. I have always done so. For a very long time, I believed there was no other choice. You took from me the only thing I ever wanted, and I believed I had lost it forever. I made myself believe it, I think, because otherwise my life became unendurable. I was a boy then, though, and I believed myself alone in the world. I am a boy no longer, and Miss Connolly never forsook me. This grasping woman you speak of knew nothing of the earldom, as no one else knew, and yet she waited for me. She loves me still, and I love her. I *will* marry her."

A taut silence filled the room. It was oppressive, like the heaviness in the sky and the still, thick air that precedes a thunderstorm.

"How touching," Derby said, his sneer of derision making Luke itch again to hit him, to sink his fist into that supercilious expression and break his damn nose. He watched as Derby took a breath, composing himself before adding, "But there's no need to be so hasty."

Luke felt no reassurance at the softening of the man's features, by the easier tone of voice, rather his disquiet grew.

"You are thinking like the boy I pulled from the mire, Luke, not the man I raised you up to be. You are no longer a nobody, a mere *Mr* Baxter, you are the heir to an earldom. Once Trevick and I are out of your way, at least," he added with a wry smile.

Luke did not smile at the man's tawdry joke. That Derby was itching to be Trevick did not escape him, but his devotion to furthering the line was no less evangelical than the present earl's. It would change nothing for Luke. The brothers were of one mind as to his future, and that of the family's fortunes.

"I do not mean to keep your Miss Connolly from you," he said, the rather confiding man-about-town note sliding into his voice with ease. "If she is so dreadfully important to your happiness, then we must all accept that. All men have their vices and she is clearly yours. So, marry Lady Frances and take the chit as your mistress. We can arrange something discreet and satis—"

He didn't get to finish the sentence as Luke knocked him down.

Luke watched the big man—who had terrified him so as a boy—sprawl on the floor at his feet. He didn't look quite so large or as intimidating as he used to. Luke hadn't even hit him that hard, aware that he was much younger and fitter than the man before him.

"I am sorry, sir," Luke said stiffly, a little appalled by what he'd done, though he didn't regret it in the slightest. It had felt bloody marvellous. "But I warned you."

Mr Derby stared up at him, the shock in his eyes chilling to something less savoury. "That... was a mistake."

"Perhaps," Luke said, amazed by how calm he sounded, how in control. Trevick *had* done him some good with all those lessons. "But I am a gentleman, and I must keep my word. Miss Connolly was correct. I asked her to marry me and, what's more, I meant it. It's a promise I intend to keep."

He leant down and offered Mr Derby his hand, but the man refused him, getting up by himself. Though he was approaching seventy and his heart was not as strong as he'd wish, the man looked a great deal younger. Luke wondered if he should feel guilty for hitting the fellow. After all, whatever he looked like, he was not a young man, but after so many years of holding back it had felt so good.

"You're willing to destroy her, then, this woman whom you love so deeply?" Derby said, a glitter in his eyes that boded ill.

"You will leave her out of this," Luke said, a sick feeling of trepidation rising in his throat.

"Don't be a fool," he said, shaking his head. "This is something you have never grasped, boy: the difference between being born to lead and merely shown how. You will do as we wish, no matter what we must do to achieve the outcome we desire. If you persist in this idiotic desire to have your cake and eat it, Miss Connolly will pay the price."

Luke's hands clenched, and he wished he'd hit the man harder now, wished he'd broken his damn nose or brought on the fatal heart attack the doctors had warned him of.

"I'll not let you hurt her," he said, his heart racing now as the enormity of what he was facing came home to him.

It had seemed so simple when he was with Kitty, so easy; but it wasn't easy, and it wasn't simple, and he was putting her at risk.

Mr Derby laughed and returned a pitying look. "I tell you what I'll do, Luke," he said, with the condescension of a man to a boy he feels lacking in wits and experience. "I'll give you a week to enjoy your Miss Connolly. Bed her if you must, and perhaps you'll come to your senses when that particular itch has been scratched. After that, you will come to heel, or I will make you."

"She is a lady, sir," Luke said, wishing he could forget himself and propriety, and the fact he was a guest in this house, and throw Mr Derby out the bloody window and have done with it. "She is not a lightskirt. I will not have you speak of her with such disrespect."

"As you wish," Derby said, taking a moment to adjust his cravat, his tone indicating that the subject bored him. "You have my terms, which are more than generous. I suggest you heed them, or your beloved *Kitten* will pay the price."

Chapter 9

Dear Matilda,

We shall be with you at Holbrooke House on the 22nd. I'm so excited! Though I must say I've had a fine time with Ruth. We have been staying at her father's new property which he has extensively modernised. It's wonderfully vulgar which puts poor Ruth all on her dignity though I've assured her I don't care a fig. I do care that it's comfortable and delightful to live in though, as I didn't hesitate to explain.

How many eligible men will be there? Please, tell me there will be droves. I have had a letter from Morven demanding to know when I will return and accept Gordon Anderson's proposal. I must do something drastic to escape such a dire fate. Give me hope, dearest Tilda. Tell the handsome and wealthy young men that they <u>must not</u> fall in love before I get there!

—Excerpt of a letter from Miss Bonnie Campbell to Miss Matilda Hunt.

22nd August 1814, Holbrooke House, Sussex.

"Good morning, Miss Hunt, Miss Stanhope. How lovely you both look this morning."

Matilda turned and smiled as Mr Burton approached them.

He looked very fine, dressed for riding, his tight-fitting breeches a thing of beauty as they hugged his powerful thighs. A man in his prime. Matilda knew he ought to make her heart pitter-patter with anticipation and felt a surge of irritation with herself when it failed to do so. The stupid thing must be defective.

Burton grinned at her and Harriet, an almost boyish expression of enthusiasm on his suntanned features. His hands were large and rough, she noted as he toyed with the crop he held, those of a man who worked for a living, not the elegant hands of an aristocrat. That ought to be a point in his favour too. Though she knew most of her ilk would strongly disagree, Matilda felt a great deal of respect for a man who had accomplished success through hard work and determination. Her brother was such a man.

"You are looking forward to our outing, Mr Burton?" she asked, addressing him with warmth and seeing at once the pleasure in his eyes.

"I am, and why ever not? Our unpredictable English weather is as perfect as one could hope for, a ruined castle the most romantic of settings, and all to be enjoyed with such pleasant company. A man would be churlish indeed to be anything other than delighted."

"I'm sure you are right," Matilda replied, finding his enthusiasm infectious.

St Clair had arranged an outing to Bodiam Castle. It lay about an hour and a half south east of Holbrooke House and some of the guests had elected to ride, while others would travel by carriage. A picnic awaited them at their destination along with a tour of the ruins, before the journey home.

"You are not riding, though, I take it?" Mr Burton asked, his disappointment evident.

Matilda shook her head. "I'm afraid I'm a very poor horsewoman and would only hold everyone back. I am resigned to travelling in the luxurious comfort of the Countess St Clair's barouche, with fortitude however, I assure you."

"How good you are, Miss Hunt," he said. He meant it as an amusing remark, she knew, but it was said with rather too much intent, the look in his eyes too warm, and Matilda blushed and looked away.

She was relieved when the rather breathtaking sight of Lord St Clair and his brother joining the assembled group on horseback drew their attention.

They were both glorious specimens of male beauty, and cast even Mr Burton's good looks into the shade. Beside St Clair, his younger brother was made in a similar but not identical mould. St Clair's hair was a touch more golden, his shoulders just a little broader, his features the perfection of a Greek god.

Jerome Cadogan's countenance held a mischievous glint, everything about him suggesting he'd take off at any moment, probably to cause a riot. His features were not *marred* by a broken nose exactly, for though he could no longer match his brother's classical beauty, it added a certain roguish charm which was very appealing. It was also a prime example of why he caused St Clair so many sleepless nights.

The story of the broken nose was well known and one of many. It was attributed to a fight over a Cyprian, for which St Clair was forced to fork out a staggering sum to the injured party in damages. Sadly, Jerome had begun the fight in his opponent's home, which contained several very breakable artworks. Needless to say, they did not survive the encounter.

"Where is everyone?" Jerome demanded, his eagerness to be off palpable. "What slugabeds we have staying."

"Jerry, please do not insult our guests," St Clair murmured. "Or our mother, as she also seems to be absent."

"Well, of course she is," Jerome replied with a sigh. "Mama has never been on time for anything in her life."

"Mr Burton," St Clair said, gaining the man's attention. "Norton over there has your mount, if you would care to avail yourself."

"Thank you, my lord," Mr Burton said, winking at Matilda in a shockingly familiar manner before striding off to take his horse from the groom.

"He's making no bones about his interest in you, is he?" Harriet said in her ear, her tone suggesting she did not entirely approve his overconfident manner. Matilda experienced a surge of unease herself, though she supposed it was normal for a man to flirt openly with the woman he hoped to marry. Still, the sense of unease lingered.

She met Harriet's eyes and returned a crooked grin. "It would appear not."

"Oh, look, there's Kitty."

Matilda turned in the direction Harriet indicated and smiled as Kitty gave a jaunty wave. She was on horseback once more and looked perfectly at ease, her smile wide and confident. The girl had been incandescent with happiness last night. Her beloved Luke had been restored to her, and he loved her still. It was like a delightful fairy story, except that Matilda didn't believe in fairy stories, and her nerves crackled with apprehension.

Mr Luke Baxter appeared a few moments later with his cousin, Miss Sybil Derby, riding beside him. She was a rather insipid young woman, with whom Matilda had struggled to converse. Not that she was unpleasant, more like she lived in terror of venturing an opinion on anything, even whether to accept a cup of tea. With a father like Mr Derby, it didn't seem terribly surprising. Mr Derby was notable by his absence.

At last, the remaining guests appeared: Lady Frances and Mrs Drake, Prue and her husband, the Duke of Bedwin, and the Countess St Clair.

Lady St Clair had invited Matilda, Harriet, and Prue to travel with her in her new barouche, an elegant open carriage of which she was clearly very proud. The duke had elected to ride, which left Lady Frances and her companion to travel in their own carriage.

As far as Matilda was concerned, the journey to Bodiam was delightful. It was a warm day, bright with only a few delicate puffs of cloud to hinder the wide blue sky. The slightest breeze rustled the lace at the edges of her parasol and kept the heat from becoming uncomfortable and her cheeks too heated.

Mr Burton, rode beside her for much of the journey and made no secret of his admiration. Prue, who sat beside her, adopted an enquiring look on one of the brief occasions he rode ahead with the other men.

"Have you given him leave to court you, Matilda?" she asked in an undertone, though Lady St Clair and Harriet were deep in conversation.

"No," Matilda said, smiling a little. "But he's very insistent," she added, frowning for a moment before pasting a smile to her face and adding. "Not to mention handsome, charming, kind, and wealthy, so I probably will." She laughed and tried to sound happy about it, about marrying a man she wasn't in love with.

"That seems like a shopping list of pros to convince yourself of something you know is a bad idea."

Matilda frowned, surprised despite her own concerns about the match. "A bad idea?" she echoed. "How strange that you would say so, when everyone else is suggesting he's perfect for me."

Prue shook her head and reached to take her hand. "I did not say he wasn't perfect for you," she said, with a brief squeeze of her fingers. "I do not know him other than by reputation though I know Robert respects him. I do know you, though, Matilda, and I can see you lack anything approaching enthusiasm for the idea."

Matilda could feel Prue's gaze upon her face as she stared out over the countryside in bewilderment. She had believed she'd made every effort to *appear* vivacious and enthusiastic to Mr Burton's suit. Had she appeared unenthusiastic?

"You forget that I've seen you flirt with men before, Tilda, dear," Prue said, an unmistakable edge of laughter to her words. "You're very good at it, even when it's rather half-hearted and just done for fun, but I see none of that spark between you and Mr Burton. Strange, I admit, for he is everything you have said he is, but I cannot see that you find his presence in any way compelling, or discover any attraction on your side, or am I wrong?"

A surge of something close to impatience made Matilda feel at once prickly and defensive. "Just because I feel no immediate surge of desire for the man is no reason to suppose he would make a poor husband. Quite the opposite. How many women fall into bad marriages by following their baser instincts, I wonder?"

"No doubt," Prue said with an easy smile. "I'm not suggesting that is a path you should follow either, only... don't settle, darling. A good marriage... it's worth waiting for."

Matilda hesitated as panic rose in her chest, the idea of spending her life alone, childless, a spectre that only ever grew larger on the horizon. "And what if I wait too long and lose any chance I have?"

Prue nodded and patted her hand. "I know, love, just think carefully about it. There's no going back if you get it wrong."

Matilda laughed at that. "Good heavens, Prue, you actually believe I think of anything else?"

Prue gave a sympathetic sigh and changed the subject. "Tell me about Kitty and Mr Baxter."

***

They paused for a while at the pretty twelfth century church of St Giles in the village of Bodiam to take a walk about the gravestones. High above the castle, upon a wooded hillside, the church overlooked the River Rother. The main attraction here was a medieval brass of a knight in armour, thought to be one of the de Bodeham family to whom the castle owed its name.

From here, the party walked to the impressive moated castle that dominated the tiny village. St Clair's servants had come on ahead and, by the time they reached the castle, they had prepared a lavish picnic for them in the blessed shade of the castle walls.

"Goodness, isn't that Bonnie?" Matilda exclaimed moments after they'd settled themselves down to the mouth-watering feast provided for them by their generous hosts.

Prue and Harriet looked up, both squinting into the sun and laughing as they saw one woman begin waving like a lunatic and jumping up and down.

"Yes, it is," Matilda said, answering her own question with an amused smile.

Bonnie and Ruth were greeted with pleasure and excitement from the Peculiar Ladies, who hurried to introduce them to everyone they'd yet to meet before settling them down among in their company.

"We reached Holbrooke House far earlier than we expected," Ruth explained, "and the dowager countess was kind enough to leave instructions as to your plans for the day, on the off chance we arrived in good time, so… here we are!"

"How wonderful it is to see you all," Bonnie said, filling her plate with a generous helping of everything and beaming at everyone. "Though I hope this isn't the sum total of eligible men, or the single ladies must fight over St Clair and his brother, Mr Baxter, and Mr Burton."

"Bonnie!" Matilda scolded, trying not to laugh. "Do keep your voice down."

"Yes, and your hands to yourself," Kitty added with a smug grin. "Mr Baxter is mine. We're engaged."

Bonnie gaped, and at once demanded details which naturally took up the rest of the picnic as the romance of the story captured everyone's attention.

Matilda forced back her concerns, not wanting to dampen Kitty's obvious happiness, nor Mr Baxter's, come to that, who had moved to join them once it became clear he was the topic of discussion.

"Are you telling dreadful stories, Kitten?" he asked, his voice so full of affection that Matilda told herself she was worrying over nothing.

The romance Kitty had told her about was every bit as strong and true as she had believed, that much was obvious to all. Yet, when the conversation lulled and he thought no one was observing him, she saw tension in Mr Baxter's eyes, and she knew she had not been wrong. There was still trouble ahead.

***

Once everyone had eaten, the company dispersed to investigate the ruins. Kitty was not about to listen to a boring lecture on the history of the castle, not when there were far more interesting things to do.

"Luke!"

Luke turned as she called his name, a low whisper designed to reach only him.

From her secluded position, Kitty grinned as he searched for her. His eyes lit up as he found her, peering around a doorway and gesturing for him to hurry up and come. With amusement, she watched him check no one was looking before he moved. Luke would do nothing as foolish as not look thoroughly before he leapt, as he had always scolded Kitty for doing.

As he joined her, she grasped his hand and tugged him through what had once been the kitchen and on to the south tower, before climbing the narrow, winding staircase. Most of the other guests had joined a tour provided by a local historian, but Kitty would not lose an opportunity to be alone with Luke. Halfway up the tower she turned, discovering she was eye-to-eye with him as she stood on the step above.

She threw her arms about his neck and Luke grasped her waist, though his expression was reproachful.

"Kitty, you devil, we can't—"

She cut the words off by the expedient move of pressing her mouth to his.

He groaned and pulled her closer, his arms closing around her, and Kitty sighed as the sound of his pleasure shivered through her. He was here, not a dream, not a figment of her imagination as she'd sometimes feared he was. She'd longed for him for so long and so badly that her memories of him had taken on a gilded, dreamlike quality that had begun to frighten her, but this was no dream.

Luke was here and flesh and blood and the absolute perfection of being in his arms made every moment of those years of longing and loneliness worth the pain.

He kissed her with slow, decadent kisses, allowing her the time to follow his lead, to learn this new intimacy that their childish affections had known nothing about. Kitty was all too eager to learn, this and everything else they had missed. They had wasted so much time thanks to a wicked old man and his ambitions.

She sank her hands into the thick warmth of his hair, pressing herself closer, aware of the hardness of his body, of the way his hands wandered, the rapid beat of his heart.

"Kitten," he said, a warning to the words she had no intention of heeding. This was Luke, the boy she'd known like her own soul and she trusted him implicitly. "Kitty, we must stop ..."

She illustrated what she thought of that idea by sliding her hands under his waistcoat, enthralled by the heat of his skin through the fine linen of his shirt, by the shape and feel of a man beneath her fingertips. There was so much more of him now than she remembered, and every inch hard and warm and so tempting.

He made a sound of desperation and kissed her harder, his hand at the back of her neck as he held her still. Kitty was giddy with it, with the delight of this new pleasure, and just like everything else in life she ran at it full tilt, heedless of the consequences. She forgot her ideas about the value of waiting, of anticipation, too caught up in the moment, in him.

His hands roved over her and she gasped as he found her breast, the heat of his hand burning through the fine muslin of her summer gown. He cupped the soft flesh and then squeezed.

"Oh," she said, pulling away to stare at him, wide-eyed with surprise. "Do it again," she said, wonder in her voice.

"Hell's bells, Kitty, you'll be the death of me," he said, sounding torn between laughter and despair. Nonetheless, he did as she asked, with both hands occupied this time as he pressed kisses down her neck.

Kitty sighed and smiled, covering his hands with hers and seeking his mouth. A few more moments passed with the delicious feel of his hands on her, and increasingly heated kisses.

"No," he said, the word wrenched from him as he took a step back. He ran a hand through his hair, disordering the heavy red locks in a most delightful way. Kitty thought his hand didn't look entirely steady, which was reassuring as her knees had turned to blancmange. "No," he said again. "Stop. Enough, Kitty. We must go back before we're missed. This was a dreadful idea."

Kitty pouted a little but knew better than to tease him, besides which she knew he was right. "Oh, very well. If we must."

"We must," he said, his tone stern and commanding.

She paused, a little shocked, staring at him.

"That's an odd look," he remarked, taking a moment to straighten his cravat and smooth his tousled hair.

"I didn't know you for a moment," she said, blinking at him. "You sounded... rather lordly." She laughed a little, shaking her head. "There's so much about you that's changed, and yet you're the same, too, it's... a little disconcerting sometimes."

"Yes," he agreed dryly. "I know just what you mean."

He took her hand and she followed him back down the stairs, admiring as they passed the narrow windows the sun glinting on his red hair, with shades of copper, gold, and auburn. "You sounded like St Clair when he's being all stiff and formal," she said, realising that was why it had struck her as being so foreign. "Like a man used to being obeyed."

Luke gave a dismissive snort. "Well, it doesn't come from experience, I can assure you. Between Trevick and Mr Derby, I'm nothing more than a chess piece, a lowly pawn manoeuvred back and forth as they see fit."

Kitty tugged him to a halt at the bottom of the stairs and waited for him to turn to her. "What happened last night with Mr Derby? I wish you'd tell me. I know you're afraid for me. Please, don't be. I can face anything as long as I have you. I promise you it's true."

His face darkened and she knew he'd been hiding his concerns, not wanting to spoil the day, perhaps, but hiding from problems never made them go away.

"Luke," she pressed when he didn't answer.

He sighed and leaned back against the stone wall. They could hear the soft drone of the guide, his voice echoing around the ancient walls he spoke about. These walls had seen wars and intrigue, fights to the death, courage and cowardice... what significance could their little romance have in the face of such history?

Kitty wasn't certain if that was a reassuring thought or not.

"He's given me a week," Luke said, his expression grim. "The fool thinks I can overcome my feelings for you in that time and go on to marry Lady Frances."

"I see," Kitty said, sounding calm and composed, whilst in her mind's eyes she conjured up half a dozen fitting punishments for the vile man. "No doubt he thinks you should take me to bed and get me out of your mind that way?"

"Kitten!" Luke said, and she couldn't help but smile at his shock.

She'd always enjoyed startling him, saying something outrageous and making him blush. Not that he blushed now, though she didn't doubt she'd struck close to the mark. Derby viewed her as less than a lady and believed she didn't need to be treated with the respect he might afford others. Though, if she were honest, she doubted he respected much besides the title he coveted so much.

"He suggested I take you as my mistress," he admitted, and he did blush at that, though she could see it was anger making his colour rise rather than embarrassment. "So I knocked him down."

Kitty stared at him, torn between fury at Derby's insolence and delight that Luke had hit him in her defence.

"Oh," she said, feeling the strangest rush of desire at imagining Luke thumping the despicable man and knocking him to the ground.

"No," Luke said, wagging his finger at her and taking a step back, interpreting the look in her eyes with perfect accuracy. "No, Kitty, behave...."

She bit her lip and moved towards him.

Luke hurried away and was laughing when they turned the corner back into the vast, echoing kitchen area and almost ploughed into Lady Frances.

"Oh," he said, all his good humour vanished in an instant. "I beg your pardon."

Lady Frances looked cool and beautiful today in a soft green muslin gown. Her companion, Mrs Drake, stood a little behind her, her expression unreadable. Lady Frances gave Kitty a dismissive glance before turning back to Luke.

"Luke, dearest, I appreciate men like to behave badly with women of a... certain class, but do try to stop short of making a fool of yourself. Papa won't like it."

Luke stiffened and Kitty moved closer, sliding her hand into his. She'd known they ought not be alone together, but only now did she realise how foolish she'd been. No doubt Lady Frances would delight in tattling about this to everyone, and Kitty's reputation would be shredded. Not that there was much doubt of that happening, after her revelations the night Luke had arrived, but she was going to hell at quite a rate now.

"Lady Frances?"

Both Luke and Kitty turned as Matilda's voice sounded behind them.

"I hope you are not implying that Mr Baxter would be so lost to propriety as to seek Kitty's company alone?" she said, an edge to her voice not entirely directed at Lady Frances. "I assure you, myself and Miss Stanhope have been here the whole time, so everything is quite as it ought to be." Kitty could have hugged Matilda. She must have followed them in for this express purpose and was staring at Lady Frances, her gaze icy. Harriet stood beside her, avoiding everyone's eye. No doubt she was furious at being involved in such a scene.

Kitty resigned herself to the inevitable scolding.

"I'm not sure that *you* are an appropriate companion, Miss Hunt," Lady Frances returned, and Kitty winced.

"You take that back—" she began, furious on Matilda's behalf, but Tilda shot her such a fierce look that she clamped her mouth shut.

"Quite so, Lady Frances," Matilda said, with a placid smile. "But Miss Stanhope here is above reproach as is Lord St Clair, who has not yet descended the tower. Shall I fetch him for you, and you can interrogate him too?"

Lady Frances stared back at Matilda with obvious hostility. "That will not be necessary. Come, Mrs Drake, let us continue our walk."

"Wait."

The two women paused as Luke addressed them and he hesitated before looking to Matilda and Harriet. Understanding, they withdrew a little. He glanced at Kitty too, but she wasn't going anywhere, and he sighed as he understood it was hopeless to remonstrate.

"Lady Frances," Luke said. "I must apologise for any difficulty that has arisen over these past days, but you know as well as I do that Trevick and your father alone have pushed for our marriage. I have made no formal offer and I do not intend to. This is no reflection on you, I assure you. We have met only three times, spent little more than an hour in each other's company, and I do not believe you have formed any strong attachment, any more than I have."

Lady Frances wore a less than encouraging expression, but Luke ploughed on.

"I love Miss Connolly," he said, and Kitty heard the defiance in the statement, knew just how much trouble she would cause him, and her heart clenched. "I have loved her for many years, and whilst I would have done my duty when I believed her lost to me, I cannot marry another when my heart is engaged. Surely you can understand—"

"You're a fool, Mr Baxter," Lady Frances said with obvious impatience. "This is about power and money, Trevick and Lymington, two ancient houses that will only grow stronger by alliance. There is a great deal at stake here. What has love to do with it?"

Luke said nothing and Kitty knew he understood what she meant all too well, that this idea had been drummed into him since Mr Derby had taken him away. She could see the guilt in his eyes, but she also knew such an idea would repulse him. There wasn't an avaricious bone in Luke's body.

"Do you not care to fall in love, Lady Frances?" Kitty asked, unable to stop herself though she knew she ought to keep quiet. Keeping quiet when appropriate was not her forte.

Lady Frances didn't even look at her, but kept her attention on Luke. "I don't care whether or not you love her. I am a sensible woman, one raised to wed a powerful man. I am not some silly child with romantic notions. I have no desire to interfere with your life or your mistresses. I believe Mr Derby has suggested as much."

Kitty felt Luke stiffen, tension singing through him.

"That is quite enough, Lady Frances," he said, and Kitty heard again the rigid, haughty man she'd glimpsed for a moment earlier, the man whose hand she held. "I'll not have you insult the woman I intend to wed. She is a lady, her family likely older and more distinguished than either Trevick or Lymington, despite their change in circumstances, and she has done nothing but remain steadfast in her affection for me. I don't believe there is anything more to say, so I will bid you a good afternoon."

Lady Frances stared at him for a moment longer, before turning and sweeping from the room with all the majesty of a queen.

There was a tense silence.

"Kitty Connolly, I could wring your neck."

Kitty turned and gave Matilda a sheepish smile, at which Tilda looked singularly unimpressed.

"You'd best hope St Clair is still outside the castle walking with his mother," Harriet added, exasperated. "*And* well out of sight, or we're all in the basket."

"Sorry, Tilda," she said, avoiding Harriet's incredulous gaze, and steeling herself for a lecture.

Chapter 10

Dear Lucia,

How I miss you, my dear friend. I feel like the mother hen you once compared me to… and all my chicks are determined to get eaten by foxes!
—Excerpt of a letter from Miss Matilda Hunt to Lady Aashini Cavendish.

22nd August 1814, Bodiam Castle, Sussex.

"There must be something we can do to help, Jasper."

Jasper glanced down at his mother who had taken his arm and insisted he accompany her for a walk.

"Help?" he repeated, though he was aware of what she was talking about.

His mother had a romantic streak a mile wild. She was more than tender-hearted, and he and Jerome had been dreadfully spoiled as children. She was an adoring parent who indulged her sons and blithely ignored their faults. As a result, they both adored her equally, but Jasper was aware that her generous nature could sometimes cloud her judgement.

"Don't be obtuse, darling," she scolded. "Miss Connolly and Mr Baxter." She sighed, holding her hand over her heart. "Such a romantic story, don't you think? Imagine falling in love as children and still feeling the same way years later."

Jasper felt her gaze on him and fought a blush. He cleared his throat and made a noncommittal sound she could take how she wished.

"Well, I have done what I can," he said, moving the conversation on. "And have consequently made enemies of Trevick and Mr Derby."

"Oh, Derby," his mother said with a scowl. "Odious man. Do you know, he tried to get me alone on a balcony when I was sixteen?"

Jasper ground to a halt and stared at her in outrage. "He did *what*?"

His mother gave a delighted trill of laughter and a misty look entered her eyes. "It was at a family party, too. I wasn't even *out*! I had only just met your father and fallen head over ears for him. He saved me, of course and gave Mr Derby *such* a set down. I remember it like it was yesterday."

Her voice caught a little and Jasper felt his heart ache. His mother and father had been one of those rare couples who'd tumbled into love in a matter of days and had remained that way until the day his father died, seven years ago. It had devastated them all, but his mother was not the fragile, brainless beauty some people believed her to be, and she'd rallied for the sake of her sons, pulling them all out of misery and back into the living world.

Jasper raised her hand to his lips and kissed it, smiling as she sent him an adoring glance.

"I miss him," he said. "He'd know what to do for the best."

His mother nodded and held Jasper's arm a little tighter. "I miss him too, darling, but you are very much like him, you know, and I have the greatest faith in you putting everything to rights."

Jasper choked with laughter, giving her an incredulous look. "Much as your faith in me touches my heart, Mama," he said, giving a sad shake of his head. "One can only presume you are queer in your attic."

His mother huffed and smacked his arm. "Don't be rude! I'll have you know I'm perfectly serious, and I'm never wrong about such things."

"Never admitting you're wrong is not the same as not *being* wrong. This is something I could never get across to you with any success."

"Now, Jasper," she began, but he spoke over her.

"I can't believe Mr Derby behaved so badly towards you, he must have been well into his thirties, and you a child! What an utter b—"

"Jasper!" his mother said hurriedly, glaring at him. "Yes, he was certainly that, and yes, he's an odious man, which is all the more reason to help poor Mr Baxter marry Miss Connolly. Derby has always been a manipulative bully, and Trevick is even worse. I shudder to think how that poor boy has suffered at their hands."

Jasper sighed. "You can see why Trevick opposes the match, though," he said, needing to play devil's advocate for a moment if only to ensure his mother fully appreciated the difficulties. "What if it were me?" he asked, wondering how she would take it. He stopped walking and turned to look at her. "What if it were me wanting to marry Miss Connolly, with her Irish merchant father, when I was all but engaged to Lady Frances?"

His mother looked back at him and wrinkled her nose, a look of distaste settling over her lovely features. "Jasper! *Really?* Need you ask? I would only ever want you to be as happy as your father and I. Dear me, a woman like Lady Frances would never do for you. She's all ambition and calculation, dear me no. Though, Miss Connolly wouldn't do either. Not because of her family; she's just far too excitable for you. You need a steadying influence, dear. I've always thought it."

Jasper rolled his eyes, but still saw the glint of determination in his mother's expression. Too late to take evasive action, he recognised the danger. He walked on again, eager to avoid the coming conversation, looking wildly about, searching for someone to save him, but they were alone.

"No, don't roll your eyes at me like that. It's true, and it's about time you did something about it too." His mother tugged him to a halt and forced him to look at her. "It's high time you married and set up your nursery, young man. At your age, your father already had you and Jerome on the way, so do stop wasting time and find yourself a wife."

Jasper groaned. "Mother, please…."

"No, Jasper, it must be said. If your father was here, he'd have a man-to-man chat with you, but you've only got me and I'm no good at such things, so I'll do the best I can with a mother–to–son talk. Isn't there anyone… anyone you would *like* to marry? If there *were* such a creature, I'd do everything I could to help you, you know."

There was an intensity in her eyes that made the hairs on the back of his neck stand all on end, and Jasper cleared his throat, avoiding her gaze. "I'll… give it some thought. I promise," he said in a rush, hoping that would placate her for now.

It seemed to do the trick, and she patted his arm fondly.

"Good boy. That's all I ask," she said with a smile, and Jasper smothered a sigh of despair.

By the time he'd returned to the castle, it seemed high time to gather everyone up for the return journey. Jasper looked around and wondered why his mother so enjoyed entertaining large groups of people.

Mr Burton had his head bent towards Miss Hunt, his expression intent and somewhat possessive and Miss Hunt's smile seemed just a little strained. Miss Connolly had clearly done something she ought not, as Harriet had hauled her off to one side and appeared to be in the middle of a lecture. The young woman appeared to be bearing it stoically enough. Lady Frances and Mrs Drake were cross as crabs, no doubt something to do with the lecture, and Luke was giving everyone a wide berth and staying deep in conversation with the guide.

Then, there was his wretched brother.

"Oh, Lord," Jasper muttered.

He'd noted Jerome and Bonnie Campbell together at Green Park. She was not at all Jerome's type, as he went for the fragile, blonde beauties, and Jasper well knew the fool was only being his usual amiable self.

Jerome was far too familiar, however, and did not distinguish as carefully as he ought to between the less than respectable ladies he adored spending time with, and those gently bred virgins of the *ton*. Not that there was anything very gentle about Miss Campbell, but nonetheless she *was* a lady. The fool would find himself leg-shackled to someone entirely unsuitable if he wasn't very careful.

Miss Campbell was exactly the excitable, hoydenish type of creature that would lead his brother gaily into ruin and scandal. He didn't doubt they'd have a marvellous time on the way, but they'd no doubt expect Jasper to pick up the blasted pieces and bail them out.

He groaned as Miss Campbell gave a squeal and stole Jerome's hat. His lackwit brother tore after her with a bark of laughter, chasing her in and out of the other guests.

"Devil take it," Jasper said in an undertone, but his mother only laughed.

"They're just having a bit of fun, Jasper," she said, thoroughly enjoying their antics.

Jasper snagged his brother's arm as he tore past in pursuit of his quarry. "Pack it in," he growled, at which Jerome just stared at him, burst out laughing, and carried on his merry way.

Miss Hunt met his gaze, complete understanding in her expression. She gave a helpless shrug and smiled. Jasper smiled back, and then discovered Mr Burton watching him with a frown and looked hastily away.

***

Luke turned his head as Lord St Clair rode up.

"Have you enjoyed the day?" Jasper asked.

Luke had been lagging a long way behind the others, lost in thought and barely noticed St Clair turning his horse riding back to meet him until he was by his side.

"Certainly," Luke replied with a smile, not about to voice the anxious thoughts clogging his poor demented brain. "The castle is wonderfully atmospheric and the company charming," he said politely. "Though I ought not have eaten so much, but it was impossible not to. I think old Zeus here is sulking about the extra weight."

He patted his mount's neck and St Clair laughed.

"Lady Frances looks like she swallowed a wasp," Jasper added companionably.

Luke started, a little surprised, but Jasper had taken him into his confidence about Miss Stanhope, and he could hardly pretend he didn't understand the comment.

He grimaced, knowing he'd been a bloody fool to take such a risk. "She nearly caught Kitty and I alone together. If not for Miss Hunt and Miss Stanhope, we should have been in quite a pickle. Oh, and you were there too," he added with a rush of guilt at involving the man. "Miss Hunt added your name, as it appears her own is—"

Jasper nodded his understanding and waved away Luke's obvious concerns.

"Where was I?"

"Up in the south tower."

"Well, that explains a great deal about the atmosphere I returned to," Jasper replied with a chuckle.

"I don't know what to do," Luke said, the weight of responsibility weighing him down. It was all well and good for Kitty to say she'd face anything for him, but what if she became the centre of some terrible scandal because of him? Mr Derby *would* punish him for his disobedience and he'd use Kitty to do it.

"Tell me."

Luke sighed with relief and did just that. He told Jasper of Mr Derby's threats, the week he had given him, and about the scene with Lady Frances.

"They could ruin Kitty with such ease, and the wretched girl will help them do it, if today is anything to go on." Not that he was in any way blameless. He needed to force her to behave, not run merrily behind her as she ruined herself. Yet the aching desire to be alone with her, to kiss her... well, it had addled his brain, clearly.

"Why don't you just elope?" Jasper suggested.

Luke gaped at him and he shrugged.

"Once you're married, it's done. The scandal of the elopement will be minimal as no one knows who you are, as yet. Trevick has kept you such a secret that a Mr Baxter marrying a Miss Connolly will hardly raise any eyebrows. Once it's done, Mrs Baxter is perfectly respectable. No doubt there will be other forms of retribution, but she'd be legally yours and no one could change that." Jasper noticed his shock and returned a rather crooked smile. "It's what I'd do in the circumstances."

The idea took root and Luke's hopes began to lift, his heart thudding with anticipation.

"She'd be mine and there would be nothing anyone could do," Luke said, considering the question. "Not to her, at any rate, and

Trevick can't disinherit me even if he were angry enough to do so."

"Quite," Jasper said, nodding. "You'd have only Lady Frances' wrath and any displeasure of her father to contend with. Though, that's enough to give any man pause. Lady Frances is a determined young woman, and she won't take kindly to being thwarted."

"No," Luke said with a sigh. "That she won't."

Yet he couldn't consider the cons of the plan with too much despondency, as the pros were so obvious. Why hadn't he considered it at once? To elope *was* a shocking thing to do, but... Kitty would be enraptured by the idea, the devil.

"Do I take it the idea meets with your approval?" Jasper asked, as Luke realised he was grinning like a fool.

"Yes," he said, laughing now, unable to contain his excitement. "Yes, it certainly does."

"Excellent. Come to my study once you've had time to change and we'll make a plan."

"*We?*" Luke said in astonishment. "Surely you can't mean to involve yourself in such a scandalous undertaking?"

"Oh, yes I can." Jasper laughed and urged his horse into a canter. "If I don't, my mother will never forgive me."

***

Kitty lay on her bed, staring at the ceiling. She ought to get ready for dinner, but her thoughts were all a-jumble. She was deliriously happy on the one hand, but there seemed an awful lot of flies in the ointment.

As furious as she was with the Earl of Trevick and Mr Derby, she knew Luke. He was decent and honourable, and letting anyone down would grieve him, no matter his own desires. He might not give a damn for Trevick and Mr Derby any longer, but she knew he was fond of Sybil and the others, and when his mother found out she'd be fit to be tied. Kitty didn't want him hurt or unhappy or plagued with guilt, and she certainly didn't want to be the one who made him feel that way. As it was, his mother would make him wretched for the rest of her days for having thrown away the chance to marry a duke's daughter.

Yet, what option was there? Luke loved her. Despite everything she'd said to Matilda, there *had* been a doubt in her mind before he'd appeared, of course there had. Although she remembered the depths of their friendship, their love for each other and the absolute certainty that it would endure, they *had* been children. She'd heard nothing from him for so many years, they'd been apart such a long time, and they'd changed. Both of them had changed.

In the moments after she'd burst out from behind the curtains that night, she'd had no doubts. Luke had known her at once, and the years had fallen away in an instant. He'd looked so different to the fresh-faced boy he'd been, and yet in his eyes was the person she'd loved with all her heart. She recognised him, and the joy at being reunited with her shone from him now. He couldn't hide it if he wanted to. So now they had to find a way to be together, a way that would cause him as little distress as possible.

If only she could figure out what it was.

Kitty looked up at a knock at her door and clambered off the bed. Her face fell when she saw Harriet, as she'd rung a peal over Kitty earlier in the day, and Kitty wasn't ready for another scolding just yet.

"May I come in?" Harriet asked, pushing her spectacles up her nose.

She looked a little uncomfortable and Kitty sighed, opening the door for her.

Harriet came in and then dithered as Kitty went back to sit on the bed. She walked to the window, looked out, walked back, and then returned to the window again.

"Is anything wrong, Harry?" Kitty asked, hoping she'd not done anything else Harriet considered appalling in the distance from the stables to her room.

"No," she said. "Yes. That is…."

Kitty braced herself.

"I wanted to apologise."

"Oh!" Kitty said, brightening with relief. Then she frowned. "Whatever for?"

"Oh, for being such a beastly friend." Harriet moved towards her and plonked herself down beside Kitty. "I had no right to reprimand you so. You're a grown woman and I'm not even your sister, certainly not your mother. Only, I was so frightened for you when Lady Frances discovered you alone with Mr Baxter. I was terrified for what would become of you. You're so much braver than me, Kitty, but sometimes what other people see as bravery seems to be dreadfully reckless in my eyes. I'm not very good at adventures," she admitted. "In fact, *I hate* adventures. They invariably end with muddy boots and soggy clothes and no dinner, freezing to death and getting a cold in the nose… well, I'd rather go to bed with a book," she added, defiant now.

Kitty laughed and took her hand, raising it to her cheek. "Oh, Harry, you goose. How funny you are."

Harriet huffed, her shoulders slumping. "No, I'm not. I'm not the least bit funny, I'm dull and boring and… *bookish*," she added, her lip curling a little with distaste. "There's no pretending that I'm not, but I can't help it." She folded her arms, her eyebrows drawing together as she stared at her feet. "Books are easy to understand, even ones that most people think perfectly dreary and incomprehensible. It's people that get me all in a muddle. I don't understand how you can *know* you're so terribly in love with Mr

Baxter that you'd risk everything, your entire future, just for the chance to be with him. What if it's merely an infatuation? What if you change your mind? What if you marry him and discover he isn't the man you thought he was?"

Kitty slid her arm through Harriet's and rested her chin on her shoulder. "It's easy, Harry," she said, her voice soothing. "At least it is for me. When you love someone, you do just *know*. It's not a mystery, there's no complex algorithm to work out, no hieroglyphs to decipher. It's such a powerful feeling that there's no mistaking it. I've loved him for so long, and I know it will never go away. What else should I do but risk everything? Living the rest of my days without him is a far greater risk than anything else."

Harriet returned a sceptical expression but said nothing for a moment. When she spoke, her words were not at all what Kitty expected.

"Does that mean you'll elope with him?"

Kitty stared back at her, wide-eyed. "What?"

Harriet shrugged, pushing a brown curl out of her eyes and tucking it behind her ear. "Well, it's the logical solution, isn't it?" she said, as though it were perfectly obvious. "If you stay here Mr Derby will ruin you before polite society, and Mr Baxter's decision to marry you instead of Lady Frances becomes even more outrageous. Once you're Mrs Baxter, there's nothing anyone can do, and it's not as though there will be a vast scandal about Trevick's heir eloping with you, because hardly anyone knows that's who he is." Harriet looked up and raised her eyebrows as she caught Kitty's expression. "What?" she said. "Ooof!"

Kitty threw her arms about her neck with such enthusiasm that she tumbled Harriet backwards on the bed. "Oh, Harry, you absolute darling genius. You're right! Of course, we must elope!"

"Yes," Harry mumbled, fighting her way out from Kitty's embrace. "Certainly," she added. "But do you think you might not smother me to death before you go?"

Chapter 11

Dear Nate,

I am so delighted by your delightful news! How marvellous to be an aunt. Please give darling Alice my best love and assure her I will indeed spread the lovely news among our friends. I'm so happy for you, Nate. What a wonderful father you will be.

—Excerpt of a letter from Miss Matilda Hunt to her brother, Mr Nathanial Hunt.

23ʳᵈ August 1814, Holbrooke House, Sussex.

Luke had spent a convivial evening with Jasper planning his elopement with Kitty. He was very much looking forward to breaking the news to her.

They would leave—assuming he'd not completely misjudged her, and she refused the idea—the day after tomorrow.

With help from the countess as chaperone, Jasper would arrange a trip for himself and Luke, Kitty, Miss Stanhope, and Miss Hunt. The rest of the guests would be occupied with various entertainments and would not notice Kitty and Luke's belongings being packed and taken away.

Their bags would go to the nearest good-sized town where they could hire a carriage without drawing too much attention. Whilst Jasper was all willingness to help, he could not be seen to be aiding an elopement, and so a hired vehicle must do for the first leg of the journey.

They would leave Jasper and company early that morning, not for Scotland as Luke had first thought obvious, but for Warwickshire. Jasper and the others would carry on with their day trip, returning to the house too late to dine. Therefore, it would be the next morning before anyone noticed Luke and Kitty were missing, and there would be no chance of Mr Derby intercepting them before they reached Stratford-upon-Avon.

Stratford was the parish in which Luke had been born. That meant, as both he and Kitty were of age, they need only buy a common license and they could be married at once, a golden nugget of information that had not occurred to Luke in his distraction, but which Jasper had been quick to point out.

Stratford was also not a very great distance from Trevick Castle, where the earl ruled his own little fiefdom like a big fat spider on a vast web.

Although it was under the earl's nose, which was certainly audacious, the old buzzard seldom left his estate and Luke knew they would not be remarked upon. The tenacious old devil had kept Luke on such a tight rein that he had rarely been allowed out and about in the local area.

No one would know him from Adam.

For once, Trevick and Derby's Machiavellian plans had worked against them.

This plan would leave them with one overnight stay at Aylesbury, where Jasper had recently inherited a property. The house was undergoing a restoration project but was not so badly arranged that a comfortable night's lodging couldn't be provided both on the journey there and the return. Here Jasper would provide them with a private carriage to take them the final distance to Stratford, where they would be married.

To Jasper's surprise, Luke had informed him they would return to Holbrooke House almost at once, so that Kitty could celebrate with her friends, and so that Luke might face Mr Derby. He'd much rather get that over with as soon as possible.

Such a dismal prospect as Derby's ire could not dampen his spirits, however. They would be married in a very short time, and Luke could feel nothing but impatience for their lives to begin. It would be like it was when they were children again, but with no going home at the end of the day.

How he would endure a night alone with Kitty before they married and act like a gentleman, he had no idea, but he'd cross that bridge when he got to it. He'd defended Kitty to Mr Derby and Lady Frances, ensuring them both that she was every inch a lady, and he was damned if he would treat her with any less than the respect she deserved. The problem was, he rather doubted Kitty would give a fig for such things when they were about to be married. He'd not think on that... yet.

He didn't join the others once their plans had been finalised and—for the first time since... well, since Mr Derby had announced the impending betrothal to Lady Frances—Luke slept soundly and woke in good spirits. He was heading for the breakfast room when Kitty accosted him.

"Luke!" she exclaimed, hurrying to him and grabbing his hand.

"Kitty," Luke remonstrated, glancing around to ensure they were not being observed.

"Where were you last night?" she demanded, her dark eyes flashing with impatience. "I had so much to tell you, and you and St Clair didn't come to dinner. By the time the meal was over and I tracked down the earl, he said you'd gone to bed! How could you? I was bursting to talk to you."

Luke chuckled, remembering all too well her outbreaks of pique when she was thwarted. It seemed that, despite waiting years for him, she'd not altogether outgrown her desire to have what she wanted at once. His mouth grew dry as he realised what that might mean for their overnight journey.

"Are you blushing?" she asked, peering at him and wrinkling her nose.

"Certainly not," he said, clearing his throat. "What did you want to say to me with such urgency, Kitten?"

To his amusement, she glanced furtively around her before leaning in and whispering in his ear, her warm breath tickling his skin and making him shiver.

"We must elope!"

There was a triumphant glint to her eyes when she pulled back. The wretch looked utterly gleeful and so smug Luke wanted to laugh. Instead he adopted his best Trevick attitude, adjusted his cuffs and said in a bored voice. "Well, obviously, Kitten. There's really no need for such dramatics. We shall leave tomorrow morning."

Kitty gaped at him in stunned silence and then gave a squeal of delight, throwing her arms about his neck and kissing him.

As charmed as he was to have her in his arms, Luke could not risk them being discovered when they were so close to freedom. "Pack it in, love," he said, untangling her from his neck. "I mean it, stop that. For the rest of the day you must not be alone with me, or give anyone any reason for suspecting our plans."

Kitty stepped back at once and nodded. "Oh, of course, you're right. I'll be careful, I promise," she said gravely, then gave a quiet cheer and danced on the spot, clapping her hands together.

Luke snorted and rolled his eyes. "Heaven preserve me, Kitty. You haven't changed a bit."

She gave him an unrepentant grin, and he offered her his arm to take her down to breakfast.

"There is something else you must do for me before we leave, Kitty," he said, remembering his determination to help Jasper. "But you must swear to be discreet," he added, giving her a fierce look and wondering if she could manage such a thing.

Kitty's gaze was so adoring he felt his cheeks heat with pleasure and whatever it was he'd wanted to say dissolved into the mush she'd made of his brain. "Anything, Luke."

Luke cleared his throat and tried to get his mind off the fact she would soon be his wife, and back to everything he owed Lord St Clair.

"I mean it, Kitty. St Clair has asked me for help, and I don't want the fellow embarrassed. I spent most of last night with him and he took a deal of care and trouble planning our elopement. We owe him a great debt, so you must tread with caution."

Kitty's eyes widened. "How kind he is," she said in surprise. "Well, I will do anything I can for him, Luke, of course I shall."

"Good girl," he said, wishing he could kiss her and forcing himself not to stare at her mouth. He lowered his voice. "Well, you see the thing is, the poor fellow is hopelessly in love—"

"Oh, yes," Kitty said at once. "With Harriet."

Luke stopped in his tracks and let out a huff of amusement. "Well, I'm blowed. Though I told him you might have guessed already. How observant you are."

Kitty shrugged. "Not as observant as Matilda. She's known for ages, I think."

"You've not told anyone else?"

Kitty shook her head. "No, and I shan't. But, Luke, it's not that hard to figure out. He may believe he's hiding his feelings, but you only need be in their company for a short while to feel the tension between them. She dislikes him and makes no secret of it, and he... the poor man."

Luke nodded, experiencing a wave of fellow feeling for Jasper. How awful to love a woman who couldn't stand the sight of you.

"The problem is, Kitten, she didn't always hate him. From all I can gather, it stems from years ago, when she was sixteen."

"Oh?" Kitty said, her interest obvious. "You know what happened?"

Luke shook his head. "No, and neither does poor Jasper. He told me he kissed her and… and that she was certainly not unwilling but… the next time he saw her she was as cold as ice. He's tried to apologise, to discover if he overstepped the mark or took too much for granted or whatever it was he'd done, but she'll not explain. She'll have none of him."

Kitty fell silent for a moment, and Luke slowed his steps as they approached the breakfast room.

"Harry thinks St Clair is only interested in her because he can't charm her. She says if she were to act as though she liked him, he'd lose interest at once, but she won't do it because she refuses to give him the satisfaction."

"I don't think that's true," Luke said, stopping to regard her.

"No." Kitty shook her head thoughtfully. "Neither do I, but you must admit, his reputation would make any reasonable person think she had a valid point. He's not what you'd call a rake, exactly, but—"

"Not far from it," Luke finished for her. He couldn't disagree.

"Well," Kitty said, brightening. "I will do my best to uncover the mystery but, for now, I want my breakfast. I'm famished."

***

"I have the most marvellous news," Matilda said in a whisper to Harriet and Prue, who were sitting on either side of her. "Alice is in an *interesting* condition."

"Oh!" Harriet exclaimed, beaming.

"I knew it!" Prue said, triumphant. "Didn't I say?"

Matilda laughed and nodded. "Well, I don't think it's the most surprising news, but it is wonderful to be sure. I'm to be an aunt!"

She refused to dwell on the fact she'd woken in the early hours of the morning and indulged in a good cry. She felt awful for having done so. Her happiness for Nate and Alice's news was genuine and heartfelt, but... she had the terrible feeling that her time was running out.

Matilda would be six and twenty in a few short weeks, and she was no closer to being settled. She'd believed herself, if not resigned to remaining a spinster, then at least not to be facing the idea with complete terror. Her feelings in those lonely hours between midnight and the first glimpse of the sun had proved that to be an utter lie.

What if you never marry? The shrill voice in her head demanded. *What if you are too old to have children even if you do?*

There seemed to be some angry clock marking time inside her and the insistent tick of the days flying past got louder and louder, making panic bubble up and swallow any reasonable arguments with which she tried to calm herself.

Mr Burton, the voice said urgently, *you must marry Mr Burton. He's your last hope for marriage and children, for security and respectability.*

The panicky feeling rose once more, but this time at the idea of marrying Mr Burton. Why, though? He was a good person, a kind one. Surely she could find some measure of happiness with a man like him. It was evident he'd be a doting husband... but that was half the trouble.

She found his devotion suffocating which she knew was unreasonable of a man she was considering marrying.

What was *wrong* with her?

There had to be some fault in her, some terrible failing in her character that could not appreciate his charms and thank her lucky stars that he had not only noticed her, but wanted to make her a respectable offer. She'd received enough less than respectable offers to know just how valuable his interest was.

Unbidden, another man's face filled her mind, and she cursed at her own stupidity. There it was: the fault, the part of her that would send her to the devil with glee. She would *not* let it win. It was her baser instincts at work, nothing more; an animal urge that called to her perverse desire for a man who valued her no higher than an exclusive whore.

"Don't you think?"

Matilda started in shock as Prue's voice filtered through her abstraction, blushing as she realised the path her thoughts had dragged her down. She came back to the conversation with difficulty as Prue put down her toast, a searching expression in her eyes that made Matilda squirm.

"You haven't heard a word I've said, have you?"

"I-I...." Matilda stammered. "No. I beg your pardon. I was wool gathering, imagining what Nate and Alice's child might look like," she said, improvising wildly.

Prue snorted. "And I'm supposed to be the one with an imagination," she said. "You were thinking nothing of the sort. A blush like that can only be caused by thoughts of a wicked nature, nothing to do with babies. Well...." Prue added with a grin and a waggle of her eyebrows.

To her intense relief, Matilda was saved by Lady St Clair, who announced that there would be an archery contest in the gardens today.

"Harry, you're with me," Jerome shouted across the table, before his mother could finish her explanation of the event. He grinned, looking pleased with himself as Harriet rolled her eyes.

"Devil!" his mother exclaimed, laughing. "Now you're bound to win."

Matilda glanced at Lord St Clair to find him attacking a slice of bacon with quiet ferocity.

"Harriet is the best shot among us. At least she always was," Jerome said to the table in general. He leaned forward to interrogate Harriet. "Tell me your wicked skill with an arrow hasn't diminished over the years, Harry."

"How should I know?" Harriet replied, regarding Jerome with amusement. "I haven't shot an arrow in… oh, I don't know how long."

"Eight years," said Lord St Clair.

He didn't look up, but Matilda saw Harriet stiffen at his words.

"Good Lord, as long as that?" Jerome said, a little less certain now. "Well, natural talent will win out I should imagine. What say we get some practice in now?"

Harriet set down her half-eaten slice of toast and wiped her fingers, before returning an indulgent look of the kind one might bestow on an impatient five-year-old. "Well, I shan't get any peace unless I do, so very well then," she said, though there was laughter in her eyes.

She got to her feet and Jerome moved to follow her.

"I'll come too," Kitty said. "I want to see this wicked skill in action."

Matilda watched them go, until Bonnie's voice caught her attention.

"If Jerome has snared Harriet, I will secure Lord St Clair," Bonnie said, blithely ignoring Matilda's glare of outrage at her audacity.

To her vexation, Matilda saw Lady Frances and Mrs Drake exchange a glance which spoke volumes about their opinion of Bonnie's manners.

"It would be my pleasure, Miss Campbell," St Clair replied politely, earning himself a victorious smile from the dreadful girl. "Though I cannot vouch for the quality of your choice. In fact, I believe I shall get in some practice too, in the hopes I won't embarrass myself."

He rose, excused himself, and strode out of the room.

"Miss Hunt, may I prevail upon you to partner me for the competition?"

Matilda looked across the table to where Mr Burton had been trying to catch her eye for the past ten minutes. "Of course, Mr Burton," she said, with what she hoped was a pleased smile. "I should be delighted to."

Chapter 12

Dearest Papa,

Yes, the journey to Sussex was exceptionally comfortable in the new carriage. Poor Bonnie doesn't always travel well, but she was excessively pleased that she didn't feel the slightest bit nauseous, so you can congratulate yourself on a fine choice.

Holbrooke House is every bit as ancient as you supposed, but I do not believe Lord St Clair would entertain rebuilding as you suggested. It may well be draughty in the winter, but it is very beautiful and the history dreadfully romantic. The family is most attached to it so I should not raise the subject if you ever meet the earl. He might take offense, no matter how generous the benefit of your advice.

—Excerpt of a letter from Miss Ruth Stone to her father, Mr George Stone.

23rd August 1814, Holbrooke House, Sussex.

"I had no idea you had such a lethal talent," Kitty said with admiration as Harriet sent yet another arrow sailing down to *thunk* into the centre of the straw target. "Who taught you?"

Harriet squinted down the length of the archery field to see where her arrow had landed and adjusted her spectacles before answering. "Lord St Clair," she said.

"When was that?" Kitty pressed, unsurprised by the answer and hoping this might give her the opening she required.

"Oh, years ago," Harriet said with a shrug as she selected another arrow.

"Was he a patient teacher?"

There was a disgusted snort. "As a boy of twelve? I think not. I was lucky not to be tied to the target."

Jerome laughed and took his place as Harriet stepped to one side. "Jasper loved to torment poor Harry," he said, raising his bow and taking aim. "He was quite single-minded about it. I'm certain she only practised so faithfully because she was determined to be better than he was, unless it was with the intention of shooting him if the opportunity arose. That's equally likely."

"Sadly, it did not," Harriet retorted. "Too many witnesses."

The women watched, admiring the picture the earl's younger brother made, with his broad shoulders and athletic physique. A soft sigh was just audible, and Kitty turned as Jerome let the arrow fly to see Bonnie had joined them and was staring at Jerome with a look Kitty recognised. She grinned as Bonnie realised she was observed, and flushed scarlet.

"What?" Bonnie said, defensive now as the *thunk* of the arrow hitting the target drew their attention back to Jerome.

"Well, dash it!" Jerome exclaimed in disgust as his arrow had hit the straw circle but far wide of the bull's eye. "What a hopeless shot."

Kitty went to take his place, but Jerome shook his head and waved her away.

"No, no, I'm sorry Miss Connolly. That simply won't do. I refuse to be beaten by a lot of girls."

"I'm on your team, Jerry," Harriet remarked dryly as Jerome sent her an impatient glance.

"That's entirely beside the point and you know it," he retorted, and took aim once more.

The arrow went sailing towards the target and, whilst not a bullseye, was only a couple of inches to the right of it.

"Hmph," Jerome said, still disgruntled. "Better, I suppose."

"Well, we are here to practise," Kitty said, grinning as Luke and Jasper arrived together. She felt her heart leap at the sight of Luke, his red hair glinting in the sun. How handsome he was. That he would be her husband in a matter of days made a strange and giddy feeling bubble up inside her like champagne. It wanted to overflow, to burst from her in a wild gale of laughter but she couldn't allow it, too aware that they must not draw attention to themselves.

Luke caught her eye and smiled; a smile that made her heart do a foolish little dance in her chest before he looked away. *Not long, not long,* it said, jolting around like a mad rabbit, *not long and he's all yours.*

Kitty turned away and did her best to stop the daft expression that threatened to break out and turn her into a lovesick girl for all to see.

The practising went on for another hour, until Lady St Clair called a halt and said the competition proper would start after a short break. Whilst they'd been busy practising, the servants had been occupied in setting up a seating area in the shade of an ancient oak tree for those who were waiting to play and those who chose to watch the competition in comfort.

A table had been set up with refreshments too and everyone adjourned for a glass of lemonade before the contest began.

Harriet had sat on the grass beneath a beech tree some distance from the others and appeared to have her nose buried in a book. Luke caught Kitty's eye as she observed this, and jerked his head.

Kitty snorted and made her way to sit beside Harriet, taking her a glass of lemonade.

"What are you reading?" she asked, eyeing the tome in Harriet's lap with trepidation.

"Plato," she said, without looking up.

"Oh," Kitty replied, impressed. She handed Harriet the glass of lemonade and sipped at her own.

"*The Republic*," Harriet added, turning to look at Kitty, her eyes large and owlish behind her spectacles. "I'm reading *The Allegory of the Cave* at the moment. Do you know it?"

Kitty shook her head.

"Is that why you don't get on with St Clair?" Kitty said, returning to their previous conversation. Time was short, and she'd best try to get to the point.

Harriet blinked at her in obvious surprise. "Because everyone can only see his shadow?" she asked, looking profoundly interested.

"What?" Kitty said, bewildered. "No, because he tormented you when you were children."

"Oh," Harriet said with a disappointed sigh, setting the book aside. "No, of course not. He was a boy, boys are obnoxious. They can't help it; it's their *raison d'être*."

"So, what did he do?"

Harriet sighed and cut her a look. "Why are you all so interested?" she demanded. "Not everyone has to like each other, you know. St Clair and I are very different people. He's chalk, meet cheese," she said, gesturing to herself. "It's really very simple."

Kitty stared at her and Harriet held her gaze for a long moment until she blushed and looked away.

"It isn't simple at all, though. Is it, Harry?"

Harriet huffed out a breath and began plucking at the grass, tearing it up by the roots.

"He's… all on the surface. Shallow," she said, frowning down at the little pile of grass she'd made. "I thought for a while it wasn't the case, that there was a more serious man there, one who felt things deeply, one who cared… but he doesn't care at all—about anything much. Oh, superficially he does, but you don't have to scratch very deep to discover there's nothing beneath the veneer. We see the shadow he casts, not the reality of who he is."

Kitty tried to reconcile her words with what she'd seen of St Clair.

"That's not the man I've come to know, nor does it match everything Luke has told me. He's done so much for me, for both of us. He didn't need to involve himself in our little drama, but he did. He seems pretty solid to me, not shallow, not shadowy."

Harriet's face darkened, and she shrugged. "I never said he was a bad man, Kitty. He's more than capable of being kind and thoughtful, but that's the danger, don't you see? He does these things and you think it means something… but it doesn't. Not really. Not like it did to… to whoever he's been kind to. He'll drop you the next moment and not even realise he's done it."

Harriet got to her feet and brushed down her skirts, before bending to reach for her book. Kitty took hold of her wrist as she did so, forcing her to meet her eyes.

"I think he hurt you," she said softly, ignoring the fact that Harriet had stiffened, ignoring the stony look behind the spectacles. "I think he hurt you badly, but I don't think he has the slightest idea how or what he did. You owe him an explanation, Harriet. It's not fair to keep punishing someone for years and years without giving them a chance to redeem themselves. You said yourself that boys are obnoxious—that they can't help it—but he's not a boy any longer, Harry, he's a man, and I don't think you realise how much you hurt him when you act so coldly."

"Is that all?" Harriet asked, her voice dull. She'd turned her face away a little, but Kitty could see the colour high in her cheeks, feel her desire to tug her wrist free.

"No," Kitty said. "You scolded me and much of what you said made a deal of sense, I accepted it, and now you must accept my words. Promise me you'll think about it, at least. You are an intelligent woman, one ruled by logic—so you tell me—but your behaviour towards the earl is illogical. If you take a moment to think about it, instead of perpetuating this unkindness out of habit, you'll see that."

Harriet paused for a long moment before meeting Kitty's eyes. There was something that might have been surprise there, and Kitty wondered if maybe she'd got through.

"Very well, I shall consider your words."

"Promise," Kitty urged.

She watched as Harriet took a deep breath and then let it out again, no doubt praying for patience. It was a reaction Kitty was familiar with and she took no offence.

"I promise."

Kitty grinned and leapt to her feet, hugging Harriet tightly. Harriet was stiff and unyielding for a moment, before she relaxed a bit and patted Kitty's back somewhat awkwardly.

"Come along," she said, pushing her spectacles up her nose. "Or they'll start without us."

***

Matilda gave a huff of frustration as her arrow buried itself into the grass in front of the target.

"Never mind," Mr Burton said, grinning at her, before carelessly letting off an arrow and watching it hit a bare inch above the bullseye.

"Easy for you to say," Matilda observed. "We shall lose horribly, despite your talents, and I shall feel wretched."

"Nonsense," Mr Burton said, laughing as he moved away for the next competitor to take his place. "It is the taking part that counts. I couldn't give a fig if we win or not."

"You really don't, do you?" Matilda said, smiling at him. "I thought all men to be dreadfully competitive."

Mr Burton shrugged. "It depends what's at stake. In business, I assure you, I am not to be thwarted, or… if there is something I truly desire. Then… I would fight to the death." He made a theatrical flourishing gesture with the new arrow he'd taken as if it were a sword and then grinned at her, a boyish expression that was endearing when set upon his very masculine features.

She laughed, amused by his antics and the boyishness faded away, a different light in his eyes now.

"You're so very beautiful, Miss Hunt," he said, his voice low enough that no one else could hear. "I cannot stop thinking about you. I want you very badly, you know."

Matilda felt her heart thud in her chest, a heavy and not especially pleasant sensation.

"I know," she said, not wanting to torment the man by playing games. In her head, the voice that had disturbed her sleep and brought her to tears in the early hours began screaming at her— *time is running out, time is running out. Old maid! Old maid!*

"Have you thought any more—"

"Yes," Matilda said quickly, feeling all at once hot and breathless and nauseous. The panicky sensation grew and grew, and she feared she might do something as ludicrous as swoon. "Yes, I have thought of it but… but I…."

She swayed a little, putting a hand to her chest to quell the thundering of her heart.

"My dear," Mr Burton said at once, his expression alarmed at he took her arm. "Are you going to faint? All the colour has gone from your cheeks. Here, come out of the sun, it is growing fierce." He led her to the seating area, casting her anxious glances as he went. "Forgive me, Miss Hunt. I ought not have plagued you. I'm a wretched fool, I know it...."

"Oh, no," Matilda replied, knowing well enough that she was the fool, not Mr Burton. "That's not the least bit true. You've been all kindness."

"No," he said, once he'd settled her in a chair and fetched her a glass of lemonade. "I've not been the least bit kind. I've been impatient. I *am* impatient, but if you will tell me one thing, I swear to you I'll give you the time you desire. Is it hopeless, Miss Hunt or... do I have a chance?"

Matilda sipped her lemonade and tried to subdue her growing need to run away like a child. She wasn't a child, she was a long way from being so. That was the problem. She couldn't ignore the fact that time was passing her by and, with it, opportunities.

"It isn't hopeless, Mr Burton," she said, trying for a smile which felt stiff and unnatural.

Mr Burton's face lit up as he took in her words, such happiness softening his features that Matilda felt a rush of warmth for him and she smiled for real. Perhaps she could do this; perhaps it wouldn't be so bad.

"You've no idea how pleased I am to hear that," he said. He reached for her hand and raised it to his lips, pressing a kiss to her fingers.

"Mr Burton," Matilda admonished, glancing about to see if anyone had seen.

"Sorry." He laughed, thoroughly unrepentant. "I'm sorry, I couldn't resist."

Matilda smiled tightly and looked away. There was an ache in her throat. The touch of his lips to her skin had been pleasant enough, certainly there was no sense of revulsion at his attention, but... she felt no fluttering of her heart, no excitement at the thought of those lips upon hers, his hands on her. She felt... nothing.

She remembered another man, and the way the barest touch of his finger against hers had sent her nerves leaping, every fibre of her being aware of him, alive and pulsing for him... longing for him.

Fool.

"Miss Hunt, Mr Burton."

They both turned as Jerome hailed them and gestured that it was their turn to play.

"Back into the fray," Matilda said gaily, forcing herself to sound light-hearted and happy, like a woman who was being courted by a handsome and eligible man... like she ought to sound if she had an ounce of sense in her stupid head.

***

Jasper stood by the refreshments table, sipping a glass of lemonade and wishing for something a deal stronger. He watched with increasing unease as Jerome and Miss Campbell laughed and teased each other. They were as good-natured as puppies, their happiness infectious and their easy friendship natural and so simple. Yet it wasn't simple at all.

Jerome was ever thus, a likable easy-going fellow mostly, until he lost his temper. This was rare, it was true, but Jerome had a very strong sense of right and wrong, and if you were wrong he'd tell you so, usually with a dreadful want of tact. Sadly, his ideas of right and wrong and society's rarely coincided.

For example, he saw no reason not to enjoy his burgeoning friendship with Miss Campbell. Except that society—and in this instant, Jasper—could predict certain pitfalls.

Miss Campbell was a nobody, born of a far from an illustrious family. When her parents died she had been made a ward of the Earl of Morven and given a reasonable, if not generous dowry. Not that Jasper would stand in his brother's way if he fell head over ears in love, he wasn't that much of an ogre. The problem was, Jerome was *not* in love with Miss Campbell and was unlikely to be. Jerome was a romantic. He fell for damsels in distress, usually frail blondes with large eyes and a tendency to swoon at the drop of a hat.

Miss Campbell was... robust.

With a generous figure that was all curves and abundance, and a forthright nature that had her speaking out when she'd do better to hold her tongue, Jasper could see that Jerome looked at her in the same manner he might one of his male friends. She was someone he could joke with and tease; someone who would not take offence but enjoy the banter. This was rare in a woman and Jasper could understand the appeal. He could also read the look in Miss Campbell's eyes, a look to which Jerome was totally blind.

The blasted imbecile.

This meant that Jasper would have to intervene and explain a few things which no doubt would put Jerome's back up and Jasper firmly in the doghouse. Well, it was his permanent abode when Harriet was around anyway, he may as well get comfy there.

"That was an excellent shot, my lord."

Jasper turned to see Lady Frances had moved to stand beside him. She accepted a glass of lemonade from a footman as she watched Mr Burton go forward to take his shot.

"Thank you," Jasper replied. "I used to play all the time, but it's been a while now. I'm relieved to discover I haven't lost the knack."

"Indeed not, you are most impressive."

Jasper glanced at her and she turned her face away, shyly lowering her lashes. Alarm bells sounded. He searched about him, surreptitiously hoping to catch someone's eye and subtly indicate that he was in distress, to no avail.

So, now that Luke had made his intentions plain, she would return her attention to him, Jasper realised with a sigh. Though Mr Derby had made it abundantly clear the marriage *would* still go ahead, no matter Luke's ideas on the subject, Jasper didn't doubt that her pride was smarting, and he would make a fine conquest. How satisfying to turn to Luke and Mr Derby and tell them they were no longer required. Any earl would do, it seemed, though she had highlighted her interest plainly enough before now.

Jasper looked around to see Mr Derby and his daughter, Sybil, sitting with Jasper's mother, Mrs Drake, and Harriet's Aunt Nell. He was nodding at something Jasper's mother was saying but Jasper doubted he was attending the conversation, his attention fixed on Luke and Miss Connolly. Happily, the pair were behaving just as they ought... perhaps too well, as everyone knew how they felt about each other. The sooner they were far from here the better. He hoped the plans he'd made with Luke last night would serve them well.

He sighed as he realised he envied them, running away to be together against all the odds. That was something worth fighting for. Good grief, he really had to get a grip, or he'd start letting his hair grow long, wear ridiculous neckcloths, and write dubious poetry.

"I was looking at the picture gallery last night," Lady Frances said, drawing his attention back to her.

He'd knew he'd been rude to have ignored her and not spoken for so long, but he was somewhat bereft of small talk and didn't wish to make the effort. What a wretched fellow he was becoming.

Her voice was soft and musical, the well-modulated tones of a perfect young lady.

"Indeed? I'm not a great connoisseur of art, not like my father was," he said, trying his best to be a good host but not encourage her flirtation. "But even an ignorant devil like me can see there are some wonderful paintings there."

"Oh, there are, but I refuse to believe you the least bit ignorant. You are funning, my lord, I know. What a marvellous painting of your father by Reynolds, though. Quite his finest, I think. I studied it for the longest time. There's a strong resemblance between you."

"Is there?" Jasper asked, genuinely surprised. "I confess I've never found one, and I have looked. Both Jerome and I favour our mother."

"Oh, yes certainly," said Lady Frances, her blue eyes grave. "But if one looks carefully you *are* like your father too. It's in your bearing, in the breadth of your shoulders, and a…" A smile played over her rosebud lips and she sent him another hesitant glance. "A certain *je ne sais quoi*."

"I know what it is," Harriet said, making him jump as she came up behind them and poured herself a glass of lemonade. For once, he'd not heard her approach.

"Oh?" Lady Frances replied, snapping open her fan and giving Harriet a cool glance from behind it.

"Yes," Harriet said, taking a sip of her lemonade and regarding the selection of cakes and biscuits laid out for the guests. "I was here when that was painted."

Jasper watched her peruse the extensive assortment. *Ginger,* he thought, and watched as she reached for the spicy treat with a smile.

"Don't you remember?" she asked, surprising Jasper again by addressing him directly. "He'd eaten a great deal too much rhubarb compote and had terrible indigestion. I made him mint tea, but it was days before he was comfortable again. I always thought Reynolds caught his rather pinched expression. I noticed the other night you have a fondness for rhubarb yourself. No doubt you've got the same constitution as your father and Lady Frances has remarked the same expression of discomfort." She took a bite of her biscuit, sighing with pleasure before adding. "You should try one of these, my lord. Ginger is noted for being good for the digestion."

Harriet sauntered off again, biscuit in hand, and Jasper stared after her for a moment in quiet awe before giving a bark of laughter.

"Well," Lady Frances said, looking outraged. "How dare she say such things about you? I've heard nothing so insulting in all my life."

Jasper looked at her with disbelief. "Really?" he said, unable to hide his amusement. "Have you not been paying attention? She's been insulting me since she got here. That was an excellent one I admit, though she can do far better when I've annoyed her, I assure you."

She stared up at him, her confusion at Jasper's humour apparent, not that he cared.

"But she insulted your father, too, not to mention that fine portrait."

Jasper frowned. "No, she didn't. She adored my father. What she said is quite true. If my father were here, he'd be in fits. He always appreciated her sharp tongue," he said, allowing himself a wistful smile. He gave Lady Frances an amused nod, noting her utter bewilderment, and walked away, smiling.

Whether or not she had meant to, Harriet had saved him from Lady Frances, and Jasper was in an excellent mood.

Chapter 13

Dear Father,

I received your letter and quite understand that your studies will keep you abroad sometime longer. However, could we not return home? I know the work to the house was more serious than you expected and is not yet completed, but surely the entire place is not reduced to dust and rubble.

It's not that I dislike remaining with St Clair until summer's end, and he certainly won't mind a bit. Harriet is not comfortable here, though, and this news will not please her. You know how prickly she is when she is not pleased.

Could I respectfully ask you to reconsider?

—Excerpt of a letter from Mr Henry Stanhope to his father, Mr William Stanhope.

23rd August 1814, Holbrooke House, Sussex.

Luke laughed as Henry groaned and rolled his eyes when they announced the winners. Not that there was much surprise. Miss Stanhope and Jerome had won the trophy with ease. Jasper and Miss Campbell had taken second place, Miss Stone and Henry third, with himself and Kitty tying with Mr Burton and Matilda for last place.

Luke was astonished he'd got a single arrow to hit home, to be honest. All his attention had been riveted on Kitty, even though he'd forced himself not to look at her too closely or too often. He was simply aware of her, as aware as of his own heart beating; he didn't have to feel it pound to know it was doing so, but he'd know if it stopped quickly enough.

Waves of nostalgia assaulted him when he allowed himself a moment to watch her. Her thick black hair was escaping its pins, and more of it tumbled loose with each passing hour. His fingers itched to touch it, and he remembered the silky feel of it, how it looked when it was free and unbound as it had been when she was a child. He'd been fascinated by it as a boy and had often wound her curls about his finger, tugging them and watching them spring back around her face like magic.

She'd seemed a wild thing from the first, like some tricksy fae come to tempt him into her realm where he'd be kept a prisoner for the rest of his days. She had done just that, he thought with a smile. He'd been hers from the start, bewitched by those dark eyes and the touch of her hand on his cheek.

"I've found you, and you've found me, and so… we shall be together, and never alone again."

Her words echoed through him, making his heart ache. They had been alone for far too long, but it hadn't been her fault. She'd searched for him, waited for him, when he'd believed his life was over and had given up, crushed beneath the power of the family who'd taken him.

Kitty would never have been crushed, he thought, experiencing equal parts pride and guilt at the idea. He'd been weak to allow others to trample his dreams, but he was done with such weakness. He'd made Mr Derby and Trevick promises and commitments, but they had wrung those promises from a boy they had bullied into submission and moulded into their perfect heir. Well, he'd learned his lessons. He'd learned how to be like them, and whilst he had no intention of being like them, he knew he was strong enough to defy them now. He would take their teachings and play by their rules, which was to say with his own best interests at heart.

With Kitty at his side he felt like a knight on a quest, like they had as children when they planned their next great adventure. Now, the greatest adventure of all lay before them, and Luke was beside himself with excitement. Now that freedom was in his grasp, he realised he had been imprisoned all this time. The future which had loomed on the horizon like a great hungry beast, ready to devour him, was now an open expanse of possibilities. The weight that had sat upon his shoulders had lifted and he was as hopeful and optimistic as he'd been when a boy, before Derby had stolen his life and his hopes, and locked him into the cage made for Trevick's last living heir.

All Luke's boyish dreams returned to him, but he was a boy no more, and he had something to fight for, something to believe in. There was no prison of Trevick's devising that could hold him now.

After they had presented the trophies, there was a deal of congratulating and commiserating, and Luke made himself scare for a while. If he stayed, the temptation would be to steal away with Kitty and he dare not risk it.

"Luke."

His heart sank as he heard Mr Derby call after him. The dratted fellow had caught him just as he was about to enter the house, and he forced Luke to a halt.

"What in the name of heaven did you think you were doing?" he asked in a fierce undertone, as he took Luke's arm and yanked him to one side. "Telling Lady Frances you would not offer for her? I've reassured her as best I can, but she's already dangling after St Clair again. If you're not very careful, you'll burn your boats."

"I believe I set the fires with intent, Mr Derby," Luke replied with outward calm though his heart thudded in his chest.

Not that he was afraid any longer, but he would let nothing interfere with his plans. Whilst he would not tell an outright lie— that would be dishonourable—he must not give himself away, must not give Mr Derby an inkling of his intent.

"I shall not marry Lady Frances," he said, holding Mr Derby's gaze unflinchingly.

"You still intend to marry the chit, then?" Derby sneered.

Luke paused, considering his options. On the one hand, he wanted very badly to break Mr Derby's nose. On the other, tomorrow he would run away with Kitty to get married, and he'd not let anyone stop him. Assaulting Mr Derby, whilst satisfying, would not do any good.

"I'm not sure I'm ready to marry *just yet*," he said carefully, after all it wasn't a lie, he hadn't packed his belongings. If he made his intentions too obvious, Derby might guess what they meant to do. "Not *just* yet, but I cannot set aside my feelings for Kitty, that is for certain."

Mr Derby took a breath, perhaps believing he had a chance to mend the situation.

"You are young yet," he said, the jovial uncle expression flickering briefly, if unconvincingly across his face. "Perhaps we have been too hasty. Why do we not leave talk of marriage for a few months? I'm sure I could persuade both Trevick and Lymington to be a little more patient with you, if you meet us halfway. Don't make a fool of yourself over your Irish beauty. Dally with her, by all means, but be discreet. That way, if you were to change your mind… there's no harm done."

Luke regarded Mr Derby. He hadn't the slightest doubt that, after this interval at Holbrooke House, he'd be hustled before the earl and browbeaten into submission. When he'd had little interest in what happened to him, it would have worked. Ignoring with difficulty Mr Derby's less than polite ideas on how to treat Kitty, Luke gave a taut nod.

"I'll think on it, sir, I can say no more than that."

"That's all I ask," Mr Derby said, nodding gravely. "No one could ask more."

Luke forced himself not to grimace and hurried away as fast as he could. Well, at least he'd escaped without raising Mr Derby's suspicions. That was something.

***

Matilda took Bonnie's arm as they ambled back to the house, wishing she didn't feel like such a wretched nag as she tried to talk some sense into the girl. "I know he's great fun, but really, you must try to—"

"Be more ladylike, yes, I know," Bonnie said, looking so glum that Matilda's guilt only grew. It seemed so unfair to squash all the life and spirit from the girl, but she would get herself into a deal of trouble if she didn't have a care.

"Mr Cadogan is very handsome and very charming, but—"

"But he'd not marry a girl like me in a million years," Bonnie snapped, pulling her hand free of Matilda's arm. She glared at Matilda in defiance but then she took a deep breath and her face fell. "I'm sorry," she said with a sigh. "Only it's not that I don't know it, and you're hardly the first person to point it out."

"Then why—?"

"Because I'm doomed," Bonnie said, throwing up her hands. "I've not fortune enough to tempt a husband to overlook my mouth and my manners, but I'm damned if I'll pretend to be something I'm not. How awful for some poor man to marry me thinking I was sweet and docile and then to discover—" She broke off as the words began to tremble a little.

"To discover you are vibrant and witty and fun and full of joy," Matilda said, taking her arm again.

Bonnie snorted. "If you say so."

"I do."

"My time's almost up," Bonnie said, her voice dull. "I'll be married to Gordon Anderson by Christmas and banished to some isolated corner of Scotland, and I'll see none of you ever again. I'll have a dozen children, and get fat and boring, and that's about the best I can hope for." She turned back to Matilda, her expression bleak. "I just want to have some fun before it's too late, Matilda. Is that so wrong?"

Matilda felt her heart ache for the girl, guilt a heavy weight in the pit of her stomach. Surely her fears about marrying Mr Burton were nothing in the face of such a fate? She ought to be thanking her lucky stars not bemoaning the fact she didn't love him or feel any spark between them. Poor Bonnie had no say whatsoever in what happened to her, unless she could convince some eligible man to wed her. Matilda reached out to her, stroking her cheek. "No, love. Not in the least. It's only that I worry for you."

Bonnie nodded and gave a smile. "Mother hen," she said, taking the hand at her cheek and squeezing the fingers.

They walked on for a while in silence until Bonnie paused again, frowning. "What do you suppose they have got their heads together about?"

Matilda looked around as Harriet joined them.

"Does that look like plotting to you?" Bonnie said, gesturing across the gardens.

Matilda and Harriet considered the scene some distance from them, where Mr Derby, Lady Frances, and Mrs Drake appeared to be having a private *tête à tête*. They were standing in the shade of a large tree, hidden from almost every vantage point other than the one they were in at this precise moment.

"Yes," Harriet said. "Yes, that looks very much like plotting to me."

"They are going to try to keep Mr Baxter and Kitty apart," Bonnie said in a harsh whisper.

"They might just be talking," Matilda said, though even she could see there was something clandestine in the gathering, something furtive in the way they stood, the way they stole glances about them.

"No," Harriet said, pushing her spectacles up her nose. "Bonnie is right. They believe Mr Baxter means to ensure he marries Kitty, and they intend to thwart him before it happens."

"Ensure how?" Bonnie demanded, staring at Harriet. "Harry, do you know something?"

Harriet shrugged. "I know lots of things, but no, nothing that I can tell you. I do know trouble when I see it though. We must watch the three of them closely."

"Oooh," Bonnie breathed with delight. "An intrigue. How exciting."

Harriet rolled her eyes before turning back to them. "We must all get ready for dinner as fast as possible. I'll watch Lady Frances. Bonnie, you take Mr Derby. Matilda, you watch Mrs Drake. Whatever it is they're plotting, we must stop them."

***

Kitty was like a cat on hot bricks for the rest of the evening. She had said nothing to her friends about the elopement, though she suspected Harriet must have guessed, as she'd suggested it. She would not tell them anything until they'd left—apparently for their day out—and it was too late for anyone to accidentally give her away or try to dissuade her.

Whether any of them *would* try, she didn't know. Harriet would have been the most likely if she'd considered it, but it had been her idea. Matilda wouldn't like it, Kitty guessed. She would

165

worry, bless her. Kitty smiled. Dear Matilda, she worried about all of them, but she'd do better looking after herself. Kitty had hoped she would be happy with Mr Burton courting her, which he was doing whether or not Matilda had agreed to it. Happiness was not what Kitty saw in her eyes, though. All the sparkle had gone out of her, and she seemed dull and listless.

Somehow, Kitty made it through dinner and up to her room without incident. She'd retired far earlier than usual, not staying to drink tea and wait for the men to return to them after their port, but pretending the archery contest had worn her out… as if!

Now she lay on the bed, staring at the ceiling. She would spend tomorrow night with Luke, and the night after, and all the nights to come. A smile curved over her mouth and she wanted to laugh with the joy of it.

She felt quite at peace, with the pleasant thrill of anticipation humming in her blood. It reminded her of so many nights as a child. She would lay awake for hours, too excited to sleep as she'd made plans for a grand adventure with Luke, and the morning could not come soon enough.

A memory returned of one such day. They'd met not long after dawn, as a soft mist still curled over the countryside and the sun shone through it like candlelight through silk. The world was cast in rose and gold, and it had appeared to be a fairyland. She had made Luke laugh by suggesting they look for a unicorn, for surely one must live in such an enchanted place. Far more prosaic Luke had suggested newts were a more accessible target, and they had headed for the river.

They'd spent hours paddling and catching sticklebacks, lying on their bellies and searching for newts and frogs. Jewel-coloured dragonflies had darted back and forth, their wings whirring and clicking as if they were made of paper.

They'd picnicked on what they'd filched from their kitchens: doorstop slices of bread, a hunk of cheese and a slice of apple pie, and bilberries they'd gathered on the way. After lunch, poor Luke had fallen into the river trying to retrieve Kitty's hat, which had blown away. Amazing to think she'd taken one. She usually didn't, for she thought them a nuisance, though not as much of a nuisance as Luke had thought that one.

He'd squelched out of the water, sopping and festooned with bright green weed.

"Kitty Connolly, you wretch," he'd said, glowering and holding her mangled hat by the ribbons. "Why is it always me who gets soaked to the skin?"

Kitty had run to him and kissed his cheek. "Because you're my brave knight," she said, laughing. "And you never let me down."

He'd laughed then, his bad temper forgotten at once, and they'd lain in the sun while he dried, until it was time to go home.

Kitty closed her eyes, reliving the memory and so many others like it. Their lives wound together like the strands in a tapestry, all the colours and textures of their adventures threaded in and out to make the picture she'd seen in her heart, one where they would always be together.

***

"Harry, Tilda, look," Bonnie whispered, as Lady Frances and Mrs Drake got up to take their leave.

Kitty too had retired unusually early. There was the strangest sense of anticipation in the air, Matilda thought. She couldn't quite put her finger on it, but something was afoot. Despite herself she experienced a shiver of excitement.

"We'll follow them?" she asked, and Harriet nodded. Even serious Harry appeared just as gleeful as Matilda felt, and she knew playing detective must appeal to her.

"Yes, as soon as they've left the room. We must hurry, though, or we'll lose them. Bonnie, you stay and keep an eye out for Mr Derby."

Bonnie huffed a little at being left behind, but she could hardly go looking for him, so she nodded and Matilda watched the two ladies slip out of the door before she followed Harriet and went after them. Lady St Clair turned from her conversation with Miss Derby and Harriet's Aunt Nell, and looked somewhat perplexed that her guests had all chosen to have an early night, but let them go without questioning them.

They had taken tea in the blue drawing room, one of a line of connecting rooms of such splendour it was impossible to take everything in. From the blue drawing room they walked directly into the Roman room, so named for the incredible scenes painted all around them from famous episodes of Roman history. On the ceiling, mythological figures and beasts stared down, the vast size of the room and the powerfully painted deities and monsters making any visitor feel somewhat insignificant.

Once outside, Harriet put her finger to her lips, indicating Matilda should stay still and listen. They could hear the low murmur of voices and the rustle of fabric from the next room and waited until it grew faint. Harriet moved, hurrying to the end of the Roman room and peering into the next.

"The men took their port on the terrace tonight as it's so stuffy," she whispered to Matilda as she drew back into the room. "So, I think they'll either go straight into the blue drawing room via the glass doors from outside, or some might go to the billiard room."

The billiard room was further down this row of rooms, Matilda knew, though where exactly she wasn't certain.

"What do you think they're plotting?" Matilda asked, even more enthusiastic about the idea now than she had been. Her heart was thudding, and she felt rather breathless. It was exhilarating.

"Lady Frances tried to ruin Kitty, but that didn't work because we got to them in time," Harriet said thoughtfully. "But what if she turned that about? What if a man were caught with a duke's daughter, in a compromising position?"

"Oh, but Mr Baxter would never—"

"No," Harriet interrupted, impatient. "But he wouldn't have to. He'd only need to be *seen* to be in a compromising position."

"Oh!" Matilda said, wide-eyed. "He'd have to marry her. There would be no getting out of it if there were witnesses. My goodness, Harry. Where would they choose?"

Harriet bit her lip, her expression intense and serious. She knew this bewildering and cavernous building better than most. Lady St Clair had even said Harriet knew it better than she did, and Matilda could believe it.

"The yellow saloon," she said at length. "It's one of the family's favourite rooms because it's smaller than the others and cosier. It's relatively close, but perfect for a seduction as, with company here, it's empty and you don't have to traverse any other rooms to get in or out of it. There's also a secret passage to it," she added, with a chortle of delight. Grasping Matilda's hand, she towed her along in her wake. "Come along," she said. "We must hurry."

***

Luke leaned on the balustrade that looked out over an immense expanse of land, all belonging to the behemoth of a building they stood before. A sickle moon gave little light, but the sky wasn't entirely dark yet and the silhouette of woods and hills was backlit still. He wondered if he preferred it to Trevick and couldn't find any strong feelings either way. Trevick was just as grand, though even older and draughtier, and less convenient.

He could never think of Trevick as belonging to him, despite so many years of preparing for his role as the earl. It still seemed preposterous, like some wild story Kitty had made up and somehow he'd become trapped in the telling of it. Still, if it was a story of her devising, she'd turn up to rescue him at any moment. A smile curved over his mouth as he realised that was exactly what she'd done.

"Luke."

Luke turned as Mr Derby addressed him.

"St Clair has challenged Mr Burton to a game of billiards. I'm going along to watch them. Will you have a game with me when they're done?" His face darkened, a frown tugging his eyebrows together. "I know we've been at odds of late but… I always enjoyed our games after dinner and, well, I suppose I owe you an apology for… for the things I said about Miss Connolly. You're disrupting all my plans, boy, and that's hard to come to terms with, but I ought not have spoken so harshly."

Mr Derby put out his hand and Luke stared at it. Suspicion crawled up the back of his neck, but for the life of him he couldn't see what the old devil had to gain from his apology, or from the game. That he'd agreed to play Mr Burton was also odd, Derby would think him an encroaching mushroom.

Luke gestured to his glass of port. "I'm not done yet, and—"

"Oh, no rush, no rush. I think St Clair and Mr Burton are fine players, equally matched. I shall enjoy watching them. Will you come when you've finished?" He held out his hand again and, though Luke knew there was something wrong, it seemed churlish to refuse him.

"Very well," he said, taking Mr Derby's hand. "I'll be along presently."

He watched as Mr Derby walked off towards the main entrance. He'd not want to go via the drawing room where the ladies were gathered in case he got waylaid and forced to drink tea. It was a longer way around but with less peril of being trapped en route. Luke finished his cognac and followed him a few moments later. There was no point going to see the ladies, as Kitty would have long since retired for the night. He imagined her lying on her bed, wide awake, waiting for their adventure to begin with her usual impatience. Luke chuckled to himself and went back into the building, heading for the billiard room.

"Oh, Mr Baxter, Mr Baxter, thank heavens!"

Luke spun around, startled by the panic in the voice that echoed through the entrance hall.

"Mrs Drake... what—?"

"I think she's dead!" the woman cried, clutching at his lapels and shaking him. "Lady F-Frances.... She fainted and I-I c-cannot wake her, she's dead... oh, oh...." Mrs Drake began to cry hysterically.

"Where?" Luke asked, appalled. Surely a healthy young woman couldn't simply drop dead?

"In t-there...." Mrs Drake sobbed, crumpling to the floor in a flurry of silk skirts as she put her head in her hands and moaned.

Luke didn't wait to see if she would swoon, Mrs Drake was breathing at least, but hurried to the door she had indicated. The room was barely lit, just a single candelabra illuminating the shadowy space, but sure enough there was a figure laid out on the chaise longue, unmoving.

"Lady Frances?" Luke said, hurrying to her.

She didn't move, didn't appear to be breathing, and he knelt beside her and patted her cheek. Nothing. He shook her a little, but she didn't stir.

"Lady Frances?" he said again, panicked now. As much as he didn't want to marry the woman he bore her no ill will, and to die... like this....

He lowered his head, placing his ear to her chest as the steady thump, thump of a normal heartbeat became audible. Hands slid

171

into his hair and curled about his neck just as voices sounded at the door behind him. Mr Derby and Mr Burton's voices….

Luke reared back but Lady Frances held onto him, her grip remarkably strong. The door opened and—

"Luke!"

Mr Derby's horrified voice reached him as he stumbled away, just in time to see the bastard staring at him with reproach, with Mr Burton and Lord St Clair looking on in astonishment.

"Oh," said Lady Frances, gasping and putting a hand to her mouth. "Oh, Luke, I knew I ought not to have met you alone like this…."

For a moment Luke felt the ground tilt beneath his feet. He was sick and hot and cold all at once. A trap, his stupid brain told him, though his heart was thudding so hard he couldn't think straight, his mind disoriented, and so… so bloody angry. He opened his mouth to rage at them for doing this to him, but then—

"But you weren't alone, Lady Frances."

He turned, to see Miss Stanhope and Miss Hunt, shadowy shapes standing by the fireplace, just out of the glow of the candlelight.

His breath caught, praying they'd understood what had happened.

"You see, Mr Baxter, we saw Mr Derby, Lady Frances, and Mrs Drake conspiring like *Macbeth*'s witches earlier today and realised something wasn't right," Miss Stanhope said, her voice cool and detached. "So we followed Lady Frances here, and we heard and saw everything."

"You used the passage from the priest hole?" Jasper said, his voice full of admiration.

Miss Stanhope nodded, taking a moment to remove her spectacles and clean them on a delicate lace hanky. "We heard Mrs

Drake's hysterical scene and how she told you she believed Lady Frances was dead, we saw you come in here and try to help her, and we saw her grab a hold of you and hang on to look as though you were embracing."

She turned to give Lady Frances a hard stare and Luke followed her gaze to find the young woman rigid with humiliation. He let out a breath, so stunned and so bloody grateful he could have kissed Miss Stanhope for the joy he felt. No wonder Jasper was so in love with her—she was a marvel!

"What utter nonsense," Mr Derby said in disgust.

"I think not," Jasper said, the words hard. "Your story of having left your heart medicine in here was a flimsy enough pretext to bring us this way, and I know Mr Baxter's feelings for Miss Connolly well enough to know he'd never have met Lady Frances here alone, not under any circumstances. I'm afraid you've misjudged." His expression was grim and far from the usual hail-fellow chap that Luke had seen till now. "This is underhand, Derby, even for you. I won't have it. I want you gone from here—"

"How dare you? How *dare* you," raged Mr Derby, his face contorted with fury, his mouth working though no sound came out.

He clutched at his chest, grasping at the door frame as he fought for breath.

"Hell and damnation! It's his heart," said Luke, hurrying towards him.

Jasper and Luke half-carried, half-dragged Mr Derby to the chaise longue Lady Frances had now vacated as Miss Hunt hurried to the bell pull and rang ferociously to bring the servants running.

Luke untied Mr Derby's cravat, resisting with difficulty the urge to throttle the man with it and finish the job.

"You… you… ruining… everything," Derby gasped, clutching at Luke's arm.

"Shut up and tell me where your medicine is," he snapped, too angry to feel the least bit of sympathy.

Mr Derby indicated an inside pocket of his coat and Luke searched for the small paper packet.

"Bring some water," he said, and a moment later Miss Stanhope handed him a glass.

A servant appeared, and Jasper gave instructions that the family doctor be called at once, Mr Derby's valet summoned, and footmen readied to carry the man to his room.

Luke poured the powder into the water and swirled it about until it dissolved, pressing the glass into Derby's hand. "Drink it," he said, before getting to his feet. He moved to Miss Stanhope and Miss Hunt, noting without surprise that Lady Frances had made herself scarce.

He knew well enough that Jasper would hold his tongue, and he suspected the ladies too if he asked them, but he didn't know about Mr Burton. As angry as he was with Lady Frances, he wouldn't have her ruined when he knew who the instigator of the scene they'd just been treated to was.

"Miss Stanhope, Miss Hunt, I… I don't know how to thank you for what you did this evening. You saved me from…." He let out a breath of laughter. "I can't even begin to put into words what you've saved me from."

Miss Hunt smiled and patted his arm. "It was our pleasure, though I can take no credit I'm afraid. Miss Stanhope here was the one who figured it out."

"You were magnificent, Harry," Jasper said with admiration.

Luke looked around to see Jasper and Mr Burton standing beside them, now Derby's valet was tending to his master.

Harriet blushed and pushed her spectacles up her nose. "It was Miss Campbell who noticed something was amiss. It was easy enough to figure out how they might contrive to force a marriage between you. I couldn't have Kitty's heart broken all over again, not after so many years apart."

"It *was* most intrepid of you," Mr Burton said, sounding troubled. "Though I cannot help but think you ought to have come to us, rather than trying to deal with it yourselves."

"We didn't *try,* Mr Burton," Miss Hunt said, her tone brittle. "We succeeded."

"Yes, yes, of course," he said at once, soothing now. "Only, I should have saved you such an ugly scene if I could."

"I shouldn't have missed it for the world," Miss Stanhope said, turning to Miss Hunt and taking her arm. "Did you see Lady Frances' face when we appeared from the shadows? I thought she would swoon for real."

"I did." Miss Hunt gave a triumphant smile. "It was marvellous. Well, there is nothing more for us to do here, so we shall bid you gentlemen a good evening."

"Wait," said Luke. "Forgive me for detaining you, but… please may I ask that you—all of you—keep this to yourselves. I think Lady Frances is humiliated enough. I should not like to see her ruined for her part in one of Mr Derby's distasteful schemes."

"How good you are, Mr Baxter," said Miss Hunt with approval. "Of course we shan't breathe a word, shall we, Mr Burton?"

Mr Burton returned a slightly taut smile but inclined his head. "Indeed not, Mr Baxter. You may rely on our discretion."

Luke gave a sigh of relief. The ladies and Mr Burton retired for the night and, soon after, Mr Derby was carried off to his room to await the physician, leaving Jasper and Luke alone to enjoy a well-deserved nightcap.

"That was a near thing," Luke said, as Jasper led him back to his study and poured a drink.

"Thank heavens your Mr Derby was unaware of our friendship, or of just how observant and tenacious the female members of our party are," Jasper said, raising his glass in a toast.

Luke let out a low breath of laughter "I'll drink to that." He glanced up at Jasper's rather rakishly dressed bear and smiled. "Are you going to leave him like that?"

Jasper stared at the bear, who looked to have enjoyed a far more convivial evening than they had.

"Certainly. At the very least, until I discover why they did it," he replied.

Luke grinned and took another drink before he said, "I've no idea what the reason was, but I can tell you one thing: Kitty made it happen."

Chapter 14

Dear Mother,

By the time you read this I shall be married ...

—Excerpt of a letter from Mr Luke Baxter to his mother. Left in Lord St Clair's keeping.

24th August 1814. Holbrooke House, Sussex.

The next morning Luke rose early and hurried to get news of Mr Derby. Though he was desperate to leave with Kitty, and didn't feel he owed the blasted man an ounce of consideration, Luke could not go if he was dying. He was not such an unfeeling bastard. For all Trevick and Derby's machinations, for all their manipulation and determination to shape him in their image, he would not become them. He was a man of principle, of honour, and perhaps he'd not had courage enough to act on that honour as he ought have these past years, but he wouldn't fail to do so any longer.

As he hurried towards Mr Derby's room, his cousin Sybil greeted him, he had the feeling she'd been waiting for him.

"Mr Baxter," she said, taking his hands. "How relieved I am to find you. I was so anxious to speak with you alone."

Luke looked at her with interest, aware of a sense of urgency about her which was quite out of character. He was fond of Sybil. She had tried hard to be a friend to him, a sister of sorts, but Mr Derby had known that having friends and companions would give Luke strength, possibly the strength to defy him. Perhaps he had believed the same true of his daughters, especially Sybil, for he had taken care to keep them apart, and they saw little of each other. Still, Sybil had been kind, as kind as she dared, though she still dared not address him as *Luke*, as her father had forbidden her to do years ago.

Her father had crushed any spirit she might have had, and she was a faded creature now, afraid to speak unless she must, so her determination to converse with him alone was alarming.

"Is it your father?" he asked. "Is his condition worse?"

"No," she said, shaking her head with such vigour that Luke's surprise only deepened. "No, Father is well enough, better than he deserves to be, and that is why I wanted to speak to you."

Luke stared, astonished. He had never heard her voice the slightest criticism of her father.

"I… I overheard Papa talking to Lady Frances." A tinge of colour rose on her pale cheeks. "And… and I got the impression that perhaps you and Miss Connolly were… were thinking of eloping."

Luke stiffened, and she reached out, grasping the sleeve of his coat.

"*Go*," she said, shaking his arm with surprising force. "You love her, and she loves you. If you don't go, someone will stop you. Lady Frances, or her father perhaps, if not my own. They'll do something, they'll ruin everything. Don't feel sorry for him, don't change your plans. Go now and don't look back."

"Sybil," he said, stunned by her outburst, for though the words had been spoken in a hushed tone, coming from Sybil they may as well have been screamed from the rooftops.

He was dumbstruck.

She gave him a tremulous smile. "I count on you, Luke. I count on the fact that one day Trevick and Father will be gone, and you will set us free. We need you, Luke, all of us. You are our only hope for any shred of happiness in the years to come, but how can we be happy if you have lost the woman you love, the woman you've loved all your life?"

Luke felt his throat grow tight. "He'll go mad when he discovers it. It might—"

"Go," she said, her face taut with determination, more strength behind that one word than Luke had heard from her in all the years he'd known her. "Father has made his choices, made his bed… now he lies in it, as he lied and schemed and manipulated you and my mother, and my sisters and me. Go, Luke, go and marry your beloved Kitten, and don't you dare spare a moment's thought or concern for that… that monster."

She was trembling now, her eyes filling with tears, and Luke leaned forward and pressed a kiss to her forehead.

"Thank you," he whispered, giving her a brief hug. "I won't forget this, and I will see you happy too, Sybil. My word on it."

Sybil let out a little breath of sound, somewhere between and sob and a laugh, and then made an urgent shooing motion. Luke did as he was told and hurried downstairs.

Breakfast was a rushed affair, though no one said it must be, but everyone seemed conscious of the need to get out of the house, and to do it quickly. Kitty did not know of last night's debacle, that much was clear. He wouldn't tell her either, not yet. There was time enough for such revelations. He assumed Jasper had not told his mother, as she had long since retired when they'd gone to bed last night. Miss Hunt and Miss Stanhope spoke to him warmly, and he knew they would not have told a soul, just as they'd promised.

Luke had blushed a little when Lady St Clair greeted him at breakfast, thoroughly aware she knew what he was about. The lady was gracious, though, and did not tease him; she just received him with a warm smile, her beautiful face full of mischief.

What might it have been like to have a mother like that, he wondered? It was obvious Lady St Clair regarded her children as the sun and the moon. From what the other guests had told him, her sweet nature hid a ferocious maternal instinct, and you criticised her beloved sons at your peril. Did Jasper and Jerome have the slightest idea how lucky they were?

His parents had ignored him, sending him away to boarding school at the first opportunity until the scandal which had found them banished to Ireland. He'd not realised how lucky he was then. He'd enjoyed school and done well there. There were rules he understood and could follow, and he'd had lots of friends. His home was a place where little made sense and his parents were either screaming at one another or ignoring each other. He'd never been certain which was worse. The screaming was interminable, and his mother's weeping worse still, but then being sent back and forth with brittle messages, *tell that insipid creature I married that…* or *tell your brute of a father that…* was not a great deal more comfortable either.

He'd thought perhaps his mother might be happier when his father died. She'd wished him dead often enough, so it was a reasonable supposition. She wasn't happier. With no one else to focus on, all her bitterness and dissatisfaction had been aimed at Luke, and things had become unbearable.

Kitty had saved him. Kitty had told him he was her knight errant and they would have a thousand adventures together. Sometimes, when Luke had crept from his home before his mother woke and decided she must tell him how woefully life had treated her—for the tenth time in as many days—Luke would think that it wasn't him that was the knight at all, it was Kitty. It was she who took him on adventures and he merely followed in her wake, a lowly squire. He hadn't cared a jot. He'd followed her then, and he'd follow her now, wherever she led… well, within reason.

Luke smiled as he realised he was no longer the biddable boy he'd been then, not by a long chalk, but he would never squash Kitty's sense of adventure. It was why he loved her so. He would, however, make certain that neither of them drowned.

Jasper was on horseback today, as was Miss Stanhope. Lady St Clair, Kitty, Miss Hunt, and Luke were in the barouche. They were going to a picnic at Mitcham Priory—or at least the others were, once Luke and Kitty had left their company. This was a rare treat for them as the reclusive Baron Rothborn owned the place, which was an historic and romantic building. He rarely tolerated visitors, but was a friend of Jasper's and allowed him to visit with guests if Rothborn was not in residence.

They'd left bright and early and were making excellent time, yet impatience sang in Luke's blood. He wanted to be far from Holbrooke, far from Mr Derby and Lady Frances.

"How fortunate we are to be allowed to visit the Priory," Miss Hunt said, drawing his attention back to the conversation. Her smile was brighter than Luke had seen it since they'd arrived. "I've heard so much about it. It's dreadfully ancient, but Lord Rothborn detests visitors and rarely leaves the place."

"Yes, he's a prickly character," Lady St Clair agreed. "But once you know how to deal with him, he's not so bad."

"Don't they call him Solo, on account of him preferring his own company?" Kitty asked, to which Lady St Clair smiled.

"Not entirely," she said with a soft laugh. "His name is Solomon, but it is rather apt all the same."

"Lord St Clair?"

Luke glanced up at the sound of Miss Stanhope's voice, she'd been riding a little behind Jasper since they departed, but now she moved up beside him.

"This isn't the way to Mitcham Priory," she said, giving him a puzzled look. "This takes us into Tunbridge Wells."

"Ah," Jasper said, giving Luke a rueful smile. "Shall I explain, or will you?"

"Oh!" Miss Stanhope said, as her face cleared. "You're eloping *today*! Yes, of course Tunbridge Wells makes sense, then.

You will no doubt hire a carriage there?" Her easy acceptance of their plan made Luke blink and perhaps accounted for the slight delay before Miss Hunt exclaimed.

"*Eloping?*" She stared around at everyone, and a rather indignant expression settled upon her lovely face as she realised no one else was surprised. "Oh! Am I the only one who didn't know?"

"No," Miss Stanhope said with quiet calm. "Though I suppose I knew they *would*... just not that it was happening now."

"Guilty," Lady St Clair said, though she didn't appear the least bit guilty.

Luke thought she was thoroughly enjoying herself.

Miss Hunt looked from him to Kitty and then leant forward, taking Kitty's hands. "You're sure, darling?"

"You know I am, Tilda," Kitty replied, such a look in her eyes that Luke felt his throat tighten.

"Oh!" Miss Hunt said, waving a hand in front of her face as tears sprang to her eyes and everyone hurried to find her a handkerchief. "Sorry," she said, as Lady St Clair thrust one into her palm. Miss Hunt sniffed, dabbing at her eyes, laughing and crying all at once. "I don't know what's got into me but... but it's so romantic. Oh, Kitty, darling... I'm so happy for you."

She threw her arms about Kitty's neck and hugged her, nearly toppling them onto the floor of the carriage. It made them both laugh, which was a relief to everyone.

"So, we are to be your alibi?" Miss Hunt asked, smiling now.

Luke nodded. This part of the plan had made him uncomfortable. "I'm afraid so. I do hope it does not cause you any distress or difficulty. Mr Derby will not take it well."

"What news of him, Mr Baxter? Is he recovered this morning?" asked Miss Stanhope, and then blushed as Jasper shook his head at her.

"Recovered?" Kitty echoed, looking at Luke with a frown.

"He had a bit of a turn last night," Luke said in a rush. "Nothing to worry about. Miss Derby said he was much better this morning."

Jasper looked sharply at Luke now, a puzzled expression in his eyes, but he said nothing.

Miss Hunt snorted and gave a shrug. "Well, I suppose we *must* be pleased he is recovering," she said, though she sounded sceptical. She cast Luke a mischievous glance. "And I'm sure we can come up with a story that makes us appear quite innocent. Whether or not he believes it is neither here nor there."

Luke grinned at her. "That's just what Jasper said you'd say," he replied.

Miss Hunt raised her eyebrows. "I had no idea you knew me so well," she said, laughing as Jasper touched his hand to his hat in a wry salute.

Luke watched this and glanced at Miss Stanhope to gauge her reaction. There was the slightest frown upon her face, but she was a rather serious girl, so perhaps it was nothing. He wondered if Kitty had made any headway with discovering why she was so brittle with the earl, and then noticed that Lady St Clair was also studying Miss Stanhope with an avid expression.

Noting that she herself was being observed, Lady St Clair returned a bland smile and looked away.

***

The post chaise rocked into motion and Kitty's breath caught. It was happening. It was really and truly happening.

"No regrets?" Luke asked her, his eyes grave and worried. "We will create a bit of a stir. Even if no one cares about Mr Baxter marrying Miss Connolly, your parents will have something to say about us eloping."

Kitty laughed at that and shook her head. "Oh, Luke, you ninny. You'll be the Earl of Trevick one day. My father will fall at your feet in gratitude for taking me off his hands, and then ask you to invest in his new mill."

Luke's countenance darkened at that. "It might be years until I'm earl, you know. Trevick is too damned spiteful to die and Derby has attacks like last night's often enough, and always recovers, looking hale and hearty. Until then I've really very little to offer you. In fact," he added, rubbing the back of his neck and sounding somewhat sheepish, "the only thing that belongs to me is the house in Ireland. Trevick gave it to my father when he banished us, so I inherited it, for what that's worth."

"You own the house next to ours?" Kitty exclaimed, astonished.

Luke nodded. She gave a squeal of delight and leapt from her side of the carriage to sit beside him and fling her arms about his neck.

"Oh, but that's perfect! We can go home, we can make the place ours like we always dreamt of."

He laughed but gave her a rueful smile. "Yes, it's ours, for what that's worth. It's been empty since I left, Kitten. It will be in a shocking state and I've only got a very little money put away. Not nearly enough to do everything required."

Kitty stared at him and gave a sad shake of her head. "You're being a ninny again. I have a generous dowry."

Luke glowered. "I know, Kitty, but a fellow doesn't like to live off his wife, you know...."

"Oh, fustian," she said with impatience. "It's not like you're going drinking and carousing with it. You'll be investing in our home, our future, and anyway, the land is fertile. You can grow flax and sell it to my father."

Luke gave a low laugh and kissed her nose. "Figured it all out, have you?" he said, putting his arms about her. "Well, I had realised that much, my love, but there will be a deal to do before the fields can be planted, and no income until the crop is sold. It won't be done overnight, and we have to live somewhere."

Kitty gazed up at him, into vivid blue eyes she'd dreamt of so often she'd wondered if she'd made up the intensity of their colour. She hadn't. "Luke Baxter, surely you're not thinking I'm afraid of a bit of hard work or a few spiders, even rats? We shall get a cat and go to work, and have the place spick and span in no time."

He stared down at her and she could see his misgivings before he opened his mouth. Dear Luke, always worrying about every little detail. If she hadn't threatened to go without him, he'd have worried himself out of a good many of their adventures. Not that he didn't sometimes have reason to worry. She had to admit that much, remembering some scrapes she'd gotten him into.

"You shouldn't have to work, Kitty. I hate that I can't provide for you, but I promise it won't be for long, and I won't sit about waiting for Trevick and Derby to turn up their toes, either. I shall make the estate viable, I shall look after you, and you shall live like the lady you are."

Kitty reached up a hand and touched his cheek. "Only if you promise we can still go on adventures. I shouldn't like to be a lady if I must sit at home behaving myself, drinking tea and embroidering handkerchiefs all day."

Luke snorted at the idea. "Kitty Connolly, you can't sew to save your life, so don't give me that. Of course, we shall still have adventures, and we shall begin with this one, a grand story that we can tell our children and our children's children, and they can wonder at how shocking the old people were."

She stared at him, her heart bursting with delight at his words. Her hand slid from his cheek to the back of his neck and it only took the slightest pressure to encourage him to lean towards her. His lips touched hers and she sighed, melting into his embrace.

"This is the best part of being grown up," she murmured as he pressed soft little kisses over her skin.

He kissed her nose again, her eyelids, along her cheekbones and back to her mouth, his hands cupping her face gently, as if she was of infinite value. She opened her eyes and looked up at him, and Luke made a low sound.

"Don't look at me like that, love. Not until our wedding night, at any rate."

"What?" she said, sitting up straighter now. "But tonight—"

"Tonight, I shall hand you into the care of St Clair's housekeeper and sleep at the other end of the house," he said, his tone dark. "Well, I shan't sleep a wink, I know, but still."

"Oh, but Luke," Kitty protested. "We'll be married the next day!"

"Exactly," he said, somewhat severely. "We've waited this long and I'll have no suggestion of impropriety... no more than can be helped when we're eloping," he added.

Kitty scowled. "That's silly."

Luke glanced at her mutinous expression and smiled. "You've no idea how pleased I am you're as impatient as I, but it isn't at all silly. I love you, Kitty, and I want to do this properly. It's been so long since I allowed myself to think of you, to dream of you, but my dreams were always of you as my wife. You could at least let me have things my own way this once."

There was no possible way of being cross with him after that, so Kitty relented. It was only one night, after all.

"Very well then," she said, pretending to still be annoyed with him. "I shall be patient, but... only if you kiss me again."

She bit back a smile as he tutted at her. "Blackmail. I might have known. Well, I suppose if I must...."

"Wretch!" she exclaimed, but before she could say anymore, he'd gathered her into his arms and there was nothing to consider except his lips, the silky warmth of his tongue, and the feel his powerful arms around her. He was so much bigger than she remembered; there was so much more of him, and she revelled in his size and his strength, pressing closer and demanding more.

"I think we'd best stop," he said, his voice rough, but Kitty sighed and tugged him back to her.

He didn't refuse. His hands began to explore, sliding over her until he cupped her breast and squeezed. Kitty arched into his touch and heard a low growl, a masculine sound of pleasure that sent her insides quivering with anticipation.

"Stop," he said, a little firmer, but then his eyes dropped to her mouth and he kissed her again, frantic this time, his mouth hot and urgent and Kitty felt like she was on fire, like she was melting inside, felt....

A huge jolt, heard an ear-splitting crack and the sound of splintering as the horses gave a dreadful shriek... and suddenly the world turned on its side.

***

Luke groaned and put a hand to the back of his head, wincing as he discovered a lump the size of a hen's egg.

"Kitty!" he said, as soon as his wits returned to him.

A muffled sound reached him, and he felt about the dim interior until he came across something struggling and cursing.

"Oh!" Kitty exclaimed, as she flung her pelisse to one side.

She'd taken it off when the journey began, as the carriage was rather snug and stuffy, and the wretched thing must have fallen on her.

"Kitty, darling? Are you hurt?"

"No, no, I'm fine," she said, quite matter-of-fact, as though this was an ordinary occurrence. "I just dislike being smothered, that's all. I'm not the least bit hurt. Well, perhaps a little bruised on my softer parts, but nothing to signify."

Luke let out a sigh of relief and forced himself not to consider her softer parts for the time being.

"Oh, but you, Luke? You're not hurt?" she said, struggling to her knees.

He shook his head. "No, but do keep still, Kitty, there's glass everywhere."

"Mr Baxter, sir?" They both looked up to where the carriage window was now above their heads. The postillion peered down at them, worry etching his face. "Are you or the lady hurt?"

"No, we are in one piece, just about. What the devil happened?"

"The wheel broke, Sir. This stretch of road is in a shocking state, been saying it for years, but nowt gets done, and now this. I don't know what we pay the blasted tolls for, it's criminal it is. I'm right sorry, sir."

"Oh, well, never mind that. Get that door open and help my wife climb out."

It took a bit of effort and manoeuvring but soon enough, they were both on solid ground and the right way up.

To Luke's relief the horses were unharmed and the postillion—whom they'd picked up in Uxbridge when they changed horses—though shaken, was a pragmatic soul. He'd eyed Luke with a somewhat suspicious air, no doubt surprised that such a well-heeled couple should travel without a footman, but he didn't seem inclined to dig and had said nothing. He'd charged them a pretty price, mind, and Luke had paid up, too impatient to quibble.

Now the man stood, regarding the mangled carriage with an unhappy countenance.

"Where exactly are we?" Luke asked, wondering what the chances were now of reaching Aylesbury before nightfall.

"Tatling End, sir," the postillion said, his expression sour. "I must go back to Uxbridge to get someone out to fix this pile of matchsticks."

"I can't wait for it to be repaired," Luke exclaimed. "It could be three or four hours before you even return, and then the thing isn't fit for use with the windows all smashed. You must have another sent out for us at once."

"Aye, well, normally I would, sir. Except as how there's nowt available today. A right busy day it's been. I told you as how you was lucky to get me. You thought I was trying it on and you paid over the odds, I know, but there's a big race meeting at Newmarket. It's on three days, and there's a fair and the like. The world and his wife started out at the crack of dawn this morning. Not to mention this heatwave sending the last of the quality off to the country. Every carriage is hired out, and the horses too."

Luke muttered an oath and fought the urge to roll his eyes to the heavens just as the sound of voices reached his ear. He turned to find Kitty having an animated conversation with a couple in a horse and cart. Kitty beckoned him over.

"Mr Baxter, such a stroke of luck we've had," she said, her Irish accent far stronger than he'd heard it since their childhood days. "This is Mr and Mrs Scripps, oh, and this adorable creature is Master James," she added, cooing over what Luke was certain to be the ugliest baby he'd ever seen. "You'll never guess, but Mrs Scripps was born in Ballymena."

"Ah," Luke said, comprehending the accent. "What a coincidence to meet a countrywoman from the Emerald Isle at such a moment."

"Ach, and it's fate, 'tis what it is," Mrs Scripps said with a placid smile.

She was a comfortably rounded woman in her late twenties, with the pink glow of a well-fed new mother, and she was regarding Kitty with the fond warmth of a beloved sister.

"And the both of us having wed Englishmen too!" she added with a peal of laughter as she slapped her husband on the back in a jovial gesture.

Mr Scripps glanced at Luke, or at least Luke thought he did as he turned his head in his general direction. The man had bushy black eyebrows of such luxuriant growth that they appeared to be pulling his broad forehead down to somewhere in the vicinity of his nose. Luke assumed his eyes were beneath them, but they were not immediately visible.

"Where to, lad?" the fellow asked with a sigh, clearly deciding to cut to the heart of the matter.

"That's very kind of you, Mr Scripps," Luke replied, eyeing the cart with some misgiving. It was serviceable rather than elegant, and certainly not built for the comfort of passengers. It held crates of chickens and ducks, and smelled vile. "We were on our way to Aylesbury, but if you could get us somewhere we might hire another vehicle, that would be most appreciated."

"Ooooh," said Mrs Scripps, leaning over to address Kitty as if Luke were not there. "A fine gentleman is he nae?"

Kitty grinned and took his arm. "That he is, Mrs Scripps. We're going to see his poor mama, sick she is, and not a soul but servants about her. His older brother is the heir, but he's a bad'un... *the bottle,*" she said in a whisper from behind her hand that they'd probably heard in Uxbridge. "He cares for nothing but spending his inheritance, and my own dear husband won't get so much as a farthing, though it's him his mama loves with all her heart. Obadiah, I said—that's his name see—Obadiah... we must tend to her ourselves, for 'tis our Christian duty."

Luke stared at Kitty, realising with the fatalistic calm of one who'd been here many times before, that she was taking them on an adventure.

Half an hour later, with a lurid past established that included a villainous father, a rake for a brother, his mama at death's door and a mad grandmother he'd been blissfully unaware of, they were on their way. They had crammed their luggage in among the unhappy fowl, and Kitty and Luke sat on the back of the cart, their legs swinging over the end as the road rumbled beneath their feet.

"Wretch," he murmured, as Kitty turned her unrepentant dark eyes on him. "Obadiah, indeed."

She lifted her chin and shrugged. "Well, at least we've still a chance of reaching Aylesbury today. I should thank my lucky stars if I were you."

"Yes, but then I must tend my poor mama as she slips from this world, and deal with my wicked brother who is bound to shoot me dead the moment he sets eyes on me. That is, if my mad grandmother doesn't cut my throat while I sleep tonight," he said with a mournful sigh.

Kitty sniggered and leaned into him.

"Well, it's the least I could give them for their kindness, as they wouldn't take any money. Now Mrs Scripps will have a fine tale to tell all her friends when she gets back home."

Luke cut her a look. "Don't give me that," he said, knowing his beloved far too well to fall for it. "You'd begun that story before you even knew they would take us, let alone if they'd accept any money for it."

"Well, and they'd have never taken plain old Mr and Mrs *Dull* from *Not Very Interesting*, in *Boring* along with such alacrity, now, would they?" she retorted.

"We're not the least bit dull," Luke said, stung. "We're childhood sweethearts, reunited after years of separation by a villainous earl, *and* we're eloping!"

Kitty tucked her arm into his and gazed up at him in such a way that Luke felt like a king, despite the fact he was sitting on the back of a foul-smelling farm cart, and a chicken was pecking at his sleeve.

"So we are," she said with a happy sigh.

Luke grinned.

Chapter 15

My Lord St Clair,

*We arrived safely at Chesson Manor after a
journey which I will tell you more of the next
we meet. Suffice to say there were a host of
interesting characters along the way, whom I
know you will find vastly entertaining, and
that's without even mentioning the crocodile.*

**—Excerpt of a letter from Mr Luke Baxter to
The Right Honourable, The Earl of St Clair.**

24th August 1814, Amersham.

After a heartfelt goodbye with Kitty and Mrs Scripps hugging
and wiping their eyes for longer than either Luke or Mr Scripps
seemed to think necessary, they parted company with their kind
companions. Mrs Scripps waved baby James' chubby fist at them
in farewell as the cart rumbled away, and implored Luke to watch
out for his wicked sibling.

Luke sighed and led Kitty inside The Saracen's Head at
Amersham. They had stored their luggage here and would stop to
eat before trying to find transport to take them onto Aylesbury.
Amersham was a bustling little market town some fifteen miles
from Aylesbury and the private rooms at The Saracen's Head were
already taken, it being long past midday. So, they settled
themselves down in the common dining room and enjoyed a
splendid repast of chops and roast potatoes, followed by fruit and

cheese, and a home-brewed ale of such quality that Luke felt himself well content with life.

"Right, I'm going to enquire about hiring a post chaise," he said, setting down his empty tankard with regret.

It was tempting to stay the night here, but every delay meant another night before Kitty was his wife, and increased the chances that Mr Derby might have recovered enough to come after them. He gave Kitty a warning look.

"Don't get into mischief while I'm gone," he said, eyeing her innocent countenance with misgiving.

"As if I would," she said with a sniff, folding her arms as though affronted at the very idea.

Luke chuckled and left her sitting at the table to speak to the manager.

A short and frustrating ten minutes later and the postillion's words returned to him The world and his wife were at or on their way to Newmarket. It looked as if they'd be forced to stay the night after all.

With annoyance at the delay, Luke hurried back to the table and found himself not entirely surprised to discover Kitty deep in conversation with two middle-aged women. Though one was a deal larger—in all aspects—than the other, it was clear they were sisters.

"Oh, and here he is," Kitty said, beaming at him. "Mr Derby, dearest, this is Miss Anne Quick and Miss Sarah Quick. Ladies, my husband, Mr Derby."

Mr Derby?

The ladies nodded politely and then the larger and older of the two addressed him.

"Well, Mr Derby, a pleasure to meet you, and I understand you are a missionary man, just returned from Africa?"

Luke remained very still for a moment while he gathered his wits before forcing a smile to face and replying with remarkable calm. "For my sins, madam."

The ladies tittered.

He glanced at Kitty, who bit her lip and stared at her hands with a fixed expression, refusing to meet his eyes. Oh, he would make her pay for this.

"Your wife tells us you are on your way to Aylesbury to nurse your poor mama," Miss skinny Quick—as he'd mentally labelled her—said with a sympathetic smile.

"I am, though it will be something of a trial, as dear Mama *loathes* my wife," he said, taking Kitty's hand and squeezing it a little too hard. "She never forgave me for marrying you, did she love? She always thought you'd lead me to the devil, and here I am, *a missionary man.*"

Kitty looked up at him, and he knew she well understood he was going to murder her.

"Yes," Kitty said, looking as innocent as the maid she was as she turned her dark, beguiling eyes on the two ladies. "But my papa would have killed him had he not after we had been meeting in secret for *so* long…"

She lowered her lashes coyly as the ladies gave Luke a sharp and disapproving glare.

Luke blushed. Damn, she was good at this.

"Yes, well, I always intended to," Luke said in a rush. "It was only that Mama didn't like me marrying so far above myself. She felt sure you'd spend my money and leave me in ruins."

Both Miss Skinny Quick and Miss Plump Quick were riveted by this back-and-forth, and Luke was therefore quite prepared when they offered to take them up as far as the Walton Turnpike.

"How kind you are, ladies," Luke said with a beneficent smile. "The good Lord is certainly smiling on us today."

The Misses Quick beamed at him.

***

Kitty thanked the ladies with warmth and enthusiasm as they set them down and waved them off with a handkerchief, before steeling herself to look Luke in the eyes.

As the Quicks' carriage rounded the bend and disappeared out of sight, she turned her most beseeching expression on her betrothed.

"Now, Luke," she said, observing the glint in his eyes with misgiving. "Admit that we would not be here, but still stuck in Amersham, if I hadn't secured us a place in their carriage."

"Indeed, Kitten," he agreed amicably enough. "I do admit it. I do not, however, see why it was necessary to make me a missionary man just back from Africa, of all places! I could wring your neck," he said with feeling. "I've turned my brain upside down trying to shake loose every last piece of information I've ever learned about the place, and I'm sure half of it was quite incorrect. Happily for us, I don't think they'd have known Africa from Australia, and were none the wiser."

"Oh, but the story about the crocodile was inspired," she said, taking his arm and staring up at him in wonder. "I was utterly enthralled myself, and I knew it was all a hum."

"Stop trying to turn me up sweet, you odious creature," he said, glowering at her. "Though it *was* a rather marvellous story," he admitted, unwinding somewhat.

"Oh, it was, and the bit where you saved the little dog from its snapping jaws! I wanted to weep and cheer you on at the same time."

Luke snorted and rolled his eyes. "Is this what married life will be like?" he demanded, though there was a smile touching the corners of his mouth. "I wonder at the fact I ever despaired of seeing you again, if I'd had any sense, I would have run the moment I set eyes on you."

"Oh, Luke!" Kitty cried, horrified. "Don't say it. I promise I shan't tease you anymore, I'll be good, I swear."

Luke frowned and then looked about to be certain they were unobserved. "Don't you dare," he murmured, before giving her a swift kiss. "I'm having a ball. I've missed your particular brand of madness more than I can say."

She sighed with relief and took hold of his hand, raising it to her cheek. "Love you," she whispered.

"Love you too, you little she-devil, even if you do make a fellow dizzy with your shenanigans. Still, we're not so very far from Aylesbury, so what are you going to come up with to get us to St Clair's place now, I wonder?"

Kitty resisted the urge to hug him and decided to be magnanimous.

"I think it's your turn," she said, "After all, fair's fair."

***

To Luke's infinite relief, a hackney carriage arrived at the turnpike just moments later. The coachman was returning to Aylesbury after letting off his last fare and happily took them up. It was rather old and rickety and there was a spring sticking in his thigh, but he was Mr Luke Baxter, travelling with his wife, and there was no mention of sinister brothers, mad grandmothers or any other manner of trying relation to colour their journey.

He'd meant what he'd said to Kitty, though: despite being thrust into these stories headfirst, he had enjoyed himself. It was ridiculous and dreadful, and thoroughly scandalous, and it was years since he'd felt so alive. Nonetheless, it was far more restful to be doing nothing more outrageous than eloping which seemed a perfectly ordinary thing to do with Kitty in tow.

Finally, they arrived at St Clair's place in Aylesbury. It was a fine Tudor mansion house set within beautiful gardens, and Kitty exclaimed with delight as Luke helped her down from the carriage.

"But how lovely it is," she said, staring about her. The housekeeper, Mrs Worth, was waiting for them and greeted them with warmth.

"I'm sorry we are somewhat later than we hoped," Luke said. "There was some trouble with the post chaise we hired, and our journey became a little... delayed."

"Well, you're here now, sir, and very welcome too." Mrs Worth said with a smile. "His lordship said to be certain you were made comfortable, so please tell me at once what else I can do. I've water ready for baths, and dinner will be at your convenience. If you'll follow me, I'll show you to your rooms."

Mrs Worth apologised for the state of the house and the fact that many of the rooms were closed off, but the earl was in the middle of some serious refurbishments and had set the place on its ears.

Luke, who was simply relieved to have reached their destination thanked her and allowed her to bear Kitty off to her own room. What exactly Jasper had said about them in regard to their marital status he didn't know, but her manner was warm and not the least bit disapproving, so either she knew and was a romantic, or she believed them already wed. Luke didn't much care, as long as Kitty was not made uncomfortable.

With a sigh, Luke fell back on the bed to wait for the footman who would attend him for the evening, and promptly fell asleep.

***

Dinner was an intimate affair, which Luke both appreciated and feared, as once the meal ended they were left discreetly alone, a fact of which he was all too aware.

Kitty looked especially lovely this evening in a dress of emerald green that made him remember their home in Ireland. Strange, perhaps, that he should think of it as home, as he'd not been born there, nor had he been there since Mr Derby had come for him. It was the only place that had ever been his home, though, the place where Kitty was.

The skies were dark now, and the candlelight reflected in the windowpanes. It was a warm night and the windows were still open, the curtains not yet drawn. Moths fluttered with suicidal determination towards the flames and Luke wondered what his chances were of keeping his word to himself tonight.

Desire simmered under his skin, the knowledge that tomorrow she would be his wife doing nothing to diminish his need to touch her, to reach out and pull her into his arms, and make her his. He made himself sit down instead of going to her, though he longed to put his arms around her. She was quiet now, standing and staring into the empty grate with a frown, her expression somewhat troubled. He feared perhaps she wasn't as sanguine about this adventure as he'd believed.

"What's wrong, Kitten?" he asked, watching that dark gaze turn upon him and finding his breath catch in his throat.

Memories rose behind his eyes—a hundred memories, a thousand—of looking upon this face and feeling his chest ache with happiness. This face, yet not this face; not the sweet visage of a girl, but that of a woman full grown. She had only become lovelier, the promise of beauty maturing into something that hurt his heart to look upon, for he was so very smitten.

"Oh," she said, a flicker of uncertainty in her eyes. "Nothing, really. I'm just being silly."

"Tell me," Luke said, holding his hand out to her, despite his best intentions.

She came to him at once and Luke held his breath as she sat herself in his lap without the least bit of encouragement, or any trace of embarrassment. It was simply the most natural thing in the world to her, and he ached to respond in kind as she wound her arms about him and pressed her face against his neck.

"There's a ghost," she said.

"Oh, Kitty," Luke said, trying not to laugh. "You've not been listening to servants' gossip again?"

Kitty nodded and bit her lip. "Well, it's such an old house, I thought there must be a ghost, and I was interested."

Luke made a choked sound and laid his head against the back of the chair. "This is just like the time you made me spend the night in that abandoned house," he said. "I was bloody terrified, but I did because you insisted. You spent the entire night telling me bloodcurdling stories and, though we didn't see or hear a blasted thing the whole time we were there, you still had nightmares for the next sennight, and you insisted it was my fault!"

"Well, it was," she said indignantly. "If you hadn't believed them all, I shouldn't have scared myself silly. You were supposed to scoff and say, *don't be ridiculous, Kitten, there's no such thing as ghosts*, but you didn't!"

"Well, I will now," he retorted. "Don't be so ridiculous, Kitten, there's no such thing as ghosts." He paused for a moment. "Where is this ghost supposed to roam?"

"The hallway," Kitty said in a small voice, glancing towards the door.

"The, er...." Luke cleared his throat. "The hallway?"

She nodded. "A big man, with a limp. You can hear him dragging his foot, the maid told me. She's not been here long, but she says most of the staff have seen or heard him."

Luke frowned. "Stuff," he said with vigour, forcing aside a tremor of unease. "Holbrooke House is supposed to be haunted, too, and I never saw or heard a thing there."

"Me either," Kitty said, not looking the least bit reassured. "Harry told me all about the ghost at Holbrooke; she wants to go on a ghost hunt to disprove its existence. She says they're not scientific, but anyway Holbrooke House is filled with people, and here...."

Here, they felt very much alone.

"Luke," Kitty said, her voice quavering a little. "Please may I stay with you tonight?"

Luke swallowed. His heart had leapt to his throat and anticipation thrummed through him, his body at complete attention. The warm weight of Kitty on his lap, her lovely behind nestled comfortably against his groin did not help one iota. He'd been trying manfully not to take too much notice, especially as she was in distress, but now....

He frowned.

"Wait a minute. This isn't a ruse to get me to—"

"Luke!" Kitty exclaimed, glaring at him. "I agreed to let you have your way and wait until our wedding night."

Luke snorted, unconvinced. "That was before the carriage fell on my head. If not for that, you'd have likely lost your virtue on the road to Aylesbury."

Kitty burst out laughing, her delight at his indignation quite apparent.

He sighed, once her hysteria had abated and tried again. "Are you really scared of the ghost, Kitten?"

She gave him a look which no helpless kitten ever born could have bettered and he knew he was beaten.

"Very well," he said, hoping he sounded stern. "You may sleep in my room. I'll take the chair."

"Oh, but Luke—"

"The chair, Kitty, or go to your own bed."

Kitty pouted and Luke resigned himself to a sleepless night.

***

Luke fidgeted in the chair. He'd shed his coat but not dared disrobe any more than that, now he tugged at his cravat which was strangling him. His neck hurt and no matter which way he shifted he could not get comfortable. Having glimpsed Kitty in her virginal white night gown, and knowing she was curled up in the big bed just a few feet away from him, was not helping his discomfort. Especially as the wretched creature had made it obvious he was welcome to join her if he changed his mind.

Well, he had changed his mind, back and forth a dozen or more times in the two hours since they'd retired to bed. He groaned, rubbing his face and wondering if he might be better off sleeping on the floor when a strange sound made him jolt with alarm.

"What was that?" Kitty squeaked, sitting bolt upright in the bed.

Luke tried to calm his heart as she'd startled him half to death. "I thought you were asleep," he whispered crossly.

"Don't be ridiculous, not with you fidgeting about over there. I kept thinking you were getting up to join me. I've been dying of anticipation all night."

"Honestly, Kitten," he began, and then froze as the noise came again.

"Luke?"

Luke swallowed and got to his feet, fumbling about for the tinderbox. It took him several tries to light the ruddy thing, but at last the candle flared and he lifted it up, turning towards the bed.

"Stay here," he said, his voice firm, though all the hairs up his neck were standing on end. Damn Kitty and her blasted ghost stories.

"Not on your life," Kitty shrieked, flinging back the covers and hurrying over to him. She grabbed hold of the back of his waistcoat and Luke knew better than to bother arguing with her. Instead he moved to the door, his lovely shadow padding silently behind him.

Luke cracked the door open, wincing as it creaked a little in the heavy silence.

The noise came again, a low moaning sound that had Kitty whimpering and burying her face against his back.

"What the devil is it? It can't be a ghost, I refuse to believe it," he said, as much to convince himself as reassure Kitty.

"What if it's the man with the limp?" she whispered, wrapping her arms about his middle, the warmth of her breasts pressing against his back about the only thing that could have distracted him in the circumstances.

"There is *no* ghostly man with a limp," Luke said, his voice firm now. "Come along."

He walked into the corridor, looking up and down and seeing nothing that resembled a headless corpse or whatever it was that roamed the house at night. Reassured, he headed for the stairs with Kitty clinging to the back of his waistcoat like a limpet.

He had one foot on the stairs when it came again. The first couple of times, it had been a low yowling sound that curled and echoed about the place like the soul of something long dead. This time… Luke frowned. That hadn't sounded as ghostly and undead as it had earlier.

A tad more confident, he carried on.

"It's definitely downstairs," he said, holding the candle aloft and peering over the banisters as he went.

Kitty hurried after him, squealing softly as Luke followed where the sound had come from and turned in the direction of the west wing of the house, which was still very much under renovation. He paused as something stirred, something… *scratched.*

"I-It's c-coming from in there," Kitty stammered, pointing at the door in front of them.

Luke nodded and moved towards it. He hesitated, taking a deep breath before throwing it open, and diving out of the way as an angry screech and a hiss rent the air, and something small and furry bolted past them.

"Jesus, Mary, and Joseph!" Kitty cried, stumbling back and falling on her backside in a flurry of white cotton. "W-What… w-what…?"

"A cat," Luke said, doing his best to look smug and not as if he'd just seen his entire life pass before his eyes. "See, I told you. No ghost. Unless it was the ghost of a cat, which I suppose is possible."

He gazed down at Kitty, sitting in a rumpled heap on the floor, and then exclaimed as her lip trembled and she burst into tears.

"Kitten!" he said, feeling like the worst kind of brute for having teased her. He pulled her to her feet and into his arms, hushing her softly. "I'm sorry, love. I'm sorry. There, it's all right, there's no need to cry."

Kitty sniffed, clinging to him. "I'm s-sorry," she mumbled. "The stupid c-cat scared me half to death."

Luke smiled and gave a sigh, kissing her wild dark curls. "To be honest, it put the wind up me too," he said, pulling back to give her a sheepish grin.

"It d-did?"

Luke nodded, stroking her cheek and wiping away the last of her tears with his thumb.

"I very nearly screamed like a girl. I would have done if you'd not been here, forcing me to act like a man."

Kitty's mouth twitched up as she stared at him. "Good thing I was, then," she said, staring at him with big, dark eyes.

"A very good thing," he murmured, before he could remember that he ought not risk touching her tonight, and kissed her.

She sighed, all the tension leaving her as she coiled about him, warm and willing and soft, and everything he'd ever wanted. The nightgown was fine and sheer, and the heat of her skin burned through it and set him ablaze as surely as if he'd embraced a naked flame.

Ten years of longing, of missing her and wanting her, the shock of love and desire, and the joy of seeing her again fired through his blood like a spark upon gunpowder.

The result was incendiary.

Luke backed her up against the wall, deepening the kiss as she clutched at his hair and pressed against him, so eager that he felt as if he'd die from wanting her.

"Kitten," he whispered against her neck, his hands cupping her breasts and finding the peaks of her nipples. He pinched gently and she gasped, her head lolling backwards.

"Yes," she said. "Oh, yes."

Luke reached down with one hand, snatching at the material covering her and hauling it up and out of his way until his hand could find its way beneath the hem.

"Tell me to stop," he said, his voice harsh, remembering everything he'd wanted for her, for them both. "Tell me to wait."

"Don't stop, don't wait…."

He groaned and kissed her again as his palm slid up and up, over the warmth of skin like silk, over the tender flesh of her inner thigh, until he found the downy patch of curls and stroked with the back of one finger.

"Luke," she whispered, his name spoken with such astonishment. "Oh… Oh, *Luke*."

He toyed with her, exquisitely gentle, barely touching her as her breathing became erratic. His heart wanted to burst with longing, his body ached and burned with the desire to be inside her… and yet he'd made a promise to her, to them both.

"Please," she pleaded as she looked up at him.

"I love you," he whispered, and found the hidden pearl of her sex, caressing in slow, circling movements as she clutched at him and he kissed her harder, deeper, her excitement driving him to the edge of what he could stand without giving into the desire to take her.

She grew still for a moment, her breath held as she gave him an open-mouthed look of wonder, and then her eyelids closed and she cried out and he smothered the sound of her pleasure with his mouth as she trembled and shook and finally quieted, limp and sated in his arms.

Luke held her, stroking her back in long soothing sweeps until her breathing steadied. "Come along, love," he said, his voice hoarse. "Back to bed with you."

She mumbled something incoherent and stumbled on the hem of her gown. He chuckled, pleased if painfully frustrated, and swung her up into his arms. She was asleep before they even reached her room and Luke tucked her into bed, kissed her forehead, and resolutely walked away back to his own room.

Chapter 16

Dearest Mama and Papa,

You won't believe what I've just done …

—Excerpt of a letter from Mrs Kitty Baxter to her parents.

25ᵗʰ August 1814, Stratford-upon-Avon.

Kitty stared across the aisle at her husband. Her *husband*!

She wanted to dance on the spot, to shout with joy and laugh and laugh… but the vicar was already disapproving enough of them, and she didn't want to make Luke uncomfortable. He was beaming too, however, a smile so broad with happiness that she decided she didn't care what the vicar thought and threw her arms about his neck anyway.

Luke laughed and caught her up, swinging her around in a circle.

"If perhaps you would care to sign the register first, Mr Baxter?" the vicar murmured, glowering a little.

Kitty pretended to look abashed, but poked her tongue out at the old humbug the moment he turned his back. Luke chuckled and signed his name before turning the book for Kitty to do likewise. Once all the paperwork had been seen to, and Luke had paid and thanked the witnesses he'd persuaded to attend them, they were free, and they hurried to stand in the bustle outside the church and stare at each other with wonder.

"Well," she said, and it was beyond her to stop the idiotic smile that was plastered to her face. "Now you've done it. You'll never be rid of me."

Luke let out a long, slow breath and stared at her in such a way she felt the pleasure of it right down to her toes. "Thank heavens for that," he said.

Kitty laughed and bit her lip, aware of the quality of his gaze on her, remembering how he'd touched her last night. She blushed but didn't look away.

Luke took her hand and raised it to his lips. "Come, Mrs Baxter, I think it's time to put your poor husband out of his misery."

There was a glint of mischief in those blue eyes of his, and Kitty felt her breath catch. Not that she was the least bit anxious. This was Luke—her beloved Luke, the boy she'd loved nearly her whole life—and there was nothing to fear when he was with her, certainly not him or what was to come.

He tugged her hand, pulling her into a run. She laughed, holding onto her hat, which almost bounced from her head as they hurried through the crowd. People exclaimed, tutted, and stared at them as they barged through back to the inn, and neither of them cared a fig for the stares and exclamations, too eager to be alone, too desperate to fulfil the promise of all their dreams.

They arrived at The White Swan breathless and flushed. Despite herself, Kitty blushed as the staff stared at them with curiosity. They'd booked the room as Mr and Mrs Baxter and now they *were* Mr and Mrs Baxter, so why she ought to feel shy when she'd brazened it out before made not a lick of sense, but that didn't seem to matter.

Luke caught her discomfort and chuckled, hurrying her up the stairs and pausing at the door of their room. He glanced about to see if anyone was watching before catching her up and carrying her over the threshold and into the room.

Kitty squealed and laughed as he kicked the door shut. She flung her hat to the floor, staring at him, breathless with everything to come as he put her down. They stood gazing at each other, stupid with happiness, grinning like fools.

He saw Kitty's eyes widen as she saw the bed. "Faith and begorrah!" she said, stunned as she stared up, and up, at the huge ancient bed, piled high with mattresses.

"It's the best room," he said, laughing a little. "I made certain we had use of the most comfortable bed in Stratford."

Kitty blushed, and he smiled and moved closer, sliding his arms about her waist. "At last," he murmured, the words barely a whisper. He let out a long sigh, staring down at her.

"At last," she said, reaching up to touch his cheek.

His blue eyes gazed down, serious now. "I never thanked you," he said. "I've never told you how… how grateful I was, how brave you were. You waited for me, Kitty. You had no reason to, no reason to believe in me, but you did and…." His voice trembled and he laughed, ducking his head. "I love you so much. I have loved you so much, all this time. I never stopped, Kitten. Not for a moment."

Kitty's breath caught, and she traced a fingertip along his jaw, smiling up at a face both so familiar and so different from the boy she'd loved. "I had a reason. I knew you. I knew your heart and your soul, and I knew that if you couldn't come to me, couldn't tell me where you were and what had happened, then someone had kept you from me. I knew one day fate would bring us together again. I *had* to believe it, Luke. I should have died of sorrow otherwise."

"Nothing and no one can part us now," he said, and she felt the warmth of his breath on her skin as he lowered his mouth to kiss her, and oh, what a kiss.

It was sweet at first, like the kisses they'd exchanged often in the days after they'd married in the orchard, but little by little it moved on and deepened as he held her tighter and teased her mouth open. Kitty gave herself over to it, to the touch of his mouth that seemed at once a single kiss and a thousand kisses, all tangled together and invading her soul, making her giddy with desire.

At last he pulled back and stared down at her, his eyes roaming over her with a possessive quality that made her squirm with anticipation.

"Too many clothes," he announced, a wicked quirk to his lips.

"Well," she said, trying to sound tart, and not as though she was quivering from the inside out. "You'd best take them off, then. I don't have a maid to help me."

Luke rolled his eyes. "Oh, well, if I *must*. I don't know, not married five minutes and already she's ordering me about."

Kitty huffed and forced herself to appear stern, though her lips twitched helplessly as she stood and tried not to fidget as he began undoing, unhooking, and peeling away the layers. He helped her step out of her gown and petticoats, and spent what seemed an age seeking out all her pins until her hair tumbled loose about her shoulders.

"I've wanted to rid you of these pins since the moment you burst back into my life," he said, the warmth of his words brushing the back of her neck like the silky black locks as they came free. "I wanted to see it loose, like it was when we were together in Ireland. I think we were barely tame, either of us, but you... my god, Kitty, you with bare feet and tangled hair and your petticoats hitched up and streaked with mud. I loved you so... I love you so...."

He pressed a kiss to the back of her neck and Kitty shivered with pleasure as his arms wrapped about her. She closed her eyes, covering his hands with hers and smiled, remembering—just as he was—the idyll they'd made of their haphazard lives. She sighed as he released her, and he returned his attention to her clothing.

When only her chemise and stockings remained, Kitty discovered she was just a little bit nervous. He was still standing behind her as she stared down at the thick rug beneath her feet. She felt rather than saw him move, and decided she couldn't stand to keep inspecting the carpet any longer. She glanced up.

He was staring down at her with a smile in his eyes that made any doubts vanish.

"The first time I saw you, I thought perhaps you were a Sidhe princess," he said, reaching out to coil a thick, dark curl about his finger. "One of the tricksy good folk the maids had told me about, and you would tempt me to follow you down to your fairy fort and keep me there for all eternity."

She smiled up at him, delighted by the admission. "You did? Why didn't you run away then?"

"I didn't care if you were, I wanted to stay with you for all eternity. I still do."

Kitty laughed at that, but then he got to his knees before her, his large hands curling about her ankle. He lifted her foot, caressing the curve of her instep before he rested it on his thigh. His hands moved up and up and over her calf, over her knee, up until he reached her garter. He untied it, though it took him a moment, and she noticed hands were trembling. *She* trembled beneath his touch, not with fear or anxiety but with the pleasure of having his hands upon her.

Slowly, so slowly, he drew the stocking from her leg until it passed her knee. Then he pushed her chemise out the way.

"Such a pretty knee," he said, pressing a kiss against it.

Kitty's breath caught in her throat. He carried on peeling the stocking away and then pressed a kiss to her bare calf, and then her ankle, and then her foot, bending low as if he would worship her, until the stocking was discarded, and he began over again.

When both stockings had been tossed to the side, he slid his hands beneath the chemise once more, sliding the fine fabric up as his warm palms moved over her legs. He leaned in and pressed a kiss to her inner thigh, the feel of his mouth on her so intimate and delicious that Kitty shivered and sighed. She closed her eyes, abandoning herself to his touch.

"Did you enjoy it when I touched you last night?" he asked, the words breathed against her skin as his mouth moved over her, kissing his way higher and higher in tiny, damp increments. "Did you like how it felt?"

"Yes," she said, almost swaying with pleasure. "You know I did."

"You liked my hands touching you here?"

Her breath hitched as his fingers brushed the curls between her legs, a flood of warmth pooling low in her belly.

"Yes," she said again, her voice husky now, her breathing so fast she felt dizzy with it.

"Good," he said, sounding dreadfully smug. "Then you'll like this even better…."

Kitty gasped, her eyes flying open as she realised he meant to kiss her there…. But then he had, his mouth upon her, his warm tongue toying with her as she exclaimed, the sound fading to a whimper as she reached out grasping at the bed post to stop her knees from buckling.

Luke moved back, chuckling softly before he stood, pulling her into his arms. "Perhaps you'd best lie down for this," he said, a smile in the words as he tugged at the tie fastening her chemise and loosened it, drawing it down to pool at her ankles.

He paused then, the feather soft caress of a fingertip gliding over her skin, making her shiver as his touch traced a path from her neck to her breast.

"I can't believe you are mine, Kitty. After so long wanting you…." He ducked his head as he cupped her breast and sought her nipple with his mouth.

Kitty cried out, clinging to him, holding him against her as he suckled and kissed and her body melted from the inside out. He tormented both breasts with equal devotion until she was hot and liquid, restless with need.

"Come to bed," he said, and the words were rough and unsteady.

The look in his eyes made her insides feel as if they were melting with the heat she saw there. She turned, eager to obey him and then stared at the bed, piled high with mattresses.

"How?" she asked, turning to him with sudden anxiety.

His lips quirked and took her hand. "There are steps," he said, as she followed him and climbed up, aware of the weight of his gaze on her as she went ahead of him and bounced as she laid back. She moved to the edge of the mattress and looked over, grinning as he leaned in and kissed her.

"Don't move," he warned, as he began to undress.

"I wouldn't dare," she murmured, too intrigued to see what lay beneath the layers of clothing he was discarding at speed. She'd seen he'd grown into a fine, athletic figure of a man from the cut of those clothes. It had been clear he was a superb horseman too, and she'd admired his skill in the saddle, and the way his breeches clung to his strong thighs as he'd controlled his horse with ease and finesse.

As the trappings of a gentleman fell away, however, the body beneath was revealed and she felt her breath catch, anticipation making her impatient as she longed to put her hands on him.

"Hurry up," she urged as he fumbled with the buttons on the fall of his trousers. "Oh, do hurry up!"

He stared up at her and gave a bark of laughter before pushing his trousers and drawers down in one smooth movement and then kicking his legs free of them.

"Yes, Kitty, at once," he said, his voice grave though his eyes danced with amusement.

He scrambled onto the bed and pushed her down, kissing her hard but giving her no opportunity to touch him before he spread her legs and moved down her body, returning his mouth to the wicked task he'd begun earlier.

Kitty was beside herself, drowning in pleasure and just a little shocked that his mouth was becoming so familiar with such an intimate part of her. Yet he was murmuring endearments, whispering encouragement, so clearly delighted with her that she forgot to feel embarrassed. She'd wanted an adventure with him, a lifetime of them.

For once, he'd chosen the path, and this was the most delightful escapade they'd ever had together. His mouth was hot and sinful and beyond anything she'd ever dreamed of. The pleasure he'd shown her last night began to crest once more, to tug her towards that exquisite oblivion. She rushed towards it, almost laughing as it tumbled her into a glittering world, a joy so absolute surging through her that she never wanted it to end. She sighed as it ebbed and faded, and left her in a sated puddle of abandoned delight.

***

Luke sat back, well pleased with himself as he regarded the wanton figure of his wife, spread out atop a dozen mattresses in The Swan's best bed chamber. She looked dazed, her dark eyes unfocused as she blinked up at him, finding her way through the haze of pleasure.

"Oh my," she said, with a happy sigh. "Oh my."

"How's married life, Mrs Baxter?" he asked, aware of the smug grin on his face as he stared down at her.

"Marvellous," she purred, stretching in a slow sinuous movement that made his pulse thunder in his ears.

Deciding he'd reached the limits of his endurance, he moved over her, settling between her legs and smiling as she gasped at the feel of his arousal sliding against her so intimately.

"Oh," she said, arching as he slid back and forth. "*Oh!*"

"Kitty," he said, a sudden surge of emotion catching at his heart. "Oh, Kitty, thank God, thank God you were there... I was dying without you."

She wrapped herself about him, her arms pulling him tight against her, her legs sliding over his as he pushed into her.

Kitty gasped at the sudden invasion and he hesitated, but she arched her hips, tugging him closer and he could not help but thrust deeper. He groaned as she caught her breath again and then laughed, because this was Kitty and of course she would laugh at such a moment.

He gazed down at her, at the joy in her eyes, and he was lost and found all at once. She was the wild adventure and the comfort of home all tangled together, and he didn't know how he'd endured the past years without her.

"I love you," he said, helpless to do anything but love her as his body moved inside her. "I always have, I always will."

"Yes," she said, pulling his head down to kiss her. "Yes, and yes, and a thousand times yes, my Luke, my husband."

She laughed again, and he swallowed the sound of it as he kissed her and chased the happiness he'd longed for, and found, with her.

Chapter 17

Dearest Matilda,

I have so much to tell you!

—Excerpt of a letter from Mrs Kitty Baxter to Miss Matilda Hunt.

29th August 1814, Goose Green.

"I can't believe you didn't tell me!" Kitty exclaimed for the third time as the post chaise carried them the final leg of the journey back to Holbrooke House.

They had spent a blissful two nights at The White Swan before returning to Jasper's house in Aylesbury for one night. The housekeeper had greeted them as warmly as ever and showed them to their room, not the separate rooms they'd had on the journey there. Other than that, she displayed no sign of knowing or caring that they'd eloped together, and Luke had every intention of congratulating St Clair on the quality and discretion of his staff.

Now, however, so close to facing everything they'd run away from, Luke had been unable to keep the events of the night before they'd left to himself any longer.

"Oh! I could wring her pretty neck," Kitty seethed, her cheeks flushed with fury. "How dare she? How *dare* she?"

Luke put his arm about her. "Come now, Kitten. It's all worked out for the best. Your Miss Stanhope and Miss Hunt saved the day. We owe them a great deal."

"Oh," she said, staring up at him and looking torn between wanting to throw things and laugh, which for Kitty was a not uncommon state of affairs. "Thank heavens for them. I shall never be able to thank them. Clever, clever Harriet, and Matilda... always looking out for me. Oh, how much I owe them. I shall never be able to repay them for saving you from that vile, devious, *wicked* woman. Not ever."

"Don't be too hard on Lady Frances, Kitten. Unlike you, I do understand the pressure she is under, the weight of expectation put on her by her father to marry well. What with Mr Derby whispering such schemes in her ears... well, I don't condone it, but perhaps we can forgive it?"

"Never," Kitty muttered, folding her arms, a belligerent glint in her eyes. "Not if I live to be a hundred."

Luke smiled and kissed her dark curls. "As you like, love."

She huffed, and he reached out, taking her chin in his hand and turning her face to his before kissing her hard and thoroughly. She resisted for the barest second before melting into him and putting her head on his shoulder with a sigh.

"I must thank Sybil, too," she said. "How brave of her to tell you to go like she did, when she is so afraid of her father. We will have her come and stay with us in Armoy once the house is in order, even if we must kidnap her to get her away from the hateful man."

"Yes, we must. Her and her sisters, but might I have you to myself for a while first?"

Kitty glanced up at him and tutted. "As if you need ask," she said, though she smiled and snuggled into his embrace.

They reached Holbrooke House by late afternoon and found a welcoming committee awaiting them. The moment they climbed down from the carriage there were whoops and cheers and they were pelted with rice.

Kitty exclaimed and ran to Harriet, embracing her so hard she nearly toppled them both to the ground as Harriet stepped on her own hem. St Clair caught her, steadying Harriet, who flushed and looked quite overwhelmed on all counts.

"Oh, Harriet," Kitty said, blinking back tears. "Luke only just told me what you did for him, for us. Oh, and you too, Matilda."

"And me!" Bonnie said, sounding a trifle indignant. "I was the one who spotted them plotting."

"Oh, and you too, Bonnie!" Kitty said, embracing each woman in turn and kissing them.

"I take it all went according to plan?" Jasper said, coming forward to shake Luke's hand as the women laughed and hunted for handkerchiefs for an increasingly emotional Kitty.

Luke laughed at that. "With Kitty in tow?" he said, shaking his head. "Not a chance, but we got there in the end."

"Congratulations," Jasper said, his expression so warm that Luke felt his throat tighten. "I couldn't be happier for you."

Luke reached out and grasped Jasper's arm. "I owe you a great deal, and I will repay that debt if I can," he said, meaning it. "I certainly won't ever forget everything you did. You can count on me, on my friendship, if ever you need it."

"Ah, well," Jasper said with a shrug. "Hope springs eternal. But, to other matters, I have a deal to tell you about what happened after you left. First, come inside. Mother has prepared a small celebration, and she's itching to show you both."

The small celebration was comprised of a lavish bride cake, thick with sugar icing, and copious amounts of champagne. There were flowers everywhere and Luke felt a surge of gratitude towards Lady St Clair for providing what Kitty had missed by running away with him in such a fashion.

"Lady Frances left shortly after we did that morning," Jasper said, once he had Luke's attention again. "She didn't say a word to anyone, just swept out with her head held high. She's got nerve, you must give her that."

Luke shrugged, feeling a surge of pity for the woman, despite everything. "She's a duke's daughter." He frowned, not wanting to spoil the day by speaking of unpleasantness, but he could not ignore it. "And Mr Derby?"

"Ah," said Jasper, his expression grave. "Miss Derby moved her father two days ago. She's rented a house, close to the doctor for the moment. In fact, she ought to be here...."

He turned as his butler, Temple, caught his eye and Luke saw Sybil walking behind him.

"Miss Sybil Derby, my lord," Temple said, before returning his attention to the liberal distribution of the champagne.

Sybil held her hands out to Luke and hurried towards him. "Oh, congratulations, Mr Baxter," she said, her face alight with a smile the like of which Luke had never seen from her. "I'm so, so happy for you. May I felicitate your bride?"

"You'd better," Luke said, laughing. "Though brace yourself, she thinks you ought to be in line for a sainthood, and she's drunk a lot of champagne already."

Sybil laughed and Luke felt his heart clench. He would help this woman as he'd promised, her and all the women of the Trevick line who'd been crushed and caged for far too long.

As he'd predicted, Kitty embraced Sybil like a long-lost sister and Sybil, quite unused to such displays of open affection, blushed and stammered. Soon enough, she unwound under Kitty's obvious desire to befriend her. She was bewitched by Kitty, as everyone was bewitched by her mixture of vibrant exuberance and quiet determination that all the world should be as happy as she was.

"How is your father?" Luke asked, once the two women had settled, regarding each other with pleasure and what he thought likely to become a deep friendship.

Sybil's face clouded, and he saw guilt in her eyes. "Promise you'll not be cross with me, Mr Baxter," she said, making his eyebrows go up.

"Cross with you?" he repeated, perplexed. "The only thing I shall be cross about is if you will persist in this *Mr Baxter* nonsense. You are my cousin and my dear friend. My name is Luke, I would like you to use it."

Sybil let out a breath and smiled, though it was rather a sad expression.

"Luke," she said softly. "I… I'm afraid I told you a lie. The attack that my father suffered the night before you left… it was followed swiftly by another, far, far more serious. He… he lives still, but not in any state that resembles the man he was. He cannot speak, cannot feed himself, he… is all but helpless."

Luke stared at her. "But why…?"

"Because I would not let him ruin any more of your life," she said, lifting her chin and gazing at him with such defiance he was truly shocked. "Or mine," she added. "I will care for him, as I am his daughter and it is my Christian duty. I will not mourn the loss of him, however. I have spent much of my life grieving for the kind of father I longed for. I'll not spend another moment on him. Oh, I'll wear black," she said, her face darkening. "I'm not brave enough to buck convention, but I will not pretend an affection I do not feel, and I forbid you to feel guilty for any of it, Luke."

"But…." Luke began, feeling the weight of guilt all the same. Good God, he'd hit the man just days earlier. They'd argued, and….

"But nothing." Sybil's voice was strong and her grip on his arm stronger still as she gave him a little shake. "He stole your life, and mine, and my sisters. He bullied us and used us, and he made my poor mother wretched. You stood up to him, Luke, and I am proud of you for it."

"She's right, Luke," Kitty said, taking his hand. He looked down into her dark eyes and felt the world steady about him, solid ground beneath his feet once more. "He was an unhappy man who lived for ambition. He manipulated everyone for his own ends, you more than anyone. You owe him nothing."

Luke wasn't entirely sure that was true. Yes, he'd hated the man, hated what he'd done to his life, but he owed him the fact that he was equipped for his role as Trevick. Not, perhaps, in the way Mr Derby hoped to prepare him, but Luke had still learned much of what it meant to be a man, a leader, from seeing all the ways he was *not* willing to do it.

"There's something else, Luke," Sybil said, her voice soft.

Luke turned back to her as she smiled at him.

"Trevick is dead. We heard this morning."

Luke stared at her, disbelieving. Though the man had been ill for many years, it still didn't seem possible. Luke had believed him too spiteful and wicked to do something as human as die.

"He's been bedridden for over a year," Sybil said, surprising him further. "Father would let no one know of it. I think he thought if you heard the news it might give you hope, make you more inclined to defy him." She gave a bitter laugh. "All these years, he's been torn between wanting his brother to live to keep their control of you, and wishing him dead and coveting the title, and now he's Trevick, and he doesn't know it because his mind is gone."

"I don't know what to say," Luke said, shaking his head.

"Don't say anything," Sybil replied, giving him a smile of such tranquillity he could not help but return it. "I don't think Father will be with us a great deal longer. The doctor thinks six months, perhaps a year. Soon enough you will be Trevick, and we need you, Luke. There is so much that needs your attention, so many things they have neglected, and too many of us who have no notion of how to live without being told what to do. We will need

221

you soon, but not yet. So have fun, my dearest cousin. The news is not yet public so enjoy tomorrow's ball, and don't even think of wearing black. Enjoy life and live it to the full, for you will have responsibilities soon enough."

Luke turned to look at Kitty, suddenly realising what he'd done to her. She would be his countess, and those responsibilities would be hers too.

"It's all right," she said, clasping his hand within hers. "Don't look so terrified. I would have happily swept spiders out of a crumbling heap in Ireland, but I'll go to Trevick and sweep away the bullies and the toadies with you instead."

Luke laughed, and he heard the echo of it as Sybil laughed too, delighted with her.

"I can see why you have loved her so faithfully all these years, Luke," she said, watching Kitty with obvious admiration. "And I cannot wait for us to all be together at Trevick, but... for now, be happy."

Luke and Kitty watched her go. Luke squeezed his wife's fingers and smiled.

"I think we can manage that," he said.

Chapter 18

I am so afraid of making the wrong decision, or of making the right decision for the wrong reasons. I'm so afraid of being alone and terrified of being tied into a marriage which can never make me happy. How cruel of me to marry a man I can't love, though I think he views me as a possession himself, something pretty to own and take pleasure in the owning. I wish someone would tell me what to do, for my heart is of no use whatsoever.

—Excerpt of an entry from Miss Matilda Hunt to her diary.

30th August 1814, Holbrooke House.

"I'm so excited," Bonnie exclaimed as the ladies gathered in Matilda's room.

It was the night of the grand ball where everyone who was anyone would attend from miles around. Every eligible young man and young woman of the *ton* would be there, the rich and the powerful, coming together for a celebration where they would see and be seen.

Matilda turned to her little chicks and smiled with pleasure. "How beautiful you look tonight," she said. "I wouldn't be the least bit surprised if you were all married by morning."

Harriet snorted and pushed her spectacles up her nose.

"Oh, come now, Harry," Matilda chided. "That gown is just glorious and, the way you've done your hair, I don't think I've ever seen you look more lovely."

"It's true," Bonnie said, giving Harriet a critical once over. "That shade of pink is very becoming."

"I could never wear that colour," Ruth observed with a sigh. "I blush easily enough as it is. I don't need help to bring any further attention to it."

Matilda smiled, aware it was true. Ruth was a solid young woman who bloomed with ruddy good health. She looked like she belonged in the countryside, perhaps managing some vast estate. Matilda thought she'd do a marvellous job; she was the sort who never got sick a day in her life and was never bored, but busy, industrious, and single-minded.

She glanced at Bonnie, who had gone to look at herself in the mirror. She too was at her best tonight in a deep midnight blue. Any man with eyes in his head would salivate over her, but they'd never offer her marriage unless she behaved with a little more decorum. The dress was the most daring she'd ever seen Bonnie wear, as she tended towards more conservative styles. Tonight's gown was *not* conservative. Bonnie's lush charms were in danger of over spilling the low-cut neckline, and the gown clung to her generous hips. Matilda experienced a surge of apprehension. Yet, she'd already nagged Bonnie enough about her behaviour, and felt bad for spoiling what remained of her fun. She only prayed Bonnie would not go too far and get herself into trouble.

Besides, she had trouble enough herself. Mr Burton would be waiting for her.

They looked up as a knock on the door sounded and Matilda laughed as Kitty hurried in, with Prue in tow, carrying a man's top hat aloft.

Harriet gave an audible groan and covered her face with her hands. "Oh, no, Kitty, not tonight."

"Oh, and if not tonight, when?" Kitty said, tutting and shaking her head. "Don't be such a stick in the mud."

"Come along, Harry," Prue said, sitting beside her on the bed and putting an arm about her. "Take a deep breath and get it over with."

She laughed as Harriet huffed and rolled her eyes. "Oh, very well, then. Though I want it noted that I had a hand in Kitty's dare already."

Matilda, Bonnie, and Ruth gathered closer and Harriet put her hand into the hat, the dry sound of rustling reaching them as she made her choice. Matilda saw her take a deep breath and draw out a tiny folded piece of paper.

No one seemed to breathe again as Harriet unfolded it, her hands not entirely steady.

"Well?" Kitty said, bouncing on the spot. "*Well?*"

Harriet scowled.

"What is it?" Bonnie demanded, looking as though she would shake Harriet if she didn't speak soon.

They watched as Harriet crumpled the paper in her hand, irritation in her eyes. "Bet something you don't wish to lose."

"Ooooh," said Kitty. "That's an interesting one."

Harriet appeared to be considering murdering whoever had thought up that little gem, and so Matilda hurried things on. "Bonnie, why don't you go next?"

Bonnie squealed with delight, not needing a second invitation. There was a deal of rustling once more as she stuck her hand in the hat and closed her eyes, an expression of intense concentration on her face.

"Oh, do come on," Kitty protested. "Just pick one."

With a flourish, Bonnie withdrew her hand, clasping a slip of paper. "*Voilà!*"

"Read it, then!" Harriet urged, just as impatient as the rest of them now.

Bonnie fumbled with the paper, almost dropping it in her excitement, and then beamed as she read the words. "Wear a disguise in public," she said, looking thrilled with the idea.

"Oh, Lord," Matilda murmured. "What kind of disguise?"

"I don't know," Bonnie said, delighted. "But I shall come up with something marvellous, just see if I don't!"

"Can I have a go?"

They all turned to Ruth in surprise.

"We usually only do two at a time," Kitty said, and then shrugged. "But rules are made to be broken." She grinned at Ruth and held the hat out for her. "On you go, then."

Ruth flushed, proving she really did go a remarkable shade as scarlet stained her pale skin. There was no fuss or dramatics with Ruth though, and she simply reached in, drew a slip of paper, and read it aloud.

"Say something utterly outrageous to a handsome man," she said, her dark eyebrows going up. "Oh," she said, flushing an even deeper shade. "*Oh.*"

"That's a… tricky one," Prue said, frowning a little.

"Well, there we are, then," Matilda said, clapping her hands together with a light-hearted tone she wasn't feeling, but anxious in case Kitty decided a fourth go would be a good idea. She had enough to worry about. "Don't feel you have to do them all tonight," she said, focusing on Bonnie and doing her utmost to stamp on her own misgivings. "You have weeks to complete them, remember. Now, come along, we'd best go down."

Clapping her hands like a stern governess, she herded the ladies out.

***

St Clair looked about the ballroom and sighed. It was filled to the rafters, the sound of music, laughter, and animated conversation swelling on the heated air. He sipped at his champagne, trying to resist the urge to tug at his cravat. He didn't want to be here.

Usually, he enjoyed such events. He didn't crave constant entertainment the way he had as a young man, but convivial company and dancing and a fine summer's night were nothing to turn your nose up at. He used to be far easier to please, he thought with a sigh.

Despite his best intentions, his gaze was drawn across the room to where Harriet was dancing with his brother. She was laughing, happy and carefree in a way she never was with him. Though he knew there was nothing of a romantic nature between them, he had to fight an irrational surge of jealousy. *It's not fair,* said a childish voice in his head that made him want to throw things and pitch a fit worthy of a two-year-old. Resolutely, he turned his attention elsewhere, and then smiled as Kitty and Luke approached him.

"Mrs Baxter," he said, taking her hand and raising it to his lips. "May I say how lovely you look this evening?"

It was true. She was glowing with happiness, gazing at her husband with such adoration that he could not help but envy Luke.

"You may," she replied, laughing. "You can dance with me too, if you like."

"Kitty!" Luke exclaimed, a little mortified. "You did not just ask the Earl of St Clair to dance?"

"What?" she said, all innocence though mischief glinted in her dark eyes. "You know I need to speak with him in private. A waltz is the best solution."

"Hmph," Luke replied, not looking entirely sanguine with the idea, as he quirked an eyebrow at Jasper.

Jasper was instantly alert, wondering if she'd spoken with Harriet, did she have news? "It would delight me to oblige, Mrs Baxter," he said, holding out his hand to her. "If your husband will allow it?"

Luke waved them away with a sigh and Kitty took Jasper's hand, casting an impish look at her husband before she left.

"Mrs Baxter!" she exclaimed. "I can't get over how wonderful that sounds."

"You won't have long to get used to it," Jasper said, guiding her onto the floor. "Not from what Luke told me. You'll be a countess soon enough."

Kitty shrugged. "Mrs Baxter is all I ever wanted, but whatever comes with Luke, comes with Luke. We'll make it work."

"I believe that," Jasper said, smiling as the orchestra played the opening bars.

He led her into the dance and had to bite his tongue to stop himself demanding to know what Harriet had said to her. At last she looked up at him, her dark eyes full of sympathy.

"I've not much to tell you," she said, and Jasper's hopes crashed to the floor. "Except that she's not as indifferent to you as you might believe."

Jasper snorted at that. "I never said she was indifferent. She hates me."

Kitty shook her head. "I don't think so. You've hurt her somehow, very deeply."

Pain lanced through him at the idea of having distressed her. He couldn't bear it. He'd cut his heart out before he hurt her, but he knew it was true. It must be.

"How?" he said, struggling to keep his voice even.

"I don't know. She won't tell me. She didn't tell me that much directly. I had to put the pieces together, but I'm not wrong."

Jasper's breath caught, trapped in his lungs as if he could neither draw in more nor expel it. It hurt. His chest hurt, his heart was raw, and he deserved the pain, and more besides, for ever having caused her a moment's distress.

"I told her it wasn't fair to keep punishing you when you didn't know what you were being punished for. I told her she must explain herself; she must give you a chance to explain too, and then she can decide whether or not to forgive you."

His heart was thudding in his chest, too hard, too fast. "Will she?" he asked, hardly daring to hope. At least he'd know. If he'd done something unforgivable, at least he'd know what he'd done. Perhaps it wasn't unforgivable…. Perhaps he could make amends.

"I can't say," Kitty said, her voice soft. "But she promised me she would think about it, so… maybe."

At long last Jasper let out a breath. He felt giddy, the first glimmer of hope he'd seen for such a long time beckoning on the horizon.

"Mrs Baxter," he said, smiling at her. "Your husband is a very lucky man, and I am very grateful to you."

She laughed, her dark eyes shining. "Yes, he is," she said, her smile wide. "But in all honesty, I haven't done much. Nothing very useful, at least, but I won't give up and neither should you. You have plenty of time. Perhaps you could dance with her tonight. It's such a magical evening," she added in a theatrical whisper. "Why, *anything* could happen!"

Jasper snorted, his hopes not daring to go to those lengths. "Yes, she might not throw her drink in my face, *if* I'm lucky."

Kitty laughed, and he smiled as he whirled her around the floor.

***

Matilda sipped at her drink. The evening was humid, and the ballroom hotter still with the press of so many bodies in a confined space.

A trickle of sweat made its way between her breasts and she fought the urge to grimace. So far, she'd danced with Harriet's brother, Henry, Mr Baxter, and Lord St Clair, this last while Mr Burton frowned across the dance floor at them. She didn't like that frown. It held a possessive quality that made her uneasy. She had danced with Mr Burton too, naturally, and was aware he would likely ask her again. To dance with a man twice was as good as announcing that there was something between you, however, and Matilda felt panic rise in her chest.

He had promised to give her time, not to be impatient, and yet there had been a quality to that frown that suggested his previous impatience was not simply eagerness but held a possessive, belligerent edge she'd not been previously aware of.

She took another sip of her drink and then surreptitiously pressed the glass to her neck to cool herself. The glass was no longer cool, though, the drink itself having grown tepid, and it brought her no relief. She closed her eyes on the colourful swirl of silken gowns and black evening wear as the dancers whirled before her and at once she was in a garden, a dappled walkway that gave shade and privacy.

She remembered a man handing her a glass, a cooling drink filled to the brim with ice which she'd pressed to her overheated skin. She'd felt the shock of cold as vividly as she had the weight of his gaze upon her, the heat of his desire for her searing hotter than the sun that had driven her to seek the shade.

Matilda felt her breath catch even at the memory, felt the weight of that gaze again, as though he was right there in the room. Resolutely she opened her eyes, pasted a smile to her face and went to find her friends.

***

Luke stared down at his beautiful wife as he whirled her through yet another dance. It was probably shocking of him to have danced nearly every dance with her, but he didn't care a jot. She was his, and he wanted the world to know it.

A flicker of guilt crept into his heart as he thought of Mr Derby, helpless and ill and not even understanding he was now the earl, but he forced it away. He would do right by the man. He'd have the best doctors, the finest care, but he'd not let him spoil this glorious night. Luke had never asked for or wanted the earldom, all he'd ever wanted was Kitty, and Trevick and Derby had taken her from him. Now he had her and he'd not let anyone tarnish the brilliance of his happiness.

That the old earl was dead ought to give him pause too, but Luke could feel no regret for his passing, only pity for a man who'd never learned how to be happy, who'd cared for little but power and the continuation of his great name. How fortunate Luke had been not to been born the heir. What hand of fate had been so very obliging as to put Kitty in his path, Kitty, who had taught him how to live, how to make life a grand adventure and find happiness in everything they did?

"Goodness," Kitty said, laughing and breathless as the dance came to a close. "I'm worn out."

Luke gave her a regretful look and sighed. "Oh, that's a pity."

"Why?" she demanded, curiosity in her dark eyes.

"Well, if you're worn out, I'll have to take you up to bed."

Kitty returned such a delighted glance he had to bite his lip to stop from laughing. "That doesn't sound so bad," she said, grinning now.

"To sleep, you wretch," he added, his laughter bubbling over as she pouted at him.

"What a cruel husband you've become." Kitty gave him a wide-eyed look of such sorrow that Luke could do nothing else but lean in and kiss her.

"Cruel and heartless, that's me."

He smirked and tugged at Kitty's hand, hurrying her through the crowd as fast as he could, suddenly desperate to be alone with her.

"Where are we going?" she protested, though it was half-hearted and she was laughing.

She'd been laughing all evening. Even when she wasn't laughing, it glittered in her eyes. She glowed with it, the happiness shining from her as if she was lit from within.

For me, he thought, his chest bursting with the knowledge.

"Does it matter?" he asked, his voice low. "Do you care where we're going?"

He led her onto the terrace, the sultry evening giving little relief from the heat of the ballroom as he tugged her into a dark corner.

"No," she admitted, moving into his arms with ease. "Not in the least. I'll follow you wherever you go."

"Ha!" he said, amused. "As if. It's me that does the following, as you well know, you little devil."

"Ah, no, Luke, 'tis not true at all," she said, her accent a little stronger now, in this private moment. "We take turns, is all. Sometimes I lead, sometimes you follow."

She gave him a cheeky grin, and he burst out laughing, pulling her nearer and resting his forehead upon hers. He heard her sigh and smiled.

"Happy?" he asked, even though he knew the answer.

"I might burst if I get any happier," she warned, and he pulled a face.

"Perhaps I'd better leave you alone, that sounds messy."

Kitty snorted and held on tighter. "Don't you dare." She looked up at him and his heart seemed to skip about in his chest. Would he ever get used to this, to her? He hoped not.

"I have a present for you," she said, pleasure shining in her eyes.

"Oh?"

She laughed, having heard the delight in his voice and he felt like a boy again.

"You can't have it until we go back to Ireland," she said, sounding stern now though her eyes were alight with amusement.

"Tell me," he demanded. "What is it?"

"Do you remember, Khan, my dog, the big mastiff?"

Luke rolled his eyes. "Well, of course I remember, he was the size of a small horse and followed you everywhere, and I was horribly jealous that you had a dog and I didn't."

Kitty hugged him. "I know," she said, such sympathy in her voice as she knew all the things he'd missed out on as a boy, all the things she'd tried so hard to make up for. "Well, Khan is long gone but his bloodline lives on, and Father wrote to tell me, there's a new litter of pups and one is a big, healthy male. He's mine, Luke." She looked up at him and pressed her mouth to his, a sweet kiss that still made his breath catch. "And I'm giving him to you."

Luke stared at her, embarrassed to discover his eyes were burning and his throat was tight.

Kitty reached up, stroking his cheek.

"Thank you," he managed, swallowing hard. "That's the best present I've ever had." He kissed her forehead and sighed, smiling against her skin. "Apart from you, Kitty Baxter. You were a gift of the kind I'll never be worthy of. From the first moment I saw you, I knew you'd make everything better."

"I promise to always do my best to make things better, Luke, because I love you," she said. "From that first day to whenever may be the last, when I close my eyes on the world."

"Oh, no," he said, the thought of it unbearable. "You'll go nowhere without me, not even the great hereafter."

"Ah, well," she said with a shrug. "We've years and years and ten thousand adventures to live before that last one need be thought of."

"Ten thousand adventures," he repeated with wonder. "I like the sound of that. It sounds like a recipe for a wonderful life." He pressed a kiss to her forehead. "Because I've found you, and you've found me, and so we shall be together, and never alone again."

"Never," she agreed, and pulled his head down for a kiss.

Girls Who Dare– Next in this exciting new series from Emma V Leech, the multi-award-winning, Amazon Top 10 romance writer behind the Rogues & Gentlemen series.

Inside every wallflower is the beating heart of a lioness, a passionate individual willing to risk all for their dream, if only they can find the courage to begin. When these overlooked girls make a pact to change their lives, anything can happen.

Ten girls – Ten dares in a hat. Who will dare to risk it all?

To Wager with Love
Girls Who Dare Book 5

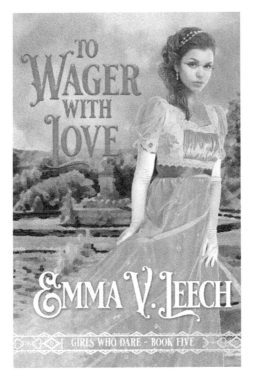

Once bitten, twice shy

Harriet Stanhope is intelligent and serious, the kind of girl who reads Plato and likes long walks in the rain. She is unsuited to ballrooms and flirting and finds the season a horrific waste of time. Once upon a time she fell in love, however, she trusted her heart to a man who kissed her and whispered sweet words … and then laughed with a friend about her having done so.

Heartbroken and humiliated, Harriet vows to use her brain in the future and never trust her stupid heart ever again.

An unrequited passion

Jasper Cadogan, The Earl of St Clair is hopelessly in love, with a woman who hates him.

Lovable rogue, Jasper, is handsome, charming, easy going and beloved by the *ton*, the most eligible man on the marriage mart, but he can't put a foot right with childhood playmate Harriet Stanhope. Though they were once close, Jasper knows he did something years ago that hardened Harriet's heart against him, but for the life of him he can't think what it was.

Jasper knows Harriet believes he's frivolous twit at best, and in awe of her superior brain, gorgeous Jasper is struggling to prove himself otherwise. Determined to discover what it was that drove Harriet away from him, he'll use fair means or foul to get to the truth.

A wager that will risk both their hearts

The Peculiar Ladies dare Harriet to *bet something she doesn't wish to lose* and when her big mouthed friend Kitty tells Jasper, she knows she's in trouble.

Too stubborn to back down, Harriet accepts Jasper's shocking wager, and plunges them both into a scandal that will risk everything, including two hearts.

Coming soon to Amazon and Kindle Unlimited!

Want more Emma?

If you enjoyed this book, please support this indie author and take a moment to leave a few words in a review. *Thank you!*

To be kept informed of special offers and free deals (which I do regularly) follow me on *https://www.bookbub.com/authors/emma-v-leech*

To find out more and to get news and sneak peeks of the first chapter of upcoming works, go to my website and sign up for the newsletter.

http://www.emmavleech.com/

Come and join the fans in my Facebook group for news, info and exciting discussion...

Emmas Book Club

Or Follow me here......

http://viewauthor.at/EmmaVLeechAmazon

Emma's Twitter page

About Me!

I started this incredible journey way back in 2010 with The Key to Erebus but didn't summon the courage to hit publish until October 2012. For anyone who's done it, you'll know publishing your first title is a terribly scary thing! I still get butterflies on the morning a new title releases but the terror has subsided at least. Now I just live in dread of the day my daughters are old enough to read them.

The horror! (On both sides I suspect.)

2017 marked the year that I made my first foray into Historical Romance and the world of the Regency Romance, and my word what a year! I was delighted by the response to this series and can't wait to add more titles. Paranormal Romance readers need not despair however as there is much more to come there too. Writing has become an addiction and as soon as one book is over I'm hugely excited to start the next so you can expect plenty more in the future.

As many of my works reflect I am greatly influenced by the beautiful French countryside in which I live. I've been here in the South West for the past twenty years though I was born and raised in England. My three gorgeous girls are all bilingual and the youngest who is only six, is showing signs of following in my footsteps after producing *The Lonely Princess* all by herself.

I'm told book two is coming soon ...

She's keeping me on my toes, so I'd better get cracking!

KEEP READING TO DISCOVER MY OTHER BOOKS!

Other Works by Emma V. Leech

(For those of you who have read The French Fae Legend series, please remember that chronologically The Heart of Arima precedes The Dark Prince)

Girls Who Dare

To Dare a Duke

To Steal A Kiss

To Break the Rules

To Follow her Heart

To Wager with Love (coming soon)

To Dance with a Devil (coming soon)

Rogues & Gentlemen

The Rogue

The Earl's Temptation

Scandal's Daughter

The Devil May Care

Nearly Ruining Mr. Russell

One Wicked Winter

To Tame a Savage Heart

Persuading Patience

The Last Man in London

Flaming June

Charity and the Devil

A Slight Indiscretion

The Corinthian Duke

The Blackest of Hearts

Duke and Duplicity

The Scent of Scandal

Melting Miss Wynter (October 10, 2019)

The Rogue & The Earl's Temptation BOXSET

The Regency Romance Mysteries

Dying for a Duke

A Dog in a Doublet

The Rum and the Fox

The French Vampire Legend

The Key to Erebus

The Heart of Arima

The Fires of Tartarus

The Boxset (The Key to Erebus, The Heart of Arima)

The Son of Darkness (TBA)

The French Fae Legend

The Dark Prince

The Dark Heart

The Dark Deceit

The Darkest Night

Short Stories: A Dark Collection.

Stand Alone

The Book Lover (a paranormal novella)

Audio Books!

Don't have time to read but still need your romance fix? The wait is over…

By popular demand, get your favourite Emma V Leech Regency Romance books on audio at Audible as performed by the incomparable Philip Battley and Gerard Marzilli. Several titles available and more added each month!

Click the links to choose your favourite and start listening now.

Rogues & Gentlemen

The Rogue

The Earl's Tempation

Scandal's Daughter

The Devil May Care

Nearly Ruining Mr Russell

One Wicked Winter

To Tame a Savage Heart

Persuading Patience

The Last Man in London (coming soon)

Flaming June

Girls Who Dare

To Dare a Duke (coming soon)

The Regency Romance Mysteries

Dying for a Duke

Also check out Emma's regency romance series, Rogues & Gentlemen. Available now!

The Rogue

Rogues & Gentlemen Book 1

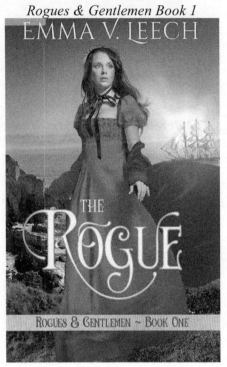

1815

Along the wild and untamed coast of Cornwall, smuggling is not only a way of life, but a means of survival.

Henrietta Morton knows well to look the other way when the free trading 'gentlemen' are at work. Yet when a notorious pirate, known as The Rogue, bursts in on her in the village shop, she takes things one step further.

Bewitched by a pair of wicked blue eyes, in a moment of insanity she hides the handsome fugitive from the local Militia. Her reward is a kiss that she just cannot forget. But in his haste to escape with his life, her pirate drops a letter, inadvertently giving

Henri incriminating information about the man she just helped free.

When her father gives her hand in marriage to a wealthy and villainous nobleman in return for the payment of his debts, Henri becomes desperate.

Blackmailing a pirate may be her only hope for freedom.

Read for free on Kindle Unlimited

The Rogue

Interested in a Regency Romance with a twist?

Dying for a Duke

The Regency Romance Mysteries Book 1

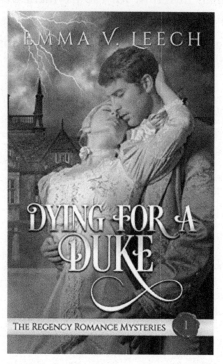

Straight-laced, imperious and morally rigid, Benedict Rutland - the darkly handsome Earl of Rothay - gained his title too young. Responsible for a large family of younger siblings that his frivolous parents have brought to bankruptcy, his youth was spent clawing back the family fortunes.

Now a man in his prime and financially secure he is betrothed to a strict, sensible and cool-headed woman who will never upset the balance of his life or disturb his emotions ...

But then Miss Skeffington-Fox arrives.

Brought up solely by her rake of a step-father, Benedict is scandalised by everything about the dashing Miss.

But as family members in line for the dukedom begin to die at an alarming rate, all fingers point at Benedict, and Miss Skeffington-Fox may be the only one who can save him.

FREE to read on Amazon Kindle Unlimited.. Dying for a Duke

Lose yourself in Emma's paranormal world with The French Vampire Legend series.....

The Key to Erebus
The French Vampire Legend Book 1

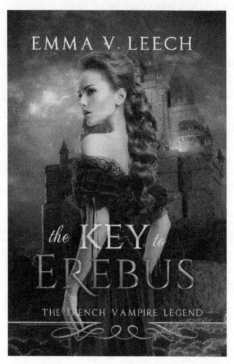

The truth can kill you.

Taken away as a small child, from a life where vampires, the Fae, and other mythical creatures are real and treacherous, the beautiful young witch, Jéhenne Corbeaux is totally unprepared when she returns to rural France to live with her eccentric Grandmother.

Thrown headlong into a world she knows nothing about she seeks to learn the truth about herself, uncovering secrets more shocking than anything she could ever have imagined and finding that she is by no means powerless to protect the ones she loves.

Despite her Gran's dire warnings, she is inexorably drawn to the dark and terrifying figure of Corvus, an ancient vampire and master of the vast Albinus family.

Jéhenne is about to find her answers and discover that, not only is Corvus far more dangerous than she could ever imagine, but that he holds much more than the key to her heart …

FREE to read on Kindle Unlimited The Key to Erebus

Check out Emma's exciting fantasy series with hailed by Kirkus Reviews as "An enchanting fantasy with a likable heroine, romantic intrigue, and clever narrative flourishes."

The Dark Prince

The French Fae Legend Book 1

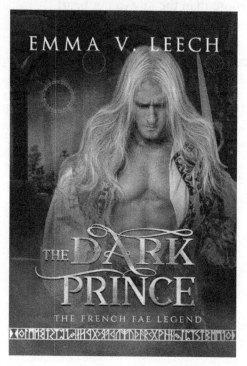

Two Fae Princes

One Human Woman

And a world ready to tear them all apart

Laen Braed is Prince of the Dark fae, with a temper and reputation to match his black eyes, and a heart that despises the human race. When he is sent back through the forbidden gates between realms to retrieve an ancient fae artefact, he returns home with far more than he bargained for.

Corin Albrecht, the most powerful Elven Prince ever born. His golden eyes are rumoured to be a gift from the gods, and destiny is calling him. With a love for the human world that runs deep, his friendship with Laen is being torn apart by his prejudices.

Océane DeBeauvoir is an artist and bookbinder who has always relied on her lively imagination to get her through an unhappy and uneventful life. A jewelled dagger put on display at a nearby museum hits the headlines with speculation of another race, the Fae. But the discovery also inspires Océane to create an extraordinary piece of art that cannot be confined to the pages of a book.

With two powerful men vying for her attention and their friendship stretched to the breaking point, the only question that remains...who is truly The Dark Prince.

The man of your dreams is coming...or is it your nightmares he visits? Find out in Book One of The French Fae Legend.

Available now to read for FREE on Kindle Unlimited.

The Dark Prince

Acknowledgements

Thanks, of course, to my wonderful editor Kezia Cole.

To Victoria Cooper for all your hard work, amazing artwork and above all your unending patience!!! Thank you so much. You are amazing!

To my BFF, PA, personal cheerleader and bringer of chocolate, Varsi Appel, for moral support, confidence boosting and for reading my work more times than I have. I love you loads!

A huge thank you to all of Emma's Book Club members! You guys are the best!

I'm always so happy to hear from you so do email or message me :)

emmavleech@orange.fr

To my husband Pat and my family ... For always being proud of me.

Made in the USA
Las Vegas, NV
16 February 2021